Anne -

Breadcrumbs changed
My entire understanding
of Middle Grade fiction.
The heart of this
book found its
voice in that
story.

Thank You!

THE TROUBLES OF

JOHNNY CANNON

ISAIAH CAMPBELL

SIMON & SCHUSTER BOOKS FOR YOUNG READERS
NEW YORK   LONDON   TORONTO   SYDNEY   NEW DELHI

SIMON & SCHUSTER BOOKS FOR YOUNG READERS
An imprint of Simon & Schuster Children's Publishing Division
1230 Avenue of the Americas, New York, New York 10020

SIMON & SCHUSTER BOOKS FOR YOUNG READERS is a trademark of Simon & Schuster, Inc.
For information about special discounts for bulk purchases, please contact Simon & Schuster Special Sales at 1-866-506-1949 or business@simonandschuster.com.
The Simon & Schuster Speakers Bureau can bring authors to your live event.
For more information or to book an event, contact the Simon & Schuster Speakers Bureau at 1-866-248-3049 or visit our website at www.simonspeakers.com.
Book design by Lucy Ruth Cummins
The text for this book is set in Adobe Garamond.
Manufactured in the United States of America
0914 FFG
2 4 6 8 10 9 7 5 3 1
Library of Congress Cataloging-in-Publication Data
Campbell, Isaiah.
The troubles of Johnny Cannon / Isaiah Campbell. — First edition.
pages cm
Summary: In 1961 Alabama, twelve-year-old Johnny tries to keep his promise to look after his disabled Pa when his older brother leaves for military service, but secrets from the past, Cuban politics, and racial tensions would make the task challenging even for his hero, Superman.
ISBN 978-1-4814-0003-9 (hardcover) — ISBN 978-1-4814-0005-3 (eBook)
[1. Adventure and adventurers—Fiction. 2. Fathers and sons—Fiction. 3. Race relations—Fiction. 4. African Americans—Fiction. 5. Amateur radio stations—Fiction. 6. Cuba—History—Invasion, 1961—Fiction. 7. Alabama—History—20th century—Fiction.] I. Title.
PZ7.C15417Tro 2014
[Fic]—dc23
2013019540

TO MY WIFE, THE REASON

THIS STORY WAS WRITTEN.

SO IF YOU HATE IT,

BLAME HER.

Acknowledgments

My best friend, Russ Conner, geeked out with me about Stan Lee, Dealey Plaza, and history in general, and the foundation of this story was laid through our late-night talks. Ladonna Friesen, my creative writing teacher at CBC, informed me of my potential and helped me commit to finishing a book, and then another. Nicole Flood was the first fan of my writing not related to me, and in many ways, I wrote this book so she wouldn't sound weird when she bragged about knowing a writer. My dad, Lattis Campbell, subjected himself to my inane interviews so I could know what life was like as a Southern boy in '61.

The fantastic people behind WriteOnCon changed my life forever when they hooked me up with my agent, Marietta Zacker. She fought for this book as we marched uphill to find the perfect editors, and I can't say enough how grateful I am that I signed with a Jedi-Amazon-Warrior-Agent. My editors, David Gale and Navah Wolfe, helped turn this book into something better than I ever imagined it could be.

Roger Thomassen, who passed away while I was writing this book, inspired me in so many ways to infuse this story with its humanity. My grandfather, Johnnie V. Campbell, gave Johnny his name and soul. My wife, above all others, believed in me when I could not believe in myself and gave me the strength to keep typing, keep pretending, and keep dreaming.

Which brings me to you, the reader. You have just made my dreams come true. Thank you.

CHAPTER ONE
BOBCAT CASSEROLE

There ain't much difference between a deer and a dog when you're shooting, but there's a world between them when one lands on your plate. If you're hungry enough, though, you won't pay no attention.

I wasn't paying no attention the day I was out hunting turkey. Took me two hours and I never could get a real good shot at one. After a while, a bobcat set himself up for me to snag. I was hungry, so I figured I might as well get a bobcat. After all, the skunks wasn't ripe yet.

Hunting was probably the greatest thing I did. I wasn't so good at school, but it doesn't matter what they tell you, sixth grade is hard, so I didn't worry too much about them bad grades. My teacher said if I didn't do better in seventh I'd be good for nothing but working at a gas station. I started practicing changing tires, but I wasn't any good at that, either.

But I was a darn good hunter. Reason was, I didn't miss.

Ever.

You might say I'm gifted like that.

You might also think I'm being cocky, but it's like my big brother, Tommy, always said, "You ain't bragging, you're reporting the news, like Cronkite."

Anyway, I was out in my favorite holler, about five miles between my house and the edge of Cullman. I was staked out underneath a walnut tree, fixing my target on that spotted bob that was just itching to be in a casserole. Had it in my sights, about eighty yards away. It was drinking from a brook, not even suspecting that my finger was starting to squeeze the trigger, and everything felt natural, from the steel in my hand to the mud on my knees.

Then a stranger stepped right out of the woods and got between me and my target, and a shot rang out.

But I hadn't fired.

No, that cat got hit by a bullet that came from the stranger's gun, a sidearm he had whipped out. Then he went running up and fired another shot. I reckoned he wasn't sure he'd aimed as good on his first one. He got it that time, right in the head.

Folks didn't cotton to strangers around Cullman, especially ones without the sense to go hunting with a rifle and stay out of the way of somebody else's. Add to that the fact that this stranger was about to go home with my dinner, and I was primed for fighting. I took off from my blind and ran down the hill, jumping over logs, dodging low-hanging branches, pounding my way so I could pound him into the ground. I wasn't trying to be quiet one bit, but he didn't turn around until I was just about on top of him.

"Howdy," he said with a wave, barely glancing back at me while he was trying to tie up the cat's legs.

Oh, great, a Texan. We'd rather have strangers in Cullman than Texans. They was about as welcome as colored folk, and the townsfolk made a sign against *them* at the edge of town. It wasn't the most polite thing in the world, but it sure was effective. Cullman was as white a town as anybody could ever hope for.

Still, Pa always taught me to return a greeting, even if you planned on walloping the giver. You didn't want folks talking about how rude the fella that hit them in the face was.

I stopped in my sprint. "Evening, mister."

He tapped his black fedora like a half-baked salute. "You're Johnny, right? Johnny Cannon?"

It dawned on me that this fellow must be a reporter or something, come to talk to me about my brother, the town hero. Cullman should have made a sign for *them*.

"Pardon the question, mister, but who wants to know?" I tried to put on every ounce of Emily Post's etiquette that Pa had beaten into my thick skull.

The fella stood up, dusted his hands off on his slacks, adjusted his tie, and ran his fingers through his mustache. "Richard Morris.

Captain. Six-five-seven-eight-two-seven." He winked at me. "Old friend of your family."

I felt the hairs on my neck bristle up. "From Guantánamo?"

"Farther back than that, from the war. I came looking for your brother, and the people in town told me you boys might be here."

I eyed him up and down. White shirt, black slacks, he didn't look like the type that would be telling Tommy to report for duty earlier than scheduled, so I reckoned he wasn't. Course, I'd read that things was changing under President Kennedy. For all I knew, they'd call Tommy in with a singing telegram. I took this fella for a baritone.

"This is the best place for hunting, that's for sure, but I come here alone these days. Tommy's got a lot on his hands, getting things ready before he ships off to Korea. In fact, I came out here to fetch his dinner." I looked over at my bob he'd tied up.

He glanced back at it himself. "Oh, right. I thought I'd save you some trouble, make a little donation to the Cannon family meat supply." He reached into his pocket, pulled out some tobacco, and crammed a glob into his cheek. "You've grown tall enough, haven't you?"

I was taller than the rest of my class, including my teacher. Just a few inches shy of Tommy, and he was six foot. I didn't reckon that was tall enough, but he didn't need to know about my dreams of looking down on Wilt Chamberlain. I decided to ignore his question.

"So, you're going to give us that bob?"

"Let's just say I owe your family quite a bit." That wasn't no shocker. I growed up with everybody owing us for something. Pa always said the more you did for others the more likely you was to get things back to you. Not that we'd had much repayment yet, but when it started coming we was going to be millionaires.

"How much you owe us? 'Cause I can think of a few other things we need around the house, and if you're buying . . ."

He chuckled. "Boy, they wasn't lying when they said you were the talker. What say we get this pussycat back up to your house? You look so hungry you'd slap your mom for a slice of bread."

He got a real sad look on his face after he said that, and I reckoned he'd remembered that I didn't have no ma.

That ain't really true, 'cause everybody's got a ma. Except maybe for sea horses. I heard they was born from their pas. But I wasn't no sea horse.

I used to have a ma, but I hadn't since I was six. I was fine with strangers not knowing about the accident and such, but this Captain fella claimed to be a friend. Not that I knew what the rules of friendship was. My closest friend was a rock I'd had in fourth grade. But I'm pretty sure he knew Ma was dead.

The Captain carried that bob up the hill to a black Chevy truck, and I followed him to make sure he was telling the truth about giving it to us. There wasn't no laws against stealing bobcats, so he could have run off without fearing no police or nothing. Once we got up there, he threw it into the bed and wiped his forehead.

"You want to drive?" he asked me while he was breathing hard.

I smiled for the first time since I'd met him and hopped in the driver's seat. Most strangers don't understand how it is in Cullman County. They don't think almost-thirteen-year-olds ought to be driving, but how else are we going to get to our fishing holes when our folks ain't up to going?

As we was driving along the dirt road, we wasn't talking about nothing. I had plenty of questions about what he was doing there and why he was hunting for Tommy, but I wasn't sure how to ask them so I kept quiet. He was acting like he had something to say stuck in his throat too, but didn't know how to hack it up, so he would cough a little and we both got more uncomfortable.

I turned on the radio to drown out the quiet and catch the baseball scores of the Reds game. Instead, the news popped on.

"As more and more Americans grow anxious regarding Fidel Castro, the enemy in our own backyard, President Kennedy fielded many questions with few answers about Cuba and the rumors of an impending invasion—"

The Captain switched the radio off with a cuss.

"Trash. You can't listen to trash, kid. It'll mess with your head."

I guess he preferred the quiet, so that's how we went as I drove us up the mountain to our house. It was gray, smaller than you'd think considering the size of our land, and it had a great big fence in front of it. It was the sort of place that a woman's touch could

ISAIAH CAMPBELL

have done a lot with, but three men living in it made it look as inviting as a free ticket on the *Titanic*.

I pulled into the driveway right behind our blue pickup. It had the hood up and Tommy was in there working on the engine. Our Chevy was almost as old as me, and trying to keep it running was his daily chore. He had to do it without buying no spare parts, too. After all, if we had money for spare parts we'd have had money to get something other than bobcat for dinner. But we didn't.

Tommy looked up when he heard the gravel crunch from the tires. He saw the Captain and he didn't smile. The Captain got out of the truck and stuck his hand out like a railroad sign. Tommy wiped his hands off on a rag and shook the Captain's like he didn't want to.

"What are you doing here?" he said to the Captain.

"And hello to you, too," the Captain said. "I remembered you learning better manners than that, Tommy."

"Hello. What are you doing here?"

The Captain grinned. "Just came by for dinner."

Tommy started to say something, but the screen door slammed open and Pa yelled out.

"Captain Morris? What in the name of all that is holy are you doing here?" Pa coughed as he talked. He'd been a Navy radio operator in the South Pacific during the war, caught tuberculosis, and they was so worried about his lungs that they missed his appendicitis. It ruptured, he got gangrene, and they ripped out most of his lungs and intestines. He'd been stuck in the military hospitals for a few years recovering, and now he walked with a cane, spoke with a cough, and couldn't get a job in town for nothing. He did get a disability check, but he called it his funny papers, cause it wasn't nothing more than a joke.

"Pete Cannon, it's good to see you," the Captain said. "You've recovered nicely."

"It's been fifteen years since you last checked me up, so I've had time to. What brings you around out of the blue?"

"I brought your family dinner," he said. "Bobcat."

Tommy looked at me and I shrugged. I'd gone out for a turkey and I brought back a turkey *and* a bobcat.

"Reckon we could set another plate for dinner?" I said.

He slammed the hood down.

"I lost my appetite," he said, and then he went inside.

Pa watched him go in with hurt eyes, but we'd both learned to let Tommy be when he got in his moods. The last time we didn't, Tommy ran off for two months and joined the Guard.

"Johnny, why don't you go see if Mrs. Parkins has her bobcat recipe handy? Me and the Captain here will get that cat ready for cooking."

"Can't I just call her?" I said. "I hate walking all the way over the mountain."

"Phone's acting up again," he said. Of course it was. Anytime he got anxious or bored, he felt like he needed to take something apart. He related better to things that was made of wires. Made me wish I was a robot. "Anyway, you can't expect her to walk all the way up here if you can't walk all the way down. Show a little respect, boy."

They took and hung the bobcat up and skinned it and cleaned the meat off. I went on over to Mrs. Parkins's house. She was the wife of the colored preacher from the main church in Colony. She'd been taking care of cooking for us for the last couple of years, ever since we lost Grandma. But we reckon Grandma will turn up eventually.

That was a joke. My grandma's dead too. I just didn't want this story to get too sad.

Anyway, Mrs. Parkins came up about three times a week and cooked whatever I'd bring in from the woods. Meat, usually. We wasn't able to give her what we should, but Tommy'd take care of their car and I'd mow their lawn to help pay for her services.

I knocked on their door and it was opened by one of the boys in the house. I always felt awkward around colored folk cause I didn't know where to put my eyes, so I stared down at the porch. It was built real good. Maybe the Amish did it.

"My pa sent me to fetch your ma to come up and cook some bobcat for us."

"She's cooking dinner for us right now," he said. "Y'all are going to have to wait."

I glanced up at him. He didn't look too happy about me being on his porch. I wasn't too happy about being there either. I was beginning to think it was built by Mexicans.

"But we got company. We need her to come real fast. I'll mow y'all's lawn extra special this week for it."

"What makes y'all's company more important than my dinner?" he asked. That was a stupid question. Our guest was a grown-up, plus he was a captain. I wasn't going to say nothing about how our guest was white and he wasn't. I'd read *To Kill a Mockingbird* a few months before, and I didn't want to be racist like how them folks was. Shooting a colored man before he even got a fair trial. They should have waited till after.

I was about to tell Willie what for, but then his ma came and stopped our conversation.

"Willie, it's okay," she said to him. "I'll come up right away, Johnny."

"Yes'm," I said, then I shot her boy my best evil eye before I headed back up to our house. I got there just as Pa and the Captain was getting the last bit of the meat off that cat. They was both covered in blood and guts and such, and they looked like they'd been having a good old time getting so messy. I was sad that I'd missed all the fun.

Our truck was gone and I reckoned Tommy'd left for a while. I didn't know what his beef was with the Captain, but I didn't much try to figure it out. Tommy had a beef with so many folks, he was practically raising cattle.

Them two men got the meat laid out and changed into some cleaner clothes. Pa loaned the Captain a fresh shirt to wear and as soon as Mrs. Parkins got up there to start cooking, they went out onto the porch so the Captain could start smoking.

Pa moved upwind so the smoke wouldn't kill him and he pulled out a loaf of stale bread to throw some crumbs to the birds. I went out and grabbed a seat, figuring I could hear some good war stories from those two vets. I always enjoyed hearing old soldiers chew the fat. That was part of why I swept the barbershop floor for a nickel every day. I could probably charge a dime and a half, but them stories was worth selling myself short. I usually skipped the corners anyway.

The Captain spied me watching him and offered me a puff on his cigarette. Pa shot me a look that said I'd be halfway to Heaven before I could even breathe out the smoke, so I turned him down. Pa didn't probably know that I did my own smoking behind the church on Sundays, cause me and the fellas kept that a secret. I traded rabbits' feet and coon tails for two smokes a week. The fellas in town couldn't catch a rabbit to save their lives, and I didn't never have the money to get my own packs. It was a good deal all the way around except for the one kid I gave a pussy willow to and said it was a foot. But he gave me dried ragweed wrapped in paper, so I reckon that was fair.

It didn't take them too long to get to spouting out stories, and I put together a bit of what past they'd had together. Captain Morris had apparently been Pa's doctor after he'd gotten sick in the Pacific, and he'd stuck by him through the whole thing. Even transferred to New Orleans to see him through to the end. Once Pa was let out to go off with Ma and Tommy again, the Captain retired. Said he didn't see no reason to keep at it with the Navy after that, since his favorite person to work on was walking out the door.

Course, all that had happened before I was ever in the picture, which was part of why it was so interesting to me. I was always trying to piece together the story that happened before my first memory, which was stepping off a plane in Birmingham a year after the accident. I blame my grandma for that nagging need to hear about history. She gave me a box of old books, like *Robinson Crusoe* and *The Count of Monte Cristo*, when she found out I didn't have no friends. She told me them stories in there was good for me, so she had me read them all. Then she told me the scars on my face was to remind me of my own story, because it was as important as any of them. But all them scars did was remind me of what I couldn't remember. It made looking in the mirror each morning like reading a German Bible.

Mrs. Parkins came and told us that she'd gotten the table ready for us, and the bobcat casserole was hot out of the oven. We went inside to eat, and Pa asked her to stick around just in case we needed something else. Her face showed that she was antsy to get back to her family, but she stuck it out anyway. The fact that Willie was probably getting inconvenienced by us made me smile to myself, just a little bit. That was what he got for being so rude.

ISAIAH CAMPBELL

We tore into the bobcat casserole, and it was real good. A little like possum pie, only with more onions. I just knew that Tommy would have thought it was the best, but he never did show up to eat with us. When he said he'd lost his appetite, he must have meant it was gone for the night. I reckoned he'd made his way to the bar in town, cause losing your appetite inevitably makes you thirsty. I wouldn't know, I had appetites to spare.

"Excuse me, Captain," I said with my mouth half full of a biscuit, "but what are you hunting for Tommy for?"

He stopped mid-chew. "What makes you think I'm hunting for him?"

"Well, you said out in the woods that you was looking for him."

He swallowed his bite. "I was hoping to see him first because I needed to clear the air between me and him. A grudge that needs to be done with, though I don't recall how it started."

Pa apologized to the Captain for Tommy running off.

"No worries," the Captain said. "That's what they train you for in the National Guard. To be an independent thinker. They think it makes their men more effective."

"Effective," Pa grunted as he chewed on some more casserole. "That's a word we couldn't use too often back in the war."

"They still can't, trust me," the Captain said. He wiped his mouth and glanced at me. "That's actually the main reason why I came here. There's a group of vets doing something I think you'd be perfect for. With radios."

Pa leaned in like a cat watching a goldfish.

"You mean there's work?" I said. "You've got a job lined up?" I was getting a bit excited.

"Well, not exactly," the Captain said. He cleared his throat and wiped his mouth. "I think we ought to speak more in private, Pete."

Mrs. Parkins shot out of there like she'd been waiting for the chance to leave, and Pa told me to head on up to bed. It was a good ways before my bedtime, and I wasn't too keen on getting treated like a little kid, but Pa had his strap handy so I went on up. I could have asked to go out and see my friends, but he would have known I was lying. That was another side effect of them scars on my face. People couldn't stop looking at them long enough to make friends. And Cullman wasn't big enough to have blind kids, so I was sunk.

While I was going up the stairs to my room, I heard the Captain say something about Pa communicating with folks all over the world. I wanted to stop and listen some more, but Pa said he was going to come check on me in a few minutes, so I had to hurry and get in my sleeping clothes.

When I got to my room, I spied Tommy sitting out in the truck with a bottle of beer and five more on the dash, watching the Captain's truck like it was a sleeping snake. I got ready for bed and kept checking to see if he was still there. He stayed out there, best as I could tell, until the Captain left. I wasn't so sure when that was, 'cause I fell asleep looking at my homework and thinking about how much work it would be to actually do it.

I knew Tommy didn't stay out there all night, cause early the next morning he was shaking me to wake up.

"Come on, lazybones," he said as he was rattling my teeth inside my head. "We got work to do. Time's a-wasting."

I rubbed my eyes and looked at my alarm clock. It said it was six in the morning. On a Saturday. Dadgummit, he was still drunk. Either that or there was a missile coming at Cullman.

"We ain't got no work to do today. At least, none that's got to be done this early."

He yanked my pillow from under my head and ripped the blanket off of me.

"We got to run the delivery. Unless you don't want to go with me," he said.

I shot up. If he was lying, I was going to punch him in the mouth.

"That's today? I thought we was doing it next Saturday. I was going to get a few more turkeys before we went."

He threw my shoes at me and I slipped them on over my bare feet. I picked a shirt that didn't smell too bad off my floor and put it on. He curled up his nose at me, which was a good sign. When folks puked at my odor, then I knew it was laundry day.

"It was going to be next Saturday," he said, "but Bob told me yesterday he'd only let us have the bird for three hours next weekend. He can give it to us for five today. Now, come on."

We went downstairs and out to the wooden shed in the backyard, where we had our deep freezer filled with all the game I'd killed over the last month. He started pulling out the brown-paper-wrapped portions and handing them to me. I filled up some cardboard boxes with them and carried them to the truck. We had to be real discreet about it, cause I had gotten a lot more than what was proper according to the hunting laws. But, when your family needs money, sometimes you got to close your eyes to the rules.

I found a marker and wrote on all them boxes NOT MEAT. That'd fool them.

We got the truck all loaded up with the frozen turkeys, rabbits, quails, deers, and squirrels and we left the house. We drove down the mountain and into Cullman, the only hometown I'd ever known. It wasn't a small town, really, cause there was about ten thousand folk that lived there. And we had a good group of different types of people. People that had their roots in Germany, Ireland, England, and a lot of other countries.

Driving through town that early was one of the few good things about prying my eyes open, cause it was quiet and you could really appreciate the town for what it was. Right at the edge of town we passed the sign that they'd put up to ward off colored folk, which told them: COLOREDS—DON'T LET THE SUN GO DOWN ON YOU IN THIS TOWN.

Pa said that was the rudest sign he'd ever seen, and he was glad we didn't live in the city for it. Tommy said Pa didn't know how things was, and he thought it was a good idea. It kept the colored

ISAIAH CAMPBELL

folk off in their own little place, a village on the other side of our mountain called Colony. Folks in Cullman called it *the* Colony, which I thought made it sound more official.

As we drove into Cullman, we passed the grocery store, where the owner was out sweeping the sidewalk and setting up his signs for the Saturday business. We passed the college, Saint Bernard, with all its trees and pretty sidewalks, where Tommy'd gotten his degree off the GI Bill and where I planned on going if I ever graduated from high school. Didn't know what I'd study. Maybe they had a degree in hunting.

We drove real quick past the Methodist church me and Pa went to on Sundays, probably cause Tommy never could stomach going in there. Not since the pastor'd told him drinking was a sin and Tommy told him being fat was too. Even the pretty white walls and tall steeple couldn't take his mind off that, so he stopped going. The only person who asked about him was Mr. Thomassen, the piano player. But they started catching up at the bar on Fridays, so they was fine.

Finally we went out the other side to where the airstrip was and we met Bob Gorman, the fella who owned the little airplane we was going to take to fly down to Birmingham.

"You're going to pay me when you get back, right?" Bob said.

"Don't I always?" Tommy said as I got to loading all that frozen meat into the plane.

"Usually," he said. "This was a lot easier back when I just took it out of your paycheck."

Bob Gorman owned the air show that Tommy'd flown for ever since he graduated from his basic training for the Alabama Air National Guard. That'd been almost three years of flying and showing off all over the South, and Tommy'd loved the fame, attention, and women he got from it. But, for the past three months, he hadn't done none of it. Just stayed at home with us to help get things in order before Korea.

"It was easier for you," Tommy said. "But you know I'm good for it. Give me the keys."

Bob fished them out of his pocket and handed them to Tommy. We got into the airplane and I took my spot next to him at the copilot's steering wheel. Tommy started flipping the switches and pulling the knobs.

"You don't let that kid fly, do you?" Bob yelled.

"Do I look crazy to you?" Tommy said, and then he started the engines on the plane. Bob yelled something back, but there wasn't no hearing it over the noise. Tommy drove the plane out onto the strip, we picked up speed, and then he eased us up into the air. I felt my stomach getting sucked up into my throat as we left the ground behind, and almost wanted to close my eyes so I didn't get nervous. But I didn't, cause I would have hated myself if I didn't watch Tommy taking off an airplane. He was an artist, like da Vinci. And when Hank da Vinci painted your house brown, it was the prettiest brown in the South.

The trip from Cullman to Birmingham wasn't a long one to fly, but it was just long enough for him to let me grab ahold of the steering wheel and fly for a bit. He gave me some tips while we was up there, but I didn't ever need them. I'd been practicing flying in my head since the first time I saw a hawk fly in the woods. I strapped a kite on our dog one time to test my ideas. Sometimes I missed Fluffy.

Tommy watched me fly in silence for a few minutes.

"So, what's your beef with Captain Morris?" I said, keeping my eyes straight ahead at the clouds in front of us like he always told me to. Fluffy hadn't done that. Pretty sure that's what went wrong with her inaugural flight.

He pulled out a bag of sunflower seeds from his pocket and chewed on a couple.

"It don't really concern you," he said. "We got a history that's been bumpy, but there ain't no reason for you to get tore up over it."

"He don't seem so horrible to me," I said.

"No, he never does." He threw another few seeds in his mouth and took hold of the wheel again. "It's time to start landing."

"Will you let me do it?"

He laughed. "Little brother, I was taught by the legendary—"

"Major Harrison. I know," I said. I had dreams of someday taking a lesson or two from that fella.

"Trust me, landing is the hardest part of it all. Someday you'll learn it, but until then I'm the man for the job."

He brought us down to the ground just as smooth as he took

us up. There was a whole group of people waiting for us with their ice chests. As soon as the plane was stopped and parked real good, they came and lined up to give us their money and take some of the meat we'd brought. I went to the head of the line and started collecting money, cause that was what I was really good at. Not so much doing the adding or giving out change, but I was real good at convincing them to give us more than what they'd planned.

"You was wanting a turkey and two rabbits? That's three dollars," I said.

"I thought it was two dollars," the old lady I was talking to said.

"It was. But we had to raise the price on account of us having to pay the colored woman to come cook for us."

"Why should I pay more cause your ma can't find time to do her job?"

"I'm sorry, ma'am," I said. "It really is a shame she died when I was six."

She got a shocked look on her face.

"Oh, I'm so sorry."

"It wasn't your fault. It wasn't nobody's fault, really. That's what I had to come to grips with while I was in the hospital." I reached up and scratched at the scar next to my nose that circled around under my eye to my ear. "I was in the car when she had the accident, after all."

"You poor boy," she said, then she put a five-dollar bill and a shiny silver dollar in my hand. "You keep the change, son."

"Thank you, ma'am," I said. I always wondered if folks thought I had a piggy bank with all that change they let me keep, and when it was full I could bust it open and buy my ma back from the store. Or maybe a bicycle. But I already had a bicycle.

That was pretty much how it went with the whole delivery. We came out with thirty dollars more than we'd planned. It was real funny how something that I barely remembered happening to somebody I never really knew could wind up so beneficial that many years later. We saved money on Mother's Day too.

Once we got all the meat sold, me and Tommy got ready to fly back out of there. He kept hesitating on getting in the plane, though, and I wasn't too sure why. But then a black car with tinted windows drove out to the airstrip we was on. I looked at the license plate; it was from Florida. They pulled up close to us and a woman got out of the passenger seat. She looked like she was from someplace in South America. She came over to Tommy and he told me to get into the plane.

I hurried into my seat and watched as they talked. She gave him an envelope and he looked inside of it, and then he nodded to her. They got closer to each other and she was whispering something to him. He had a reputation with the ladies, but she was too old for him to brag about. It was the darnedest thing.

After a while, the other door on the car opened and a short white fella with sunglasses and a suit got out and walked to where they was talking. He interrupted them talking and pointed at his watch. She shooed him away, but he only took a couple of steps off and he stood there listening to what they was saying.

I could tell Tommy was getting frustrated with him listening, cause he kept glancing at him and showing off his fighting stance. He finally went to push the short guy away. Then the short guy opened up his jacket and showed a gun.

Tommy took a step back with his hands up.

The lady said something to the short guy, and then she kissed Tommy on the cheek and headed to the car.

After they drove off, he got into the airplane. He was so interested in whatever was in the envelope that he let me go through the routines of getting the engines started. He even let me get us going down the runway, though he didn't let me do the actual takeoff. I reckoned he was still spooked over Fluffy.

"Is that some woman you've been seeing?" I said.

"Her? No. She's a friend of a friend," he said, and he stuffed the envelope into his pocket. He didn't talk about her or the envelope again.

After we was up in the air real good, I looked at his watch to see what time it was.

"It didn't even take us three hours to get this all done. Why couldn't we have done it next Saturday? Was it cause you had to meet that lady?"

He glanced down at the trees and such that was passing underneath us.

ISAIAH CAMPBELL

"I wanted to make sure everything was taken care of and that the money from the meat was ready to go to the bank on Monday. You know how to make a deposit at the bank? Fill out the slip and all that?"

I hadn't never been inside the bank before except to get the candy that the tellers kept out on their counters. Even then, it was only when I was really hard up. You'd think, with all that money, they could afford something besides peppermints.

"Why?" I said. "You can drop it off, or Pa can if you're too busy. Ain't no reason to let me screw up the deposit."

"No, you need to learn how to do it." He pulled out the wad of money we'd just made and stuck it in my shirt pocket. "And how to pay bills, too, writing out the checks and all that. Pa ain't no good with figures."

"What you talking about? He's an egghead."

"Sure, when it comes to wiring stuff or making the TV work. But his head ain't been good for handling money since the war. He gets his numbers mixed up. You're going to have to handle things while I'm gone, or else you two will be in a mess of trouble."

We was most always in a mess of trouble when it came to money. And with me at the steering wheel, we'd crash and burn faster than Fluffy had nose-dived into that tractor. May she rest in peace.

He saw my face getting worried, so he let me take over with the flying.

"You got money saved, right? From all them jobs you do and stuff?"

I nodded.

"Good. You keep it hidden, don't let yourself give in to using your money for the bills."

"But what if Pa needs it?" I said. "What if he gets hard up?"

"He's going to get hard up, and you're going to have to help him. Just not with your own money. Help him fight off the lions."

I right off got a picture of me and my hunting rifle staked out on our porch, shooting lions that was escaped from the zoo. That made me feel a bit better, cause I could hold my own better with wild animals than with wild bankers. Still, I was pretty sure I didn't have the right ammo.

"What you mean?"

He thought for a bit, staring out the window.

"Pa's in a lion's den in Cullman. Surrounded by folks, by creatures, that are aiming to eat him up. That's why we're always poor, cause it makes sense to him to feed all his money to the mouths of the lions. It's the only way he can think of to keep them from tearing him apart. And they'll tear you apart too, if you let them. So don't let them."

"There ain't no lions in Cullman. Maybe at the zoo in Gadsden, but I ain't heard of no escapes."

"It's a metaphor, Johnny."

"What's a 'meta'? And why's it for me?"

He shook his head.

"Just listen. You got to keep yourself and Pa surviving until you can get out of there, out of Cullman. That's the only way you'll be safe, when you can leave. Like I did."

"But you came back."

"Yeah," he said. "For you. But when you get the chance, you got to leave and never look back. It's the only hope you got."

Now he was scaring me.

"Why you talking like this?"

"Cause I'm leaving again soon," he said.

"Yeah, but you're coming back again."

He didn't say nothing.

"You're coming back, Tommy. Right? Ain't you?"

He took a deep breath.

"You never know, little brother. Nobody can tell the future, not even them gypsies that come in the fair. But I can tell you this, you can only come and go from the lion's den so many times before you get bit. And I've ridden my luck about as far as it'll go."

I had a lump the size of a baseball in my throat.

"Is this cause the Captain came in to town? I reckon he's either gone or going soon."

"It ain't," he said, then he paused. "And it is, I reckon. He did help me remember that we got a history in our family of bad luck. And bad luck ain't exactly something you shake, not the kind we got."

"Is he one of the lions you're talking about?" I was starting to get the meaning of what he was saying. "What in tarnation happened between you and that Captain? If it's so horrible that it's making you talk like this, I need to know."

He sighed.

"No, you don't. It's in the past, it's history."

"Mrs. Buttke at school always says if you don't know your history, you're doomed to repeat it," I said. It was one of the few lessons I really remembered, and it was why I only paid attention to history class. Math, English, and all them others just claimed to be beneficial for you. History was the only one that came with a warning label.

"Sometimes it don't matter if you know it or not. You're still doomed." He stretched his arms out, then plucked the silver dollar out of my pocket.

"Hey, that's mine," I said.

"Then you might ought to learn how to protect your things." He grinned his usual possum grin at me. "But, that's enough of all that talk. Have you picked up your comic books this month from the grocery store? What's happening in the world of Superman?"

Normally, talking about superheroes and monster stories was top of my list of favorite conversations we had. We was both the biggest Superman fans in Alabama. We was convinced that Krypton was blown up by the Commies. It would explain why red Kryptonite was so powerful.

But I didn't feel like talking about superheroes. And it wasn't cause I was sore about the silver dollar. But he didn't want to talk about nothing else. So we went the rest of our trip not talking about nothing. He landed us, gave what he owed to Bob Gorman, and we drove back to the house. I hoped the Captain was gone, for no other reason than that Tommy'd cheer up and spend his last couple of weeks having fun.

We got to the house and the Captain's truck was parked in the driveway. Tommy didn't even get out, he let me out and said he was going back into town. I said I'd go with him, but he said he was going drinking and I couldn't come. I almost wondered if the Captain owned stock in the beer business, for how much drinking he inspired in my brother. Tommy drove away and I felt that lump in my throat getting heavier and heavier. I went inside the front door.

Pa and the Captain was sitting at the dinner table with a whole mess of RadioShack catalogs and ham-radio books laid out in front of them. They was looking at radio equipment and checking the specs off of stuff in the catalogs against numbers that was in the books. I got myself a glass of water and went to sit down next to them.

When I did, I caught a whiff of the Captain's aftershave and it made me have a memory. I remembered being wrapped up in a blanket, sleeping in the back of a car while my folks drove around late at night. I tried to focus on the memory, tried to key in and see my ma's face, but I couldn't. My brain was too broken. It was funny, it was a different aftershave than what Pa used, which was why I hadn't never remembered it before. He must have changed brands after the accident.

I peeked over Pa's shoulder at the page he was looking at.

"What's that?" I said about the big box-looking thing that had the dials and knobs on top.

"It's a Collins 30S-1 linear amplifier," Pa said. "It can cover the whole frequency spectrum, which is good if you're going to be operating at different times of the day."

I took a look at the price tag.

"Dadgum, Pa! It's fifteen hundred dollars."

His cheeks got red.

"Why don't you head upstairs and work on your homework?" he said.

"Or he could stay," the Captain said. Pa shot him a look. "Sorry, didn't mean to overstep."

"I ain't got no homework," I said. Which wasn't exactly a lie. I did have homework, I just didn't have none I was going to do that day. Homework was like cheese, it had to sit for a while. Then you could throw it away.

"Well then go read your comic books or something. We can't have you down here."

I didn't see no good that could come from arguing with him about it, even though I had a bad feeling he was fixing to start shoveling our money into the lion's mouth, just like Tommy'd said. I took my water upstairs and listened to my radio for a while to catch the baseball scores. I wondered if there was any equipment in them magazines they had that could make my radio pick up better stations. Like ones that had the Reds actually winning.

After I was served a good dose of lousy news, I reread a few of my Justice League comics. I wouldn't read none of Tommy's if my life depended on it. Pa'd gone through and drawn long pants on all the pictures of Wonder Woman. He said he was protecting our minds, but Tommy said all it was doing was feeding his imagination. None of that made no sense to me, but I learned to hide my comic books in a box after that. Tommy kept his girlie magazines in there too. But they didn't have no good stories, so I never read one.

I went downstairs a couple of times to make myself a sandwich or to refill my cup of water. I offered to fetch the both of them some of Tommy's booze from the fridge, but they said they didn't drink. Which I knew was true of Pa, for the most part, but the Captain struck me as a guzzler for some reason. I reckoned I was wrong.

After a while they left together. I headed back down so I could look at their catalogs, but they'd taken the whole lot with them. So I got myself a bowl of cereal and sat on the couch to watch some TV. Of course there wasn't nothing good on except for an afternoon movie about a fella that was frozen in an iceberg for fifty years, so I watched that. I watched shows and movies for the rest of the day all by myself in the house. I must have fallen asleep on the couch, and Pa must have left me there, cause when I got woken up the house was quiet and it was pitch-dark outside. Tommy was leaving a piece of paper on the table.

"What you doing?" I said. He jumped.

"I thought you was in bed," he said. His breath stank of beer and whiskey, I could smell it from the couch. That didn't trigger no memories for me, at least none but dragging Tommy out of the bathroom after he passed out on the toilet. And I sure didn't want to dwell on that one.

"I ain't in bed, am I? What are you doing?"

He looked at the paper he had put on the table and crumpled it up and put it in his pocket.

"I'm leaving," he said.

I realized that he was in his uniform, and I saw his duffel bag by the door.

"Where you going?" I said, even though I already knew the answer.

"Montgomery. I'm reporting for duty on Monday, and then I'm shipping out."

Dadgum, that lump in my throat wasn't going nowhere.

"But, I thought we had a few more weeks before you went to Korea. You sure you ain't been drinking too much?"

He turned and looked away from me. His voice wasn't as level as it usually was.

"I ain't going to Korea. I'm going somewhere else, but it's top secret." Yeah, he was drunk as a skunk. I'd seen his papers myself.

"Where you going, then?" I reckoned his answer would be something like Mars or Wonderland or something.

"I told you," he said, "it's secret."

Narnia. That had to be it. When he'd had a pint of whiskey, he was always going to Narnia. He started toward the door. He was walking pretty straight, considering how drunk I reckoned he was. Still, if he was headed to Narnia, he probably thought our door was a wardrobe. Poor cuss.

I jumped up and grabbed his arm. He almost fell over. Yup, he was pretty drunk.

"You can trust me, Tommy. I swear I won't tell nobody."

He stared at the door. He swallowed and I wondered if he had a lump in his throat too.

"I can't. I got orders. It ain't just my secret, it's the government's." The government of Aslan, I reckoned. He looked in my eyes. "If you ever told anybody, I don't know rightly what would happen to me. Or you and Pa, for that matter."

"I swear. On Ma's grave, I swear."

He searched my eyes like he did when he thought I was lying about something.

"That ain't enough. You got to swear on mine."

I took a tiny step back. That was new. Maybe he wasn't talking about Narnia.

"You ain't got no grave," I said.

"But I will if you tell."

I spit in my hand and held it out. "Swear on *your* grave, then."

He spit in his hand and shook mine. "I'm going to Nicaragua."

I racked my brain to figure that one out.

"Is that in Oz?" I said.

"That's in South America."

Dadgum. Nicaragua. That almost sounded like a real country.

"Was that where that lady was from?"

"No, she was Cuban."

"Oh, well South America's still closer than Korea." I started to feel better. "So it ain't so bad."

"No, it's worse. I got a mission to do that ain't the safest doing. A whole mess of people are counting on me to help them out. But it's worth it, I promise you it is." His face was sweaty, like it was when he was lying. Also when he was drunk. Which he usually was when he was lying. "I just hope my luck holds up."

As soon as he said that, I got an idea. Just in case he was telling the truth. I hurried up to my room and dug under my bed until I found what I was looking for. I went back downstairs and put my Superman action figure in his hand.

"He'll keep you safe," I said. "That's what he does."

"But he's yours," he said. "I gave him to you. You can't give him back."

"Nope. I ain't giving him to you. Just loaning him." I almost got choked on something, must have been allergies. "You make sure you bring him home, okay?"

He nodded and I could tell them allergies was getting to him, too. He didn't say nothing else, just grabbed his duffel bag and started out the door. He stopped.

"You take good care of Pa, you hear me?" he said, his voice crackling a bit. He went out and closed the door behind him.

I ran out after him and he was walking out of our driveway, I reckoned down to the bus stop at the bottom of the mountain. Which meant he was really going. Or else he was in for one heck of a hangover.

"Who's going to take care of me?" I yelled after him.

He turned around and showed me a big grin on his face. He threw something at me and I caught it.

"You're Johnny Cannon," he said. "You'll take care of yourself. That's what you do best."

I looked at what he'd thrown. It was that dadgum silver dollar the lady had given me. I looked up to watch him disappear into the darkness. The lump in my throat was threatening to jump up into my mouth and blow my head apart. I had to blink a few times to keep myself from blubbering, and I finally remembered where my feet was and how to use them to go back inside.

In spite of all his flaws, Tommy was more than just my brother. He was my best friend. For the first time I could remember, I was alone. Even though Pa was there, the house was empty. Like a den just waiting for the lions to arrive.

.

CHAPTER TWO
NEVER FIGHT ON SUNDAY

I woke up the next morning to a smell that made me feel all warm and bubbly inside, so good I almost forgot about what had happened the night before. But then I saw the silver dollar on my dresser and my heart started breaking all over again. The smell even smelled sad after that.

I went down to see what it was I was sniffing, and the Captain was in the kitchen cooking at our stove. He was wearing an apron and everything. I didn't even know we owned an apron, but he'd found it. He was smoking a cigar, too, which I reckoned counteracted the frills.

Meanwhile, Pa sat at the table, looking through them catalogs again. I was dadgum curious at what they was aiming at doing. Maybe they was building a robot. If they did, I hoped they'd train it to keep the house clean. And to not kill nobody. But, if we could only pick one, I'd choose a clean house. After all, I owned a gun and it wouldn't be nothing to shoot a robot.

"What you cooking?" I said.

"Jalapeño cheese biscuits with gravy and scrambled eggs with spicy sausage, or as we call it in Texas, *chorizo con huevos*. It's my mother's recipe," the Captain said. Since it sounded like a Mexican dish, I didn't reckon she'd come up with it on her own. Unless she was Mexican. But he'd said his name was Richard, not Ricardo, so there wasn't no way.

He scraped at the red-colored eggs with a spatula and turned them over. I took a seat next to Pa. He closed the catalog and put it away.

"It smells awful familiar to me," I said.

"Your ma made it every Sunday morning when you was little," Pa said. "I imagine Tommy's going to be real excited when he gets up. It used to be his favorite. When I told Captain Morris that while we was at the grocery store yesterday, he decided to cook it for us this morning."

"To smooth things over with your brother," the Captain said. "The *other* reason I came here."

I wasn't sure how to tell them about Tommy, so I got myself some orange juice from the fridge and occupied my mouth drinking it. I must have not worn a blanket the night before, cause as soon as that juice hit my throat it burned like the dickens.

"What's the matter?" the Captain said.

"Throat hurts. It ain't nothing."

He pulled out the pan of steaming biscuits from the oven and plopped one on a plate, covered it in gravy, then scooped some of them eggs on the other side. He set it in front of my seat.

"You want me to look at it?" he said.

Couldn't he see it from where he was standing?

"Maybe later. I reckon I'm fine."

He grabbed the knife out of the butter and wiped it off on his pants.

"Here, open up. Let me have a look-see."

I clenched my teeth together. I didn't much care for folks poking around on me. That's why I never went to the doctor. Sometimes I'd go with Pa, but that was mainly to see what Goofus and Gallant was up to in *Highlights*. Them two fellas was a hoot and a half.

"Johnny," Pa said, "let the Captain look. He's a darn good doctor."

I didn't feel like fighting the both of them, so I opened my mouth. The Captain pushed my tongue down with the knife and peered into my throat.

"I can't really see." He pulled a match out of his pocket and lit it with his thumbnail. "Don't breathe," he said, and then he held the lit match inside my mouth. It was getting pretty hot, and I held my breath for fear of third-degree burns.

"You don't look so bad in there," he said after he looked for a spell. "How do you feel? Achy? Run down?"

I shook my head while I put my orange juice back in the fridge and poured myself some milk. It didn't hurt as bad as the juice.

"I'm fine, just the throat's sore," I said.

He started pushing on the sides of my neck, feeling it all up and down. He ran his finger along the three-inch scar I had just under my Adam's apple. He looked like he was hurt over it.

"That's from the accident," I said. That one on my neck was the longest, the one on my face was the most obvious, and the one on my forehead was the ugliest. I also had a few where people couldn't see them, like on my chest and in my pants, but I hadn't never had to explain those. I had a habit of keeping my pants on. Pa said Tommy should learn that habit too. "I've had my scars since I was six."

"I know where you got the scars," he said.

I was about to ask him how he knew where I got the scars since he hadn't seen my pa for fifteen years, but Pa distracted me from the question.

"I'm surprised your brother hasn't come down yet," Pa said. "I'd have thought the smell of this breakfast would drag him out of bed."

"He ain't here," I said, and then I took a bite of the eggs. Dad-gum, it was good.

"Where'd he go? Into town for something? On a Sunday?"

I sipped my milk. I knew the answer to his question was Narnia. No, wait, it was Nicaragua, wasn't it? Good thing I'd sworn to keep Tommy's secret, cause I probably couldn't tell it if I tried.

"Korea," I said. That one I'd had practice telling. "He went ahead and shipped out."

Captain Morris set a plate in front of Pa and sat down with his own.

"Was it because I'm here?" he said.

It sure was.

"No sir, I don't think so. I reckon he got called to go early."

Pa sighed and started picking at his food.

"Ain't that just like the military? No concern for family whatsoever."

The Captain was eating his food fast. Faster than me, and that was something to brag about. We sometimes had eating races during lunchtime at school, and I won almost every time, as long as Eddie, Bob Gorman's pudgy son, didn't get involved. That kid was a vacuum cleaner disguised as a twelve-year-old. Maybe *he* was a robot.

"We running late for church or something?" I said.

"Church?" he said with his mouth full of *chorizo*. "You two go to church on Sundays?"

"Yeah, don't everybody?"

Pa caught eye of the Captain's bewilderment.

"Me and the Captain ain't going today. We got a lot of work to do. But you ought to go. Why don't you hitch a ride and go with the Parkinses today?"

I laughed cause I reckoned he was joking. Then I realized he wasn't, he was dadgum serious. Which meant the person playing the joke was the Almighty Himself. He was one devil of a prankster.

"To the colored church? In the Colony?" I said. "Are you kidding?" I was pretty sure there was laws against white folk going to the Colony for anything, and especially for going to the colored church. It was for our own safety, of course. Kind of like all them hunting laws I never listened to. They was intended to keep us all civil.

"Church is church, ain't it? And I can't take you, so you should go with them."

"Maybe I could stay home. After all, with Tommy leaving and me having an inflamed throat and stuff, I'm sure it's all right for me to miss."

He stabbed his biscuit and took a big bite.

"No sir, you got to get going. To the Parkinses' church today. You'll be fine."

I ate my food as slow as I could given how good it was and how hungry the Captain looked, and then I took my time getting ready. I figured if I missed the chance to ride with the Parkinses, I couldn't be blamed for not going to church. It would have been a lot easier if I was a girl and had makeup to do and stuff. All I had to do was comb my hair and spray cologne on my armpits.

I wasn't able to go as slow with that as I wanted to, cause Pa came up to my room and was watching me with his leather strap just itching to meet up with my backside. So I got into my clean white shirt and my black pants and started working on getting my dress shoes on, when Pa saw the wad of money me and Tommy'd made the day before sitting on my dresser.

"Is this your earnings from yesterday?" he said.

I reached to grab it, but he took it first and shoved it in his pocket.

"I don't want you putting this in the offering or nothing. I'll hold on to it."

I wanted to tell him that it wasn't his place, cause Tommy'd put me in charge of the money, but I didn't have the guts to do that. That strap of his was practically humming in anticipation of getting swung at my hindquarters. I hurried out of the house and ran to the other side of the mountain. I caught Mrs. Parkins just as she was loading her kids into their big white station wagon.

"I told your pa I wouldn't never be available on Sundays," she said to me while she was helping her little daughter get into the backseat. She was a cute little girl in a white dress, probably only three years old. She stuck her tongue out at me, and I almost returned the gesture but Mrs. Parkins was eyeing me, so I decided I'd save it till later. I made a mental note so I wouldn't forget.

"I ain't fetching you to come up. He sent me to go to church with y'all."

She got as funny a look on her face as I had inside my head.

"Is this a joke?" she said.

ISAIAH CAMPBELL

"I reckon so, though it ain't one being played by my pa."

She understood that, I guess.

"The Lord does have an interesting sense of humor," she said. "Well, get on in and make room for Willie."

I wasn't enjoying the seating arrangements one bit, but I slid in next to the little girl and braced myself for Willie to squeeze in after me. He came out of the front door and I noticed, for the first time ever, that he walked using a crutch like the kids that had had polio did at school. He was carrying a suitcase under his arm and he hurried to get into the car. If we was ever putting on a show of *A Christmas Carol* with an all-colored cast, he could probably play Tiny Tim. Finding a Scrooge would be hard, though. Maybe Bob Gorman could put on blackface.

"What's in the suitcase?" I said to him.

"None of your business," he said. "What are you doing riding in our car?"

"None of your business," I said, and I reckoned that about covered all the questions.

We drove down the mountain on the opposite side of Cullman and went the ten miles into the Colony. It was small, even compared to Cullman, and it was as run down and poor looking as folks might expect of a colored town. We drove over to where the Parkinses' church was at. It wasn't all that different from the church in Cullman, except that it was older and smaller and the outside wasn't kept up as good. I didn't reckon that was the fault of any of the folk that lived over there, after all churches was kept up by the money of the people. And everybody knew that the Colony wasn't where no money was at.

We pulled up and Mrs. Parkins walked in and the kids all followed her, so I did too. The kids ran off to different classrooms for Sunday School except for Willie. He headed through two big doors into the sanctuary, carrying his suitcase with him. I was plumb curious as to what he was up to, so I followed him. Actually, he walked so slow, I just went in ahead of him and waited.

He hurried as much as he could with his bum leg all the way up to the front of the sanctuary and set the suitcase up at the foot of the pulpit. He opened it and pulled out some metal stick thing with a wire coming off of it and set it up on the wooden podium. He plugged the wire into a little hole on the suitcase and then he pulled out a couple of round things, one that had a black ribbon come off of it. I went up to see closer. I didn't think a preacher's kid would bomb his own church, but there was a first time for everything. I ate an egg roll once.

"What you doing?" I said.

He stopped and tried to hide his stuff from me.

"What I'm supposed to. Why don't you go to your classroom?"

Meeting strangers was right up there with getting eaten by a bear on my list of favorite things to do. I didn't even bother answering him.

"What is that thing?" I said.

ISAIAH CAMPBELL

He let out a sigh.

"It's a reel-to-reel tape recorder. I record my pa's sermons every Sunday."

I looked at the suitcase more closer. Pa would have loved it. It had a switch on it that said Stop/Play/Record, and there was a speaker set into the top of it. He had the two reels all ready to go, the one on the left was a thick roll of the black ribbon, the one on the right was empty. I really hoped his pa wasn't going to fill that whole tape with his preaching.

"Is that your pa's tape recorder?"

"It's mine. The church folk got it for my birthday last year so I could record the sermons." He ran the end of the ribbon from the reel on the left to the one on the right and fastened it. "Anyway, I got to get this ready. So go find somebody else to bother."

I thought about shooting back a comment at him, but since we was in a church and he was the preacher's kid, God would probably hit me with a lightning bolt the size of Kentucky, so I decided against it. I walked around the building, finding things to look at and kick around until about time for the service to start. I went in and sat as close to the back as I could, figuring I was in for another boring Sunday morning.

Boy was I ever wrong.

The first thing I noticed was different was the singing and the music that went with it. It wasn't necessarily that everyone in there was a better singer than the folks back at my usual church, but I'll be darned if they didn't sing them songs better than we did. They sang every word like it was a dadgum message from Heaven itself, and the organ that was played was like a singer all its own.

They went through a few songs, some of the women crying and darn near swooning, the menfolk clenching their eyes shut tight like they needed to block tears from popping out. I didn't sing along with them. Not so much 'cause I was embarrassed by how bad of a singer I was, but because I didn't know how to get myself worked up like that. Crying wasn't one of my skills. It was like dancing. I usually just plastered myself to the wall and ate the food.

After a while, they sat down and the preaching was set up to start. Willie went up and started his tape recorder and his pa, the Reverend Parkins, stood in front of the little metal stick on the pulpit and started preaching.

I usually took a nap during the sermons at my church. One time I'd snuck in my radio in my jacket to listen to a football game, but I got caught and whipped for it by every deacon on the board, so I didn't try that no more. I figured that I might catch some valuable sleep while Reverend Parkins was preaching.

But there wasn't no sleeping during his sermon.

He started off kind of slow, talking about Daniel and the lion's den. I thought that was a pretty funny coincidence, and it made me remember the cash Pa'd taken from me, but I tried to put it out of my mind. It got pretty easy, because Reverend Parkins told that story like he'd been in the den with Daniel. He started yelling and shouting, and the folks in the pews would yell and shout right back at him. He'd jump up and down and wiggle his finger in the air, and some of the men would stand and point at him. Occasionally, while he was getting to preaching real hard, somebody would jump, run to the front, and slap some money onto the platform, telling him to "Keep on preaching." Folks didn't do that at the white church. They was all trying to figure out how to make the pastor shut up.

Reverend Parkins kept going and going, and the folks kept getting more and more into his sermon, and I wasn't getting bored with it or nothing. The only problem I was having was that my head done started hurting, and it got worse and worse as he went on. My Sunday School teacher told me once that a guilty conscience would do that, but I was fine with all the sinning I'd been doing, so that couldn't have been it.

Instead, it felt like my brain was a fishing pole that had gotten grabbed by a big whopper in the water, and it was bending the pole in half fighting from getting reeled in. Now, I wasn't sure if the fish I'd snagged was a trout called "My Brother Just Left Town," or if it was a bass called "That Dadgum Captain Had His Fingers Down My Throat This Morning," or what it was, but I felt for sure that it was only a matter of time before my pole got yanked out of my hands. And I didn't want to be around when that happened. Too bad I probably had to be, on account of me being stuck with myself.

I was racking my brain to figure out just what exactly was going on in my head, but then Reverend Parkins said something that just about put all the ache out of my head.

"See, we're all in the lion's den with Daniel, and we're surrounded by lions at every side. But we're also surrounded by someone else. We're surrounded by angels, angels who will shut the mouths of the lions that threaten us. So you have to ask yourself, are you staring at a lion or at an angel? Are *you* a lion or an angel?"

Well, that got me to thinking. Maybe the whole point of all this was that, if I was going to protect Pa from the lions, I had to be an angel for him. When Reverend Parkins said the closing prayer, I said my own that the Good Lord would help me be strong like an angel. It wasn't a long prayer, cause I didn't do long prayers. Besides, I almost felt like I needed a brain doctor for the machine gun that was firing in my head. I wanted to get back home and have the Captain look at me again.

Folks got up to leave, Willie went and packed up his tape recorder, and I hurried to find Mrs. Parkins. She was standing with a group of women, talking with them about the week's schedule and such. I'd learned the hard way not to interrupt women when they was talking like that, back when I was just a kid and I'd spied a mouse in the church and the women all took turns twisting my ear for interrupting. Then they all screeched when they saw the mouse and blamed me for not running it off. Since I figured I needed to wait for her to get done, I headed outside for some fresh air. I'd have to settle for that, since I didn't have no rabbits' feet to trade for a smoke.

Willie and his friends was talking together and laughing at something, which was usually my clue to stay away. That's how it was with the kids at school, at least. But I wasn't sure if them clues was the same with colored folk. Somebody should have written a handbook.

Then I spied Willie's eyes and I realized that there's some things that is the same, no matter what sort of fella is doing it. 'Cause I recognized his look from all the times I'd had it myself. It was the look of a fella trying his hardest not to cry while he's acting like he's laughing.

In spite of the fact that it was the leading cause of death among cats, I gave in to my curiosity and went over for a better listen.

"Maybe we could find you a job at the front, Willie," the tallest kid among them was saying. "You could give out tickets or something. Provided we got you a stool. That'd be a long time on one leg, even for a flamingo."

All the fellas with him laughed, and Willie did too, though his laugh was a little too loud and a little too fast.

"What y'all talking about?" I said.

They all got real quiet. The tall fella eyed me all over.

"Who wants to know?" he said.

"This is Johnny," Willie said, and I could tell he was hoping time would hurry up and move on past the moment we was in. "My ma brought him."

I held out my hand, 'cause that's what manners says to do. They didn't take it none.

"Figures," the tall fella said.

"This is Russ," Willie said. "He's going to be a boxer when he grows up."

"And I'm going to give jobs to all my friends," Russ said. "Even my little crippled friend here. 'Cause that's what a good man does."

Willie winced when he said that, then pretended he'd had to sneeze. He probably fooled all them, but I spoke the language of winces real good, so I knew what it meant.

"A boxer?" I said. "Like Sugar Ray?"

"Sugar Ray Robinson, for sure," Russ said, then he put up his fists and punched at the air in front of me. "Best boxer there's ever been."

"Does that mean you're going to lose to Gene Fullmer, too?"

The whole mess of them groaned, and I knew I'd hit a nerve. A white boxer like Fullmer beating a legend like Sugar Ray was something Cullman folks was real proud of, which meant it was something the folks in the Colony was probably butt hurt about.

Russ stepped forward and his fists was clenched. Yup, they was butt hurt.

"Losing to one boxer don't take nothing away from Sugar Ray," he said.

"Except Fullmer beat him three times. Reckon that makes Sugar Ray a three-times loser."

"If they fought again, Sugar Ray'd knock him out just like he did in '57," Russ said.

"I guess there ain't no way to know, is there?" I said. "Fullmer's got too much class than to humiliate him like that again."

Russ kicked at the ground. Willie eyed me and then him, like he wasn't sure which one of us he wanted to be right.

"Well, Genie, I mean Johnny, maybe there's one way to know," Russ said. "What about you and me having the rematch for them? Right here and now?"

My stomach clenched in on me and my head felt ready to pop. I had a feeling it was the only move that was the same no matter where you was, challenging a fella to a fight. The one who gets challenged ain't really got no choice in the matter. He's got to fight or be a chicken. Even if he's the pope. That's what them crusades was all about. I think.

"We ain't Sugar Ray and Fullmer," I said.

"Of course I ain't Sugar Ray. That cat is rich and famous. But around here," he said, pointing around the yard and at them other fellas he was with, "around here I'm Sugar Ray. And there ain't but one fella that could stand in for Fullmer." He reached out and patted my chest.

"Come on, Russ," Willie said, eyeing me like he was worried I might say something I shouldn't. "He didn't come here to fight. Just let him alone."

That worked for me. I turned to get away. I couldn't help but remember what Eddie Gorman had told me once, about how colored folk was more savage when they fought than civilized white folk, which was why they was such good boxers.

Of course, Eddie was a racist. He rooted against Jim in *Huckle-berry Finn*. But he was funny, so it was okay.

Still, there was no telling if he was right or not. But I didn't want to test his theory out. I'd rather be a chicken in the Colony than a body in the hospital. I took a couple of quick steps away.

And that set Russ to laughing.

"Probably a good thing," he said. "I'd have punched him so hard, his mama would have felt it."

Now, I'll be honest with you. Folks had made fun of my ma before and it hadn't really bothered me much. And Russ probably didn't have no idea about her being dead. Heck, even the couple of times Eddie, who knew my ma was as dead as a doornail, had asked me where my ma was only made me kick his shins. It just didn't affect me too much, since I couldn't remember her none.

But when Russ said that, it was like the fishing pole in my brain that had been getting yanked and tugged by I didn't even know what all of a sudden broke right in half and I got yanked off the boat.

I spun around and I clobbered him right in the eye. I barely even realized I'd done it before my fist had already met his cheek-bone and all them other boys had their mouths gaping open. Even Willie.

Russ touched his face where I'd hit him and realized I'd drawn blood.

Then he cracked me in the mouth.

ISAIAH CAMPBELL

So I kicked him in the crotch.

He doubled over and I reckoned the fight was done. I was starting to feel like I was back in charge of the boat again, so I offered him my hand. Like a gentleman.

He reached out and grabbed my belt, yanked me around, and threw me into the wall of the church. The whole building shook and a loose shingle fell off the top.

I jumped onto him and we went rolling around on the ground. I was boxing his ears and slapping his face, he was punching my throat and I think trying to rip my arm out of its socket. Not a one of us heard the footsteps of all the grown folk coming around the corner of the church.

Two of the deacons pulled us apart and then Mrs. Parkins ran over and almost had a cat when she saw how messed up my clothes and my body was. She hurried me and her kids to the car, talking about how she didn't know how she'd explain it to my pa, and how she shouldn't have let me out of her sight. I tried my best to let her know I would have probably gotten just as beat up if she was watching me, but she didn't pay me no mind.

She drove us all on out of the Colony and back up to my house, even though I told her I could walk on my own from theirs. While we was going, Willie was trying to ask me all sorts of questions. I wasn't giving him too many answers, not 'cause I was trying to be rude or nothing, but because my head was hurting way too darned bad.

"Russ is a good guy with an ego too big for his britches. He needed to be brought down a few pegs," he whispered to me. "And you did it. That's really something. He don't usually lose no fights."

I nodded.

"I mean, you was winning, wasn't you? Gosh, how did it feel? I mean, getting in those punches? Did you feel strong? Powerful?" he said. He rubbed his bum leg while he was talking, and I got a better idea of why he was asking. I nodded again.

Mrs. Parkins was watching in her rearview mirror as he was grilling me with them questions.

"Leave him alone, Willie. Can't you see he don't feel good right now?"

I was thankful for that. My head hadn't stopped hurting, and after getting in that fight, I was realizing the prayer to become an angel was just another one that wouldn't get no answer. Just like the one asking for the Cardinals to get to the NFL Championship.

"Okay, I'll stop asking. Today." He got a grin on his face. "But, can I do an interview with you some other time? And record it, and everything, like what they did for Gene Fullmer?"

"An interview?" I said.

"Yeah. It's a hobby."

I nodded to get him to leave me alone and then I acted like I was trying to say something to his sister, who was sitting next to me again. She was asleep 'cause it was probably her naptime. I accidentally woke her up and she stuck her tongue out at me again.

ISAIAH CAMPBELL

Dadgummit, I might have to get a ledger book to keep track.

We got to my house and Mrs. Parkins got out to go tell my pa what had happened. I got out too, and I was embarrassed by our front yard. In between the time I'd left for church and then, Pa and the Captain had filled our front yard with a whole mess of empty boxes and papers and such. It looked like a homeless paradise. If homeless people used RadioShack boxes.

Mrs. Parkins knocked on our door and there wasn't no answer. Then we both heard a loud ruckus of banging coming from the backyard, so she headed that way and I followed her. And if I was embarrassed by the state of our front yard, our backyard made me want to change my name and move to Canada. And you know that's bad, 'cause there ain't no good reason to go to Canada.

Pa and the Captain had dug everything out of our shed, the lawn mower, the deep freezer, my bicycle, everything, and they had it thrown all kinds of ways out in the grass. They was inside the shed hammering and sawing and drilling, and they was laughing and carrying on while they did it like two fellas that didn't have a care in the world.

Mrs. Parkins went and knocked on the shed door that was half-way open.

"Mr. Cannon?" she said.

Pa bolted out of the shed, along with the Captain, and they pushed the door closed.

"Hello, Coretta," Pa said. "How are you doing today?" He had the kind of grin you got when you was trying to hide something from somebody and you thought it was the funniest thing ever to be doing it, but you knew if you told it to them they wouldn't think it was funny at all and they'd whip you for it. I tried to get the image of Mrs. Parkins having my pa over her knee, swatting him with a paddle, out of my head, but things like that, once it's in there, it's in there.

"I'm doing fine, but your boy here ain't doing as good."

Pa spied me and my torn, dirty, bloody shirt, pants, and face and he got as stern as a gnarled piece of wood.

"Boy, what did you get into?"

"Just a boxing match, Pa," I said.

His mouth almost crackled at the edges with the beginnings of a smile.

"Did you win?" he said.

"I reckon," I said.

He started to say something else, but the Captain cleared his throat and shot Pa a look. Pa went back to being stern.

"You know the rule about fighting." We didn't have no rule that I'd ever known, except to make sure and tell the story over dinner. "Get in there and go to your room," he said. "You done embarrassed me enough today."

I looked at the big mess he'd made of stuff. There was more boxes back there, including one that was marked with that linear amplifier he'd been looking at.

"I know how you feel," I said. "Looks like you two went shopping. How'd you pay for everything?"

His eyes got steely at me.

"That ain't your place to ask, is it?"

"Do you still have the money from yesterday in your pocket?" I said.

He looked at Mrs. Parkins and then back at me.

"I'm your pa. If I see fit to spend our money on something, I'll do it without your questions. You hear me?"

"No worries," the Captain said. "I floated him a loan. You all can pay me back whenever you can."

A loan. That wasn't much better. Whether we was devoured by a lion all at once or one bite a day over the next few months, we was still doomed to be dinner. Dadgummit.

I didn't say nothing else to Pa, I just went inside. I watched out the window as Mrs. Parkins got in her car and drove off to her house. I thought about making myself some lunch or something, but my head was hurting too bad to even think about nothing like that. It was throbbing again and all I wanted to do was lay down and rest.

I went up to my room and sat on my bed. I couldn't stop thinking about that money that Pa had thrown away on some stupid equipment. And taking a loan from the Captain, what in tarnation was Pa thinking? Most likely Pa was trying to impress him. Tommy told me that folks was the stupidest when they was aiming to impress, and they was downright brain dead when they was impressing a woman. It was a good thing the Captain wasn't a woman.

Now I had the picture of the Captain wearing a dress in my head. I wished there was a pill for that. To get images out of my head, I mean. Not to get the Captain in a dress.

The more and more I ran all them thoughts in and out of my head, the madder and madder I got. I stood up and tried to walk around my room a bit to get my anger out, but it just kept coming. It felt like a fountain that was springing up in my gut, and I couldn't explain it. I left being angry *at* anything, and I was beginning to just be angry in general.

It got to the point where I couldn't take no more, and I just had to either hit something or yell. And with my head hurting so bad, there wouldn't be no yelling or I might have a brain attack, so I turned to punch my wall. The worst that could happen was I'd get bloody knuckles, and that would be fine. It'd make me look tough at school the next day. Might even impress Martha Macker, the prettiest darn girl in Cullman County.

I punched and then my fist went straight into the wall. It made a hole in the Sheetrock, a big one that I couldn't hide or deny.

Apparently I was a lot madder than I even realized.

Madder than I'd ever been before.

But I just didn't know why.

CHAPTER THREE
CATCHING PUBERTY

Monday morning I got up with my headache half gone but the rest of my body feeling a whole lot worse. I almost thought about taking the day off from school and saying I was sick, but then I saw out my window the backyard still all messed up from Pa and the Captain's project, and I decided I'd rather leave.

I went downstairs to get something to eat first and Pa was sitting at the table with a cup of coffee, reading out of the ham radio book.

"Feeling better?" he said. "I came up to check on you last night. You was tossing like a man on a boat."

I'd had some crazy nightmares, that was for sure. I shook my head to get out the picture of the Captain in a green dress with Pa over his knee, paddling him something fierce. I grabbed some bread and put it in the toaster.

"I think I'm better today," I said. I sat down across from him and tried to think of what I wanted to talk about. I'd done decided there wasn't no point in talking to him about money, the cash that had been on my dresser or any other money issues we was having. I'd pick up a rock on my way home to talk to about that. It'd be more advantageous and less risky than filling Pa's ears with our figures.

I was still real nervous about the way I'd felt the day before, and how angry I'd been, and about punching through the wall, and that was on my tongue to talk about. But I wasn't sure how much Pa would know to tell me, or how much I wanted to tell him. He could talk transistors and circuits all day long, but it was like there was a wall when it came to flesh-and-bone conversations. He'd get so awkward you felt sorry for him, and guilty that you'd made him look so foolish.

Still, he was my pa. He had to be good for *something*.

"Something funny's happening to me," I said. "Like, I'm getting all kinds of weird feelings and such."

He looked up from the book, real uncomfortable. He coughed a couple of times.

"You got hair growing in your pants?" he said. "It's normal, part of growing up. You want to talk about it?"

I absolutely did not want to talk about nothing going on in my pants. I had to find the exit sign in this talk. Too late, he kept going.

ISAIAH CAMPBELL

"See, son, there's this thing that's called 'puberty.' You start having weird things happening to your body. You start getting hair in places you didn't before and you start to smell bad." He was twisting the book in his hands like he was wringing all them words out of his brain. "Girls have it too, but their changes are a lot prettier than boy changes. And you'll notice the girls as they're changing too. That's another side effect of puberty."

I had to make him stop. I couldn't listen to my own pa talking about these things.

"And you might start getting the rage, too," he said. "That's what my mama called it. When you start feeling like you could tackle a bear and it about drives you crazy that you can't find one nowhere."

That got my attention. Maybe he was onto something.

"So, you start feeling like you're a live wire?" I said. "And you get angry faster?"

He nodded and coughed again.

"Yeah, and your voice starts dropping."

Captain Morris picked right then to come into the kitchen.

"What are you two talking about? Puberty?" he said.

Pa said we was, and since the Captain said it too, I reckoned that settled it.

"You experiencing changes?" the Captain asked me. I didn't feel like getting into it any more in front of Pa, so I just nodded and got my toast. Still, he was a doctor.

"How's your throat feeling today?" he asked. Took me a second to remember that I'd had a sore throat the morning before. He came over and pulled my mouth open and looked inside. "Looks fine. Still, if you get any more sore throats, there might be something we can do."

"Like what? Take out my tonsils?"

He poured himself some coffee.

"Something," he said. He squeezed my shoulder and for a second I forgot what Tommy'd said about not trusting him. He looked like he really cared about me, like he was almost worried or something. I tried to shake it off.

Pa got up to get himself some more coffee.

"Hey, Captain, all these call signs they're using now, I can't make sense of them in my head. Can you look at them for me?" He glanced at me. "When Johnny goes, of course."

Well, that was practically a permission slip, as far as I was concerned.

"I'm leaving right now," I said, and I left the house. I had to go to the bottom of the mountain to catch the school bus, and normally I'd have run down there. But I had a lot on my mind, so I decided to walk it instead.

I barely made it in time to catch it before it went off. I got settled into my seat and then I tried to forget how crazy of a weekend I'd had and have a normal day. I was pretty thankful that the colored kids had their own school in the Colony, even though most

ISAIAH CAMPBELL

days I thought it was unfair. Why should they get to learn things I didn't? But, today I didn't want no reminders of how weird things had been over the past couple of days.

Things went pretty normal, too. I walked into John Cullman Middle School and everybody left me alone, as usual. Heading through the yellow halls to our classes, folks hurried past me, laughing and carrying on, hoping to get all their jokes out before the bell rang. Thing was, most of them only knew about five good ones, and they retold them every morning. And almost all of them fellas that was telling them jokes yet again was doing it to impress one girl.

Martha Macker.

I'd had a crush on Martha Macker for as long as I could remember, probably since the second grade. She'd been the first person to smile at me when I came to school as the new kid. She was also the only one to smile at me for two months after. My scars had been real dark back then, and everybody else looked away from me when I came by. She did too, but she'd try to smile first.

Problem was, every other fella our age in Cullman had a crush on her too. She had the prettiest red hair, the brightest blue eyes, and five freckles on her nose that danced when she laughed. And she wasn't like one of them girls that puts on being nice or sweet to try to get her way. Her smiles was like dog farts, they wasn't trying to hide nothing.

Once I got into our class, I found my spot two rows from the back, the seat right behind Martha, and I settled into my desk. Mrs. Buttke got us started with the prayer and then the Pledge of Allegiance. After that she had us all pull out our reading for the day, and then she started writing on the board the same thing she wrote every single day.

This Day in History:

I was maybe the only kid in the class who paid attention to that every time she wrote it. It was all 'cause I'd told her on the first day of school that I thought history was stupid, 'cause it had all happened so long ago it didn't matter. She told me that everything that's ever happened in history was as close to us as yesterday, and the reason we study it is so we can keep today from being as bad as yesterday was. That made sense to me a whole lot, 'cause there was a lot of bad stuff in my yesterday that I needed to stay out of today. From then on I wrote down everything she told us about history, especially them facts of the day, hunting for clues. I even kept track of each day's fact in a notebook. I had made a fancy cover for it too.

Johnny Cannon's Guide to Surviving Yesterday

She finished writing on the board and I copied the day's event.

March 13, 1781—Sir William Herschel discovers Uranus in Bath.

The kids behind me started snickering. Mrs. Buttke turned around and glared at them. Eddie Gorman raised his hand.

"Yes, Eddie?"

"Whose did he discover?" he said, and half the class started giggling.

She looked at the board again and blushed.

"Eddie Gorman, you despicable little child. Go immediately to the principal's office." She made him come up there and get a note, and then he went out the door. The class was still giggling. It took me a second to get the joke, but when I did, I snickered to myself.

"Johnny, do you have something to say?"

I hated when she called me out. I always wanted to get sucked into a hole in the floor and go to school with the mole people.

"No'm," I said, then I thought for a second. "Well, I guess I do. Why is it so important to know how Ur—" I stopped, 'cause I was afraid of saying the name and making everybody laugh again.

"*Your*-in-us," she said. "It's pronounced Your-in-us. Not what you foul-minded children are thinking. And Bath was the city in England where Sir William lived."

There was a couple more snickers, but mostly the class calmed down.

"And it's important," she said, "because it illustrates how long it can take for what we observe to become what we understand. Sir William initially thought the planet was a comet or a star, and even after other astronomers were convinced it was a planet, he had difficulty accepting it. It wasn't until two years later that he formally confirmed it to be the seventh planet from our sun."

I made a note next to the event in my book.

It can take a while to go from seeing to believing.

I thought for a second and wrote right underneath it.

Naming a planet for a butt is a sure-fire way to get Eddie sent to the principal's office.

Both of them was real good things to remember.

The rest of the day was filled with boring school stuff, like math, which I didn't figure I'd ever understand so there wasn't no point in trying, and English, which I'd been talking since I was a baby, so I didn't know why we had to keep learning it every year. Science was about the ins and outs of plants, which didn't matter much to me since I didn't figure I'd be a plant anytime soon. Of course we studied history and the Civil War and stuff, which was real interesting, even though Mrs. Buttke had a knack for making it as boring as Sunday School.

Right before we left, the best part of the day happened. It was when Mrs. Buttke would pass out all our homework and Martha would hand the stack back to me. I always managed to touch her hand when I took it.

"So much to do," she said every single day.

"I reckon," I said every single day.

I lived for that part of the day.

Finally the bell rang and I was super glad for it. I went real fast to the barbershop to do my daily job of sweeping up all the loose hair and stuff that was all over the floor. It was perfect for me, 'cause none of the men who came there talked to me, and I got to listen to all their stories. They liked to brag about their big hunts

ISAIAH CAMPBELL

they'd gone on recently, and I liked to compare their stories to my own. Mine were usually better.

I got to the front of the barbershop and my day went from being normal to weird all over again. Willie was sitting outside with his tape recorder, and as soon as he saw me, he called me over to him.

"Hey, are you ready to give me that interview?"

"What are you doing in Cullman?"

"My pa came to meet with the preacher from the church here. Now, about that interview."

"Why are you so all-fired determined to interview me?" I said.

He looked at me like I'd asked the dumbest question in the history of the world. Which I hadn't. The dumbest question in the history of the world is, "Will you marry me?" It narrowly beats out, "Do you think you could shoot this off my head?" and "Can I pet that rattlesnake?"

Tommy told me that joke. It's one of my favorites.

"I want to interview you 'cause you fought like a wild man yesterday," Willie said, "and you beat Russ. Got that straight from his mouth this morning. That don't happen that often. That's a news story if I ever saw one."

"So? You ain't a reporter. You're only ten," I said.

"Eleven," he said. Dang, he was small. "And I aim to be a reporter. A sports reporter, actually. Though I guess if I had to announce the big stories too, that'd be fine."

I didn't have the heart to tell him that they wasn't going to hire a colored person from the Colony to be a reporter on the radio, except maybe on the colored stations. Plus, what with him having a bum leg and all, he wouldn't probably get no jobs nowhere when he got older. If my pa couldn't get a job, there wasn't no way a crippled colored kid would. Except maybe as a professional beggar. I heard there was a union for that.

I sat down in front of him. At least talking to a tape recorder would be easier than talking to a real person. Sure, I was going to be talking to Willie, but he wasn't really like a stranger. Not anymore, at least.

"All right, ask your questions."

He got his recorder going and held the microphone in front of himself.

"Hello again, sports fans, this is Willie Parkins, your on-the-spot reporter. I'm here with the toughest kid in Cullman County, Johnny Cannon. Tell me, Johnny, have you ever fought like how you did yesterday before?"

I had to think for a spell.

"Nope," I said.

"And, what do you reckon was different about yesterday's fight? The level of competition? The setting?"

I thought for a second.

"I don't know. I wasn't feeling too well beforehand, actually. I reckon I got puberty."

He stopped the tape.

"You can't say 'puberty' on the radio."

"We ain't on the radio," I said.

"Don't matter. You can't say it," he said.

"I don't see why not. It's what I got."

"Do you even know what puberty is?"

"A headache. Right?" I said.

He snorted, and then he went and explained what in tarnation puberty was, and it was a horrifying image. It was all about body parts sprouting hair and other parts growing, and smelling bad when you sweated, and feeling funny around girls. And, what was the most disturbing, it wasn't nothing about headaches or punching through walls. And, even though I actually had been noticing some of those things happening for a couple of months before that, like the hair and stuff, and I'd felt funny around girls ever since I figured out I was a boy, it hadn't scared me none. Not like the events of Sunday had.

"So, I don't reckon you was fighting hard because of puberty," he said.

I was real embarrassed by this point, so I got up.

"Hey, ain't you going to finish the interview?" he said.

"Some other time. I got to head in there for work." I started to go, and then I stopped. "How come you know so much about puberty?"

"I got this hobby called 'reading.' You should try it."

"I read a lot. I've read every novel at the library, and I got a big history book that I read every night."

He sneered.

"Novels are made up and history's stupid."

"No it ain't," I said. "With science all you do is figure out how things is. With history, you figure out how they ought to be."

He wasn't buying that.

"How? By repeating the same stupid thing they was doing a hundred years ago?"

"Nope," I said. "By not."

I didn't feel like putting up with him no more, so I opened the door to the barbershop.

"Just let me know when we can finish the interview," he said. He wasn't going to let up about that. "Or if you need me to explain the birds and the bees."

I wasn't *that* stupid.

"I already know about them. Birds fly and bees make honey."

"That explanation will probably work till you're through with puberty," he said, and I could tell he was trying to hide his grin.

I felt like I should say something real smart back, but I was starting to believe I didn't have it in me. Worse yet, I was getting more and more convinced that my pa's horse sense was slower than mine, which meant he really wasn't qualified to be running the business of our house. I tried not to let that worry me and I went inside.

ISAIAH CAMPBELL

Mr. Thomassen, the barber who also played piano at church, said hello. He was shaving Bob Gorman. Shaving his face. Bob's head was already bald enough.

"Where were you yesterday?" Mr. Thomassen said. "I looked for you at church."

I really didn't want to answer no more questions. I fished out the broom and the dustpan from behind the waiting chairs.

"I went with the Parkinses to their church," I said, hoping that would end it.

Bob sputtered and some shaving cream went flying through the air.

"In the Colony? You went to the Tigger church?" he said. Except he didn't actually say "Tigger," he used a different word that I ain't obliged to say no more on account that I've been cutting back on my cussing. But Bob wasn't trying to cut back on nothing. "Tigger" was his favorite word, or rather, the other word was. I don't know how he felt about anything A. A. Milne wrote.

Mr. Thomassen stopped shaving him.

"Bob, I've told you I won't stand for that kind of talk in my shop." Mr. Thomassen was from up north, New York or some such place like that. I didn't know why he'd moved to Cullman. Maybe it was for the traffic. We got a new light over on Fourth Street about the same time he came.

"Yeah," I said, and I was surprised that I did. Maybe it was 'cause of my puberty or whatever. "You're supposed to call them 'colored.'" I expected Mr. Thomassen would be happy I'd taken his side. He sighed.

"That's not much better," he said, and I felt stupid again. "If you call a man 'colored,' you're implying that he's different from normal, 'uncolored' people. And I don't think any of us are normal. Or uncolored, for that matter."

Bob yanked the towel off of Mr. Thomassen's arm and wiped off the shaving cream from his face.

"I can shave myself," he said, and then he stormed out. I felt pretty bad that I'd just made Mr. Thomassen lose a customer. Especially a Gorman. Everybody salivated over their money like dogs staring at a pile of raw meat.

"I'm sorry. I didn't think I was doing nothing wrong. I hope he don't stay away for good," I said, hoping Mr. Thomassen wouldn't fire me right there on the spot.

Mr. Thomassen had an upright piano off to the side of his shop, and he went over and started playing it. He played better than anybody I'd ever heard before, and he played the kind of music I never got to listen to when Tommy was around. Jazz. That was the other reason I swept his shop for a nickel.

"Don't worry about Bob Gorman," he said. "He can't afford to be too high and mighty with me. We have a history together."

"Really?" That was downright interesting to me. "What kind?" He ignored my question.

"But I do want you to make me a promise," he said. "Get rid

of that 'colored' talk, the proper term is 'Negro.' Saying 'colored' makes you sound ignorant. You're better than that, better than all the hillbilly boobs you're surrounded with. And, comparing you to Bob . . ."

He didn't finish that sentence, but went straight into a real fast piece of piano music. I swept to the rhythm he was making and tried to not let nothing get into my head about Bob, or about my weekend, or nothing else. I got just about all that mess out of my head except for the picture of Martha handing me my schoolwork. I figured that was fine.

I got done sweeping and he paid me my nickel. He also gave me his order for meat, three squirrels so the lady that worked for him could make him a stew. I told him I'd go hunting for them squirrels that night and then I left. I had my nickel from Friday still in my pocket, so I went to the drugstore and paid ten cents for a new comic book. The only one they had that I hadn't read yet was *Star Spangled War Stories*, which had a dinosaur eating an army plane out of the sky, and the soldiers shooting at it from their parachutes. I took it and read it on my walk home.

When I got back to the house, I at first thought maybe things was getting back to normal, 'cause all the boxes was cleaned up out of the front yard. But then I saw a great big antenna sticking up over the top of the house, and I realized life was just getting weirder and weirder.

I looked in the backyard and saw all the stuff from the shed still strewn about, and the antenna was coming off the top of the shed. Pa and the Captain was connecting wires and such around the building, and when they saw me standing there, they shooed me away. I got my rifle and went out to get Mr. Thomassen's squirrels. Didn't take me too long, and after I packed them up and put them in the freezer in our kitchen, I went up to my room and read my comic book again. It was important to read things like comic books twice, once for the story and the second time for the pictures. Tommy taught me that.

And that was pretty much how the days went for the next few of them. I went to school and Mr. Thomassen's barbershop, avoided giving Willie an interview that he hounded me for every day, and then came home to see Pa and the Captain working on their new-fangled project. They stopped constructing whatever it was they was building and started going out and just staying in the shed every day. Since Pa'd pulled our freezer out, I couldn't fetch nearly as much meat as I liked when I went out hunting, so I had to stick to what would fit in our fridge. Which meant I had to hunt more often, which didn't bother me none.

Friday was Saint Patrick's Day, so we all wore green to school to avoid getting pinched. Eddie was pretending that he was color-blind that day, though, and he went around pinching whoever he could, mostly the girls. He came and pinched me at lunchtime, and I socked him in the stomach. I didn't know if it was what Saint Patrick would have done, but I wasn't Catholic, so I didn't reckon

　　　　　　　　　　　　　　ISAIAH CAMPBELL

it mattered. Got sent to the principal's office for it, though, and the principal called my home so I could get picked up. Since it was the fourth time in two months that I'd punched Eddie, I was getting sent home for the rest of the day.

I waited in the office, dreading Pa getting me. He was pretty quick on the draw with his paddle when it was regarding my school. He said if your seat didn't hurt you four or five times a week, then you wasn't learning nothing. I must have been learning more than anybody else at school.

They told me my ride was there and I started covering my butt right away. But it wasn't my pa that had come. It was the Captain. I said a quick glory-be and got into his truck with him.

"You're quite the fighter, aren't you?" he said as I closed the door. I shrugged. That fight I'd been in at the Parkinses' church was about the only real fight I could recall. I mean, sure, I'd occasionally beat the living tar out of Eddie, but that wasn't much of a fight. He was the closest thing I had to a friend at school, and our friendship was that he'd mess around a lot and I'd sock him in the gut a few times for it. I didn't expect the Captain to understand newfangled friendships.

"Just like your mom," he said.

"You knew my ma?" I said.

"Sure. She was there in New Orleans when your pa and I were there."

That made sense, I guessed. It was weird that he knew her and

I didn't, but then again there was a whole mess of folks that knew her before the accident killed her and all my memories. She was buried in a grave there in Cullman, they'd brought her up from Havana. Wherever my memories was buried, I didn't have no idea. They didn't make the trip.

"She did a lot of fighting with folks around the hospital?" I said.

He chuckled.

"She did a lot of fighting with folks everywhere she went. But she loved her family, especially her sons." He looked down the road for a bit while he drove us to my house. "I think that's why it hurt her so bad when your brother moved in with your grandma."

"Yeah, he told me about that," I said. He'd moved away when he was twelve to live with Grandma there in Cullman. I was four then. He was still living there when Pa and I moved up from Guantánamo three years later, after I got out of the hospital. "But that was long after we left New Orleans. How'd you know about that?"

He kind of stuttered for a second.

"I visited y'all a couple of times while you lived down there. Don't you remember?"

I tried, but there wasn't no use.

"I don't really remember nothing from before the accident. Don't rightly know why," I said. Then I had another brain flash. "But, Pa said he hadn't seen you in fifteen years. Didn't he remember you visiting?"

He pulled us into a gas station. There was a bus filling up at one of the pumps, he pulled up to the other one.

"Well, look at that. I need to top off my tank before I hit the road," he said. "I'm going up north. Have to meet another old friend up in Washington. We can talk all about this when I see you again," he said and handed me a quarter. "Why don't you go in there and get you a drink?"

"You got more friends up north?" I said.

"Oh, I have friends everywhere. Now, go get you something."

I hopped out of the truck. It sure seemed like he was avoiding my questions, but I couldn't make no reason why. I had Tommy's voice in my head saying not to trust him, but everything about the Captain was telling me I should. I didn't know what to do about that. I did know what to do with the quarter, though. I went into the station to get a MoonPie and an RC.

I said hello to Skippy, the fella that was working in the station. I was pretty sure he was the owner's sixteen-year-old son. He barely ever said hi back at me when I came by. He was always too busy. No matter where I saw him, he was busy working, whether it was at football, or at studying, or whatever. He acted like he had to take care of the entire world before dinner. We had a lot in common.

I got me an RC and my MoonPie and went up to the counter. Skippy was wiping down the window.

"How's your pa?" I asked.

He stopped his wiping and shot me a glare.

"What's that supposed to mean?"

I didn't reckon I was speaking in a different language. Maybe he was listening in one.

"Your pa, Mr. Dexter."

His shoulders relaxed.

"Oh, right. Folks always think that. He ain't my pa, he's just an old friend. But he's more like my pa than my pa."

He took my money and fiddled with the change.

"Who's your pa?" I said.

He double-counted the coins he'd just put on the counter. After I took them, he finally told me.

"Archie Dean," he said.

Archie was the town drunk. He was in and out of the jail cell so often he and the sheriff had started a checkers match with each other, one move a night. Archie claimed the sheriff was cheating. The sheriff claimed Archie was drunk. That story was easier to believe.

"I'm sorry," I said. "I'm sure it ain't easy having him as a pa."

"It ain't. But Mr. Dexter really took me under his wing. He's taught me how to be a man and how to take care of myself. He's helping me fill out college applications."

I looked out the window at the Captain. He saw me looking and waved. I waved back.

"So does that make Clem your brother?" I said to Skippy.

He groaned. That confirmed it.

Clem was worse known in town for drinking than Archie. He

ISAIAH CAMPBELL

wasn't smart enough to get in a checkers match, either. So he had no redeeming qualities.

"Why didn't Mr. Dexter help him out?" I said.

"Clem doesn't trust Mr. Dexter. He says he's trying to turn us into city folk. I think he started drinking more after Mr. Dexter took me in than he did before."

I understood completely. Tommy wasn't trash like Clem, but he acted like it sometimes. And Captain Morris seemed at least to be better for me than Tommy let on. Maybe me and Skippy had more in common than I thought.

"Do you read comic books?" I said.

"Never. They're stupid."

Nope, we would never be friends.

The Captain came in and paid for his gas and I got back into the truck. We headed on home, and the whole time I couldn't help but think about Skippy and Mr. Dexter. I wondered if me and the Captain could be the same as them. Maybe he could buy a gas station and I could wipe off the counters. Course, there was only two gas stations and none of them was for sale.

Dang that Cannon luck.

The Captain pulled into our driveway.

"I'd better get going. I'll see you again when I come back into town," he said.

I tried to not show how sad I was.

"When do you reckon that will be?" I said.

He shrugged.

"You never know," he said, then he got a funny look on his face like there was a mosquito stuck in his boxers. "I'm sorry. I'm terrible at good-byes. No idea what to say."

I shrugged.

"All Tommy said when he left was that I was to take care of Pa. But that's how Tommy is, always thinking about others."

He chuckled. "Right before he abandoned you two, right?"

"Well, he done that for his country. So it was noble."

His eyes got real stern-like.

"No. You don't abandon your family for anything. There is nothing more important than your family. Nothing."

His words hung in the air like the humidity and it made me about as uncomfortable, too. Then he put his truck into reverse. I hurried and got out.

"*Hasta luego,*" he said, and then he pulled out and drove off. And it felt terrible to see him go.

Pa walked around from the backyard.

"Where'd the Captain head off to?" he said.

"I don't know. He said he had to go meet another old friend."

Pa rubbed the back of his head.

"He did say he was leaving later, but I didn't know he meant right now." He must have just then noticed that I was home. "Why are you here so early?"

"Got sent home for hitting Eddie Gorman."

"Did he deserve it?" he said.

"Yup."

"Then that's fine." He started to head to the backyard. "Go on inside and watch you some TV. I got to focus on what I'm doing."

A shining example of manhood, for sure.

I started to go, but I was worried I'd spend the whole time day-dreaming about the Captain being for me what Mr. Dexter was for Skippy. Didn't want to do that.

"What *are* you doing?" I said, and I followed after him. He stopped walking.

"Oh, you wouldn't be interested," he said. "It's all real boring technical stuff."

"Come on, I want to know. You don't got to dig into the technical mumbo jumbo or nothing. I just want to see why I've been stuck in my room every day for the past week."

He thought about that for a bit, and then he agreed to it. We went around to the shed and he unlocked a padlock that was on the outside. He opened the door and let me go into it. And, I got to admit, it was pretty dadgum impressive.

It was like a whole military radio station, like what I'd seen in all them World War II movies. There was a bunch of wires and boxes with knobs on them. There was a hand-cranking generator nearby, and then there was a big thing that I reckoned was a microphone like Willie's and some headphones, all plugged into another box on a table. There was a chair set up in front of it with Pa's favorite afghan draped over the back. He had a few notebooks piled up on the table and a whole mess of pencils. I tried to see if he had any crossword puzzles, but that must not have been appropriate for radio work.

"Wow, what does it all do?" I said. He raised his eyebrows.

"You sure you want to know?" he said. "It's awful technical."

"Maybe I need to get more technical stuff in my head."

He got a big fat grin on his face at that and started going like I did when I was talking about baseball stats. He showed me the knob where he selected the frequency he'd be using and he explained how at different times of day different frequencies would work better for him. He showed me how he'd get the power going with the generator, and how it'd run for up to an hour after he'd cranked it real good.

"I've gotten to where I can talk to folks pretty far away," he said.

"How far?"

"This morning I was talking to a fella in Japan."

Well, that floored me.

"If you can talk that far with the radio, what do you need that telephone out here for?"

The phone from the living room was sitting on the desk, and the line was running out the door and all the way into the kitchen window.

"Oh, that's the best part," he said. "You see this box here?" He pointed at a little white box that had two holes on top. "I can set the phone in there and the folks I'm talking to on the radio can talk to folks on the phone."

It was one of them moments where I knew I was looking at something I should have been excited about, but I just couldn't muster up the effort. Like when I watched a soccer game.

"That's great, Pa," I said.

"No, it is, it really is," he said. "See, what I'm doing out here is, I'm connecting with soldier boys that ain't got no access to telephones themselves. They tell me their home phone number and I call up their families so they can gab a bit."

His chest swelled up and there was some tears that came to his eyes.

"Considering my own boy is off on a military base, it's sort of like I'm helping Tommy."

I was too focused in on something else to appreciate that.

"Are all them families local?" I said.

He looked confused.

"What you mean?"

"I mean, are all them calls you're making local calls?"

"No, of course not," he said. "Like, the boy this morning, his family was up in Vermont."

"Dadgummit, Pa!" I said. "You mean you're making a mess of long-distance calls? Those cost by the minute. Please tell me you're getting paid or something for all this."

His face stopped looking happy, or proud, or anything else. He only looked mad.

"I'm doing this for God and country," he said.

"All right, then which one of them should I send our phone bill to?"

He tapped his cane on the ground a couple of times, which was usually a sign I was about to get my butt busted.

"Stop your worrying," he said. "We got my disability check coming in, plus money in the bank. And you're making money too. We'll be fine. It's like Jesus said, 'Take therefore no thought for the morrow: for the morrow shall take thought for the things of itself.'"

I hated it when he quoted Scripture at me.

"That was easy for him to say," I said. "His pa could make money out of dirt."

He was done listening.

"Time for you to go inside now," he said. "I got work to do. There's boys out there that actually *wants* to talk to their parents, and with respect, too."

He turned his back to me and I knew the conversation was over. I went inside, frustrated as all get-out, and decided to watch some TV. While I was sitting there, watching *Lassie*, I couldn't shake this feeling I had. Like, as bad as things looked, it was only the tip of the iceberg. Something real bad was blooming, I just knew it. It made my stomach hurt to think of it. I tried to convince myself that it was just all them bills and dollar signs getting to me, but deep down I didn't believe it.

No matter how hard I was trying, it seemed like yesterday was marching closer and closer to blowing up in my face.

CHAPTER FOUR
THE PRICE OF A PONYTAIL

The next couple of weeks was real busy for me. What with Pa doing his thing out there in the shed, it was up to me to take care of all the things there was to care for around the house. I was cooking and cleaning and straightening up the lawn and such. We didn't have nowhere to put all them things Pa'd pulled from the shed, so I made a pile of them over against the house and covered it with a tarp. Then the tarp blew away, so I covered it with my blanket. Then I got cold, so I covered it with Tommy's. Then a stray cat had kittens in the blanket. I reckoned I should wash it before Tommy came back. Or at least shake it out.

Our meals wasn't much more than sandwiches when we ate, 'cause I couldn't hunt for no more than what was asked for by folks in town since we didn't have no deep freeze to hold it in. I also couldn't ask Mrs. Parkins to come help out since I didn't have no time to go do nothing in return. Anyway, I was avoiding Willie like the plague. Eddie'd probably say "like the Black Plague," but I'll just say the plague. Even though "Black Plague" is a pretty dadgum funny joke.

It was a Wednesday and I was on my way to school when I realized I'd been forgetting about getting the mail out of our box every day. Or maybe I'd been avoiding it, 'cause them bills downright terrified me. I got the stack of it out and took it with me. I spent the whole bus ride looking at the Sears summer catalog, thinking about all them things I couldn't afford to get. Like the grill with the blue lid on it that I could use to burn food on. It was twelve dollars. I had to decide if it was worth putting off one of the bills for. Maybe during deer season it would be.

When we got into class, Mrs. Buttke already had the board filled out.

This Day in History: March 29, 1951—The Rosenbergs convicted of espionage.

I wrote that in my book and didn't even have to ask, Mrs. Buttke got right into explaining what the big deal was. The Rosenbergs was an American couple that gave the Russians the secrets they needed to make an atom bomb. And they was real slick, too, but it didn't matter. After a while, they got caught.

She walked around the classroom to Eddie's seat and picked up his science book. She pulled out a girlie magazine he had stashed in there.

"You always get caught," she said, then she went back up to the front to start the prayer.

ISAIAH CAMPBELL

I wrote in my book: *You can't avoid what's coming to you.* I didn't like that too much.

After the pledge, she had us get out our books and I snuck the mail inside of mine so I could have something worth reading. I had to be real careful since she was on the lookout now, but it had to be done. I was responsible for taking care of Pa.

The first few pieces of mail was bills and more sales papers. Then there was an envelope with Pa's disability check in it. I figured I needed to run by the bank after school to drop it off. Maybe I could stop by Mr. Thomassen's first, let him know I'd be late, and ask him to show me how to fill out a deposit slip, since Tommy hadn't gotten around to showing me. I could pop the cap off a beer bottle with a knife, thanks to him, but filling out a deposit slip was a trick I couldn't get.

The next envelope was a notice from the bank. It said we was sixty days past due on our house payment.

Dadgum, I definitely needed to go by the bank.

A pudgy hand reached over my shoulder and snatched the letter out from in front of me.

"Well, look who's sneaking now," Eddie whispered from behind me. Thankfully, Mrs. Buttke was putting sentences up on the board for us all to work on.

"Give it back," I whispered.

"Ooh, looks like y'all are in trouble." He was reading the letter. "Got to get your act together, or you might wind up living in the Colony."

"Shut your mouth," I said, still whispering. A couple of the kids around us was looking at us. "Or I'll shut it for you."

"So? What if I tell everybody what this says? What if I tell Mrs. Buttke that you was sneaking? Socking me in the mouth ain't going to change that."

"I hear whispering," Mrs. Buttke said, her back still turned to us. I waited a couple of seconds, then I wrote a note and slipped it to him.

What do I need to do to keep you quiet?

"Five dollars," he whispered as soon as he read it. Didn't even hesitate. That was when I realized that Eddie was pure evil, through and through.

"How about one dollar?" I said.

"Mrs. Buttke?" he said real loud.

She turned around.

"Yes?"

I turned to look at him too, begging him with my eyes not to say nothing. He got a disgusting grin between his puffy cheeks.

"Nothing, ma'am. I was just wondering if you could hear me."

She muttered something about having ears like a dog and went back to writing on the board. I wrote another note.

If I had five dollars, I'd give it to you, but you already know I ain't got enough money.

He thought about that for a bit, and then he reached into his desk and pulled out a pair of scissors. He scribbled onto a note and gave me the note and the scissors together.

I'll keep quiet for part of a ponytail.

I looked back at him, praying that he wasn't meaning what I thought he was meaning. Then he nodded at Martha Macker's head, which was paying real good attention to her notebook, where she was drawing the prettiest picture of a mountain stream I'd ever seen. Her hair was pulled into a perfect ponytail that hung just below the top of her seat. The thought of cutting even a smidge off of that ponytail made my hands get all sweaty.

"I can't do that," I said.

"Then get ready for the whole class to know your family ain't no better than white trash."

I hated Eddie right then, and I hated myself for what I was about to do. But, taking care of my family was the most important thing, and I had to do what he asked. Still, the thought of cutting Martha's hair nearly made me sick, and that made my head start hurting again. I tried to ignore it so I could focus on being sneaky.

All I had to do was cut off a tiny bit, maybe she wouldn't even notice if I was real careful. Maybe she wouldn't know that the boy behind her who touched her hand every single day when she handed him his homework had mutilated her hair. Maybe this was the kind of story we would laugh about years later, remembering back when Eddie wasn't rotting in prison somewhere and we all had fun with our shenanigans. Maybe.

I leaned forward and reached up with the scissors in my hand. I only needed to cut off an inch or so to say that I cut her ponytail. I tried to go real slow. I had the spot to cut right in mind.

Dadgum, my head was hurting real bad.

I inched the scissors up to her ponytail. Only an inch, that was all I needed.

My head started pounding. I tried to swallow.

Mrs. Buttke put the chalk down. I had to do it before she turned around.

I was going super slow and focusing real hard, and I would have just cut an eighth of an inch off, but then Eddie shoved me. He put his hand right square in the middle of my back and gave me a real hard push. And next thing I knew, my scissors went all the way up to right next to her head and I panicked and closed them. I cut her ponytail all the way up at where the hair thingy was. Right at the back of her head. About a foot and a half of hair fell down onto my desk.

Martha jumped up and shrieked, then she felt for her ponytail and shrieked again. Eddie dove over his desk to grab her hair before she turned around and he dropped the bank letter in my lap. Mrs. Buttke came running back to where we was.

Martha spun and saw me holding them scissors, and she hollered at me like a banshee. It didn't sound nearly as pretty as her normal voice was. I wanted to say something, apologize and explain myself. Maybe even offer to buy her a wig or something. All I could muster out was, "It wasn't me."

She pointed at them scissors in my hand and hollered again. She still hadn't gotten around to making words, just wailing that

　　　　　　　　　ISAIAH CAMPBELL

only comes from a woman who got her hairdo butchered.

I dropped the scissors.

Mrs. Buttke grabbed me by the ear and yanked me up.

"Principal's office! Now!" she yelled, and shoved me toward the door. I tried to grab the mail I had on my desk, but she blocked me. "I said now!" She wrapped her arm around Martha, who had moved from shrieking to crying, and tried to get her to calm down.

And all the while, Eddie Gorman was grinning like a fat possum. It was a good thing for him he wasn't a possum, 'cause I was itching to shoot him.

I got into the principal's office and he didn't waste no time. He spanked me something fierce, almost broke the paddle on my backside. I had to do a lot of fast talking to convince him not to call my pa. I had to use the Dead Ma excuse *and* the Brother Away from Home excuse, with a hint of the Pa's Only Got Half a Lung excuse. But he eventually had mercy and sent me back to class.

Martha was gone for the day. Her ma had come and got her to take her home. I was kind of glad for it, 'cause I didn't want our first real conversation to be me telling her that I'd stolen her ponytail 'cause my pa couldn't pay bills good.

I slid into my seat while Mrs. Buttke was going over math problems. I snuck a peek into my English book. All the mail was still in there, so she must not have seen it. The letter from the bank was in there too. Which was weird, 'cause I didn't put it in there. I double-checked everything to see if anything was missing.

Pa's disability check was gone.

I shot a look back at Eddie, but he was busy doing the math problems in his book.

"Psst," I said. "Did you grab my pa's check?"

"Johnny Cannon," Mrs. Buttke said real loud. "That is enough from you."

I heard Eddie chuckling behind me. I was sure he did something, but I'd have to wait to find out what.

It wasn't until the end of school, when we was all leaving, that I got a chance to grab Eddie and get him alone.

"Where is it?" I said.

"Where's what?" His face looked as innocent as a skunk about to spray you.

"You know what. Where's my pa's disability check?"

"Oh, you mean this?" he said, and then he pulled something out of his pocket. And my stomach turned to lead.

He'd done cut up Pa's check into a line of paper dolls. He made them do a little dance and then he held it out to me.

"You pig-faced weaselly turd." I grabbed it out of his hand. "You've done a lot of low things, but now you're messing around with our money."

"Relax," he said, laughing at me. "Your pa's just got to call the VA office and tell them the check got messed up in the mail. They'll send you a new one. My pa does it all the time, and he cashes the both of them. They don't care."

ISAIAH CAMPBELL

I didn't have no time to argue with him, I had to get to the bank. I kicked him in the shin real good, just so he'd remember to be careful who he was messing with next time, and I took off running. I went back and kicked him one more time for good measure. I guessed we was square.

I ran as fast as I could through town to get to the bank. I didn't know what time they closed, but I figured, since they already had all the money, they probably wasn't too concerned about putting in their eight hours. I was sure relieved when I got there and the door still had the OPEN sign on.

The building was marble and the front doors had golden handles, and it was a good reminder that the folks inside there had money and the folks outside didn't. I went inside and asked for the fella whose name was on the letter we got sent. Turns out he was the bank manager, and they took me to his desk. He looked sort of like a barn owl watching mice scampering around the dirt below.

"Johnny Cannon?" he said after I sat down. "Why didn't your pa come to take care of this?"

"That's a long story, mister," I said. "What do I got to do to pay our house payment?"

He scrunched up his forehead at me and I wondered if he might let out a hoot. He reached into his desk and pulled out a big book, sort of like how the preachers said the Good Lord would on Judgment Day. I had a bad feeling that meant we was damned.

"Well, I don't like involving you, but your brother did tell me you'd be handling payments, so I suppose you'll have to do. Your family is sixty days behind on your mortgage payment. That's two month's payments of one hundred thirty-three dollars. Add the late fee of five dollars, and your total is two hundred seventy-one dollars that we need to delay any action on your house."

"What do you mean, 'action'?" I said.

"Proceeding with foreclosure," he said.

"What's that mean?"

The bell on the door dinged and Mr. Thomassen came into the bank. He walked over to the teller and started doing his business, taking some money out.

"It means that the bank will take ownership of your house," the bank manager said.

That got me right in the gut.

"How's that even possible? My family's owned the house for forever. My ma grew up in the house. I think my grandma even grew up there too."

"Your grandmother took out a loan against the property about six years ago," he said. "She did own the house before that, with no mortgage that I'm aware of."

Six years? That would have been about 1955. It wasn't like anyone in my family to ask for unnecessary help. Or even necessary help, sometimes.

"What day did she do the new mortgage?" I said. He looked in the book.

"July 17, 1955."

I felt my face's color get drained out.

"Me and my ma was in an accident on July 16 of that year. I wonder why Grandma took out the mortgage then."

He looked at some notes he had in the book.

"It says, 'medical expenses, travel expenses, and other expenses.' To Havana, apparently."

"That was where we had the accident at. In Havana."

He looked lost in the conversation.

"So, do you have a plan to get the payment made today?"

I had to get my head back on target. It was hard, 'cause I didn't like thinking that I was the reason Grandma'd needed help from the bank, or that I might be why we was about to lose our house. If I thought I felt guilty over Martha's ponytail, that wasn't nothing compared to this.

"How much is in our bank account? Can't we just make the payment?"

He told me he needed to go check and he got up and headed over to the tellers. Mr. Thomassen had finished what he was doing and he came over to where I was.

"I hope you didn't come by the shop today. I tried to call you and let you know I'm closed for personal business, but your phone was busy almost all day."

"Pa's using it." I tried to put on a smile, but instead it looked like I was constipated.

"Everything okay?" he said to me.

I shrugged. The bank manager came back over.

"You have fifteen dollars," he said. My stomach sank even lower than it had before.

"Oh, wait," I said, "I got my pa's disability check." I fished the cut-up thing out of my pocket and put it on his desk. Both he and Mr. Thomassen stared at it for a second.

"Why did you do that?" the bank manager said.

"I didn't," I said. "A rat fink named Eddie did."

"Well, I can't deposit that."

"We're going to get a new one sent to us. Can't you just take that and I'll bring you the new one?"

"That's not how it works," he said.

"Hold on," Mr. Thomassen said. "How about if I give you the money that your check would cover, and when the new one comes in you can give me the money back?"

I hated the idea of owing anybody anything, especially Mr. Thomassen, since he was my boss and all. It was a step closer to slavery, and I was pretty sure Abe Lincoln had chopped down a cherry tree to end that. I could have been wrong. We wasn't quite there yet in our history class.

"I couldn't do that. It ain't in my blood to take charity."

"It's not charity, it's an interest-free loan."

"Sounds an awful lot like charity," I said.

He thought for a bit.

ISAIAH CAMPBELL

"How about this, what if I charge you interest, but the interest can be in the form of a favor sometime, if I need one."

That was a little bit better.

"Yeah, that'll work," I said, and it seemed like we was all happy for it. "But you make sure you cash in on that favor, or else I'll be the biggest bum in town."

"Don't worry," Mr. Thomassen said. "I never forget who owes me favors." He looked at the total that was on the check and unrolled the cash he'd just withdrew and handed the amount to the manager. He had to leave right after that, but I shook his hand and told him how grateful I was.

"There," I said to the bank manager. "Are we all good now?" I got up to leave.

"Certainly, just let me know how you're going to pay the rest."

I sat back down.

"What do you mean, the rest? Didn't that cover our payment?"

"Mr. Thomassen gave you the amount of the disability check, which was ninety-eight dollars. Add the fifteen still in your account, and you're at one hundred thirteen dollars. Twenty dollars short of one month's payment, and you're down by two. So, how will you be paying the rest?"

It ain't too often that I feel like crying, but that was one of those times. Here I was, trying my hardest to take care of Pa like Tommy'd told me to, and to take care of the house and everything else, and it seemed like I was getting blocked at every turn.

I had to get away so I could think harder and make a better plan.

"I'm going to have to talk to my pa," I said, even though I knew it wouldn't do much good.

"Maybe you should have done that before you came," he said. Folks always liked to remind you what you should have done before you got to where you was, especially if you was a kid. I excused myself and headed home.

The fact that we was soon going to be losing our house and there wasn't nothing I could think of to do about it made me not feel too keen on running home. I dragged my feet, kicking the rocks and cans that was in the street as I went. I did speed up a bit when I passed Martha Macker's house, 'cause I didn't want to get into what was sure to be a long talk with her ma. Plus, I still didn't know how to explain what I did.

Eventually I got to our house. At least it was ours until the bank took it away.

I went in to look for Pa. I knew, after what he'd said before about Jesus and all, that he probably wouldn't think it was worrisome. But I was fearsome worried. He wasn't inside the house, so I reckoned he was out in the shed again. I went out there and pounded on the door.

He opened it with tears in his eyes.

"This soldier-boy in Africa is getting to talk to his baby girl in Texas for the first time," he said, and his grin was as sappy as a fella that was watching a Marilyn Monroe flick. "I tell you, there's some things that you can't put a price tag on."

"Tell that to Grandma," I said. "Did you know she took out a mortgage on this house when Ma died?" He bore some of the blame for that. He should have told her not to do it. She wouldn't have listened and would have done it anyway, but at least he could say he tried.

"Yeah," he said. "Here, do you want to listen in to this call? It's precious."

I punched the door.

"Doggone it, Pa, no! Did you know we ain't paid that mortgage for two months and the bank is aiming to take our house?"

That got him to pay attention better.

"What? How do you know?"

"I went and talked to them," I said.

He sighed. "What did they say?"

"That we need another one hundred sixty dollars or the house is theirs."

He leaned against the doorframe and sighed again. He was good at that.

"Well, I reckon we need a plan then," he said.

"I also borrowed some money from Mr. Thomassen," I said. "So we got to pay that back too."

"Reckon he might be willing to loan us some more?" he said. "I could go ask him, since I'm the grown-up and all."

Yup, Tommy was right. Pa shouldn't be trying to take care of things. I wasn't going to ask nobody else for no help, not if I could help it.

"No. We ain't asking nobody for a personal loan. We got to protect our pride."

He got mad at that.

"'Pride goeth before destruction, and an haughty spirit before a fall,'" he said.

"Oh good, God and country. That's going to fix the problem."

"I'm just saying, sometimes you've *got* to ask for help," he said.

"No, sometimes *you* got to ask for help. Ain't that what being disabled is all about?" I felt bad for that, but somebody had to say it. I think. "I still got the full use of my mind and body, and we ain't going to depend on somebody else's hand to care for us. I promised Tommy I would handle it, and that's what I'm going to do."

"Hey. Pull in your neck, boy." He looked like he wanted to whip me. I didn't care.

"Why should I? I'm doing everything around here, at least everything that's got to do with our house and our money. I reckon I got the right to stick my neck wherever I want to. You're the one who ain't got a job, or the strength to take care of the house, or the brain to figure out the bills, or nothing else. But at least you got this here shed. And God and country. I'll figure out how to make our mortgage."

I didn't give him no time to say nothing back, I just turned and ran off. He didn't try to yell after me. I wouldn't have listened anyway.

I needed to talk to somebody. Usually it would have been Tommy. He wouldn't have let us get into this mess if he was around. But he wasn't around, and I couldn't talk to him to figure nothing out.

Deep down inside, I knew there was only one person I could talk to that wouldn't spill my news to any of the kids at school, and who might have the smarts to figure something out. I hated that it had come to that, but it was the only option. I blamed Pa for every step I took as I went to his house.

I knocked on the Parkinses' door. Mrs. Parkins answered.

"Is Willie home?" I said.

She sent me back to his bedroom. His door was closed and I could hear him inside talking.

"In the darkest hour of the night, in a strange land, our hero awoke in a prison cell watched by a member of the alien race. Mercury did not flinch, nor did he fear, but he rose to his feet and, by the time he found his balance in the lowered gravity of the barren wasteland, he devised a plan to escape."

I knocked on his door.

"Doggone it!" I heard him click off his tape recorder. He came and opened the door.

"Johnny?" He was real surprised to see me.

"What was you doing?" I said.

"Nothing."

"Yes you was. It sounded real interesting, too. What was it?"

He took a second, I reckoned to see if I was being sincere.

"I was recording a radio show. A serial."

"Like the Superman and Batman ones?" I loved those shows, listened to them every Saturday I could. I stepped into his room, even though he hadn't invited me in. He couldn't do much to stop me, what with only one leg working versus my two.

"Yeah. Only I write my own. I was doing Mercury, the alien hunter from outer space. I've also got Captain Harlem, Dark Lantern, and Amazing Woman, the African Princess."

"You like superheroes?" I was surprised we had something in common like that. I looked around his room more now, and I noticed he had a bunch of comic books all over the place. He also had some covers that he'd ripped off and stuck up on his wall.

"Yeah, but I call mine 'SuperNegroes.'" He grinned for the first time since I got there. "They're better than them other ones."

"How are they any better?"

"'Cause they're black. There ain't no black superheroes out there. So, mine are better."

I was about to prove him wrong by listing all the black superheroes there was, but I realized I couldn't think of none. I could think of a few black bad guys, but I didn't reckon that would make my argument.

"Can I talk to you about something?" I had to swallow a couple times to get my pride out of my throat. "I need your advice."

"Johnny Cannon needs the advice of a crippled black kid?" He made like he was dying from shock. "Give me a second to let my pa know that hell's gotten some snow and then we can talk."

I gave him a second, but he didn't go nowhere. I figured he was joking. It wasn't funny.

I closed the door to his room and sat down with him. I told him all about what was happening with our house and the bank and stuff. I also told him about Eddie Gorman and me cutting Martha's ponytail. He laughed at that.

"This ain't funny, Willie," I said.

He started pretending he was her, screaming and hollering over her ponytail. He had a coonskin cap he pulled out, and had a quick funeral for the tail, saying that's what Martha's ma had to do.

That was funny. I felt bad for laughing, but not bad enough to stop. I went on and told him all about our house situation. He wrote them numbers down on a paper and stared at them for a bit.

"So, what do you think you ought to do?" he said.

"I don't know. I got to get one hundred sixty dollars."

He got up and hobbled over to his bed. He picked up his mattress and fished out a few dollar bills. My heart almost stopped when he held it out to me.

"I wish I had more to give you," he said.

Dadgummit. I could honestly say there wouldn't have been a day in the week that I'd do the same thing for him. I didn't use my own money to help out nobody. It took me a bit before I could talk back.

"I ain't taking your money. We ain't a charity case. I just got to figure out a way to make that money, and fast."

"Well, if there's anybody that can make money fast, it's you. I've read about all the richest folks, and they're all as tough as nails. Like you."

"Yeah. I almost wish I'd taken bets on that fight with Russ at our church."

He nodded, and then his eyes got big as baseballs.

"That's it!" he said. "I've got the idea for how you can make the money."

I tried to figure it out before he told me so I wouldn't sound dumb, but it didn't come to my head.

"You'll hold a tournament. A boxing tournament. And you'll take bets from the fellas and from the kids that are watching, and then you'll win all the money."

I had to admit, that was a good idea. Of course, I wasn't too skilled at being a boxer, but if my house was on the line, I reckoned I could channel the rage Pa'd talked about.

"When will we do it?" I said.

"In two weeks. April fourteenth, down at our church. Same spot y'all fought before."

"Which kids will we finagle into it?"

"Whoever thinks they could beat you. I'll bet Russ'll jump in. He's been talking about taking another pop at you. And any white kids you know that might like to fight too."

Well, I had a feeling that was going to go over like a lead balloon.

"You aim to have the white kids *and* the black kids at the same spot, doing the same thing, and competing for the same prize? You might be setting up a bigger fight than you think."

Willie waved that off like it was a shoo-fly.

"Sports has a way of bringing folks together. Trust me, I'm the scientist here, once they're in the thick of it, they'll be fine." He thought for a second. "But, it might be a deterrent to them actually coming. We probably shouldn't tell either side about the other. Let it be a surprise."

Well, if he felt that science was on his side, who was I to argue? If it was the only way, it was the only way.

"If you want some white kids, we can't be having it at your church, or anywhere else in the Colony."

"It's just 'Colony,'" he said. "It ain't 'the' Colony."

"I ain't going to remember that. Anyway, it's got to be somewhere in Cullman."

"Then you won't have any black kids come."

Well, I thought the fight was probably dead right then and there, but that was when I got the only good idea I had that day.

"Mount Vernon Cemetery," I said. "It's at about as equal a distance between Cullman and the Colony," I caught myself, "I mean, Colony. And it's also about the same distance from here. It's about as neutral as it gets."

He liked that idea, and we spent the next hour or so making a list together of names and how we might go about talking them into betting a lot of money against me. Willie said he'd play it up that he was going to record the fight as a sportscaster, which would probably make the kids want to do it even more. He was a lot smarter than I ever thought he was. I stayed down there at their house for dinner and everything, and it felt real good to be in a family again.

Even if it wasn't a white family.

When I went home later, I went out to the shed so I could apologize to Pa for what I'd said before. After all, it was my job to take care of him, not the other way around. It wasn't fair that I'd put all that on him.

But just when I was about to knock on the door, I heard him talking on the phone.

"Let me make sure I've got it down. Number of troops, estimated dates and times, and a preparedness ranking." He stopped and listened. "No, that's fine. I got my son's old Spanish textbooks to help me do that." More listening. "And you're sure it will be here before the date I told you?"

What in tarnation was he talking about?

"No, I just appreciate you giving me this opportunity. It'll help ease Johnny's—"

He must have gotten interrupted, 'cause he stayed quiet for a good spell.

"No, I understand. Can't tell nobody. Loose lips and all. That's fine."

I tiptoed away from the door, 'cause I didn't want him to catch me outside. Besides, all my plans of apologizing and making peace needed a window to fly out of. 'Cause now, while I was busy trying to save our dadgum home, he was busy getting tangled up in another project. A secret one, at that.

A project I was afraid had come straight from the lion's mouth.

CHAPTER FIVE
RAIN NEVER HURT NOBODY

M e and Pa hardly spoke at all for the next couple of weeks. I was too busy, what with planning the big fight and all, and picking up as many odd jobs as I could around town, and doubling my hunting orders and such. Which was both me doing my best to make more money and also me doing my best to stay away from Pa.

Pa was powerful busy too, and he was spending a whole lot more time out there in the shed. He wasn't sleeping very much, either, and it was showing in his forgetfulness. He was leaving notes around the house that I reckoned wasn't meant for my eyes. Notes that said things like

1,000 there. 230 in transit. Eight birds ready. Preparedness equals low.

Another one I found said

Target changed to Playa Girón in Bahía de Cochinos.

And that was how they all was. I couldn't make no sense of

them, partly 'cause I didn't want to try. All I knew was that Pa was staying busy and we was burning through coffee so fast I had to pick up the big can at the store. Willie suggested filling up the old one with some potting soil from his front yard, since there wasn't no way you'd taste any difference, but I reckoned it'd smell different, so I went ahead and spent the money.

That was about the only suggestion Willie made that I didn't listen to. Every step of the way in planning the fight, I did it all just like he told me. I was learning that he was about the smartest kid I'd ever met, black or white. Except maybe for the kid in fifth grade who faked a bladder infection so he could sneak into the school office every thirty minutes and set the clock ahead, that way they rang the bell a whole hour early. That kid was a genius.

But Willie was making a pretty good argument for being even smarter than that. He'd already worked out a bracket for the fight, like the college basketball tournament, and he was going to give folks their slots based on their shoe size. He said that physics showed a fella's foot gave him the leverage to pound another fella's face in, and the bigger the foot, the bigger the pounding.

Considering Tommy'd always said I had water skis for feet, that meant I was going to be ranked number one. And Willie was already working a plan to make sure I made it all the way to the final fight. It was just going to be up to me to win it.

There was one thing I was getting more and more concerned about with the tournament, besides the fact that my face might get refigured. In spite of Willie's brain for science, I had a feeling that getting paired up across the races wasn't going to sit well with either side. But Willie said it might be just what the world needed, a chance for both sides to wallop each other with a referee involved. Of course, we didn't have no referee picked out yet. But he didn't seem too worried about it.

Still, I went along with the plan and invited every boy at school that was big enough to be high on his own boxing skills. I didn't have to talk to very many, either, 'cause word started spreading on its own. Something about the winner winning a fat load of money made the fight a pretty popular talking point for most of the fellas at school. And the fact that we was keeping it as secret as we could from the grown-ups, that helped out too. But the biggest secret of all was that the winner was going to be me. Hopefully.

Me and Willie took to training for the fight every chance we could get. We went down to his pa's church and I'd box the big tree about a dozen times a day. Got to where I almost liked how bloody my knuckles was getting. Then he'd string one of his pa's preaching robes over a branch and wiggle it around, and I'd duck and dodge just like Floyd Patterson. I got to where he couldn't even touch me with a sleeve. I was pretty dadgum impressive, even if I did say so myself.

Every once in a while we'd ride with his pa to go visiting somebody that was a shut-in there in Colony. I'd sit out in the station wagon while they'd drop off a casserole or some groceries at one of them rusted trailers them folks called homes. It was so much different from how things was in Cullman, it was almost like being in a different country. Maybe even more than that. Based off the pictures I'd seen from when we was there, Cuba wasn't nearly as different as Colony.

When we wasn't in Colony and I had time to kill, we spent it in Willie's room and I'd read his comic books while he'd record another radio show about his SuperNegroes. It wasn't really like we was becoming friends or nothing, but we was becoming business partners of a sort. And anyway, I didn't want to spend no time at my house. My cooking wasn't nearly as good as Mrs. Parkins's. She found out how much I liked okra, so she cooked it every time I showed up on their porch. Plus I got to try something called hoppin' John, which was the dadgum tastiest way to make black-eyed peas I'd ever had.

I don't know how the fact that I was hanging out with Willie got found out at school, but the fellas all started acting funny about it. Where they used to didn't ever talk to me, now they would say things to me every time they passed. Mean things, sometimes, or just statements that they was worried about my choice of friends. Which was maybe the worst, 'cause it rang in with the part of my brain that was worried about it too.

The one fella who was really showing me his true colors was Eddie. It hadn't been enough that he'd done what he did to Pa's disability check. I'd sort of gotten over that when the VA office said they'd tack it on to the next month's, provided it didn't get cashed or nothing. So I was ready to forgive and halfway forget.

But Eddie kept making trouble. He started taking it on himself to point out to anyone that would listen that I was so poor I couldn't afford real friends, so I had to settle for the castoffs from the other side of the mountain. He did his best to say it loud in front of Martha, too. She didn't act like she was listening, but that's the sort of thing that girls talk about when they're powdering their noses. Combining that with the ponytail incident, and it was starting to make me think Eddie wanted to ruin my chances with her. I didn't even punch him for that. We wasn't friends enough anymore.

On the day of the race he tapped me on the shoulder at school. I didn't pay him no attention. I figured he had some stupid thing to say about me and Willie, especially since we was talking about the Civil War.

I was busy copying down that day's history fact, which was that Abraham Lincoln had been shot on that same day back in 1865, just about a hundred years before. Mrs. Buttke was telling us the story, all about how the fella, John Wilkes Booth, had busted into the president's box and shot him right behind the ear, and then jumped down onto the stage yelling a Latin phrase.

"'*Sic Semper Tyrannis,*' he yelled," Mrs. Buttke said. "Which means, 'Thus always to tyrants.' Can someone tell me what a tyrant is?"

Martha raised her hand. She'd gotten a new haircut that was

short to her head, and as far as she was concerned, I was twice dead, buried, and rotting in the afterlife. Her ma had tried to talk to Pa a few days after, but he hadn't been available. I thanked the Good Lord.

"A tyrant is a terrible ruler. Like a king," she said.

"That's good," Mrs. Buttke said. "Was President Lincoln a tyrant?"

"No, he freed the slaves."

"And that's one of the biggest reasons Booth thought he *was* a tyrant," Mrs. Buttke said. "Booth couldn't stand the idea of Negroes being citizens with rights. He thought it would take power away from the white landholders in the South."

"That's what happened, ain't it?" one of the fellas that was going to be in my fight said. "Seems like every year the coloreds get another law passed to take more of our rights away."

I heard Eddie ripping up some paper behind me, but I was too interested in the discussion to pay him no attention.

"Are they taking away our rights?" Mrs. Buttke said. "Or are they getting some for themselves?"

"My cousin was a bus driver, but he lost his job during the bus boycott in Montgomery five years ago," he said. "And that was just 'cause they didn't want to give up their seats for folks that needed it. I reckon he lost his rights from that. Maybe Booth was right."

A spit wad hit me in the neck. Eddie leaned up behind me.

"*Sic Semper Tyrannis,*" he said. I turned to look at him.

"What do you want?" I said.

"I heard about your fight. I want in."

I couldn't help but look down at his belly that was squeezed into his desk like an eighty-pound pig squeezing into a two-foot hole.

"You want to enter the fight?"

"Not in it. I want to bet on it." He glanced up at Mrs. Buttke, then reached into his pocket and fished out a wad of bills. "Fifty dollars. Is that too heavy for you?"

My jaw must have bounced off the floor.

"Where'd you get that kind of money?"

"What do you care?" he said. "Can I bet it?"

"Sure, I don't care how much money you lose."

"Or how much I win," he said. "I already know who I'm picking to beat everybody."

"Who?" I said.

He grinned.

"That's my secret. I'll tell you at the fight. Is it right after school?"

"And after I sweep up Mr. Thomassen's shop, yeah. At Mount Vernon Cemetery. Willie Parkins is going to sportscast it."

He got a funny look on his face.

"The Tigger boy that lives on your mountain?"

Him saying that made the hair on my neck stand up.

"That ain't right to say, that word."

"You sound like Mr. Thomassen now," he said. "Speaking of which, could you tell him that I'm offering fifty dollars to your fight?"

"Why? He don't know nothing about it."

"I told him about it. Of course, I lied and said you was having a race, but he told me I better throw some money in," he said, then he sat up real innocent-like and I realized that the whole room was stone quiet.

"Are you two done?" Mrs. Buttke said. I just about died. Martha shot me a look that said she wished I would.

After school I went to Mr. Thomassen's, really hoping that there wouldn't be too much to do so I could get ready for the fight. That wasn't what happened, though. Instead, he had fellas sitting and waiting for his chair, and his floor looked like he'd been cutting and trimming all day long.

"Dadgum, you've been busy," I said as I hurried with the broom.

"There's a big storm coming," he said while he shaved the fella in the chair. "All these farmers are getting their business done in town before it hits."

I hadn't even paid no attention to the clouds outside, but come to think of it, they did look pretty treacherous. I hoped it'd wait till after the fight to start raining.

"Oh, Eddie told me to tell you he's giving fifty dollars to the fi—I mean—to the race."

"Good. Bob will be glad to hear it," he said.

"Why was Bob concerned about Eddie giving me money?"

He took a long swipe through the shaving cream on the fella's face with his straight razor.

"Since I convinced him to be," he said. Then he shot me a smile. "I'm looking out for you, Johnny."

I'd never noticed how skilled he was with a blade until right then. Just as skilled as he was with the piano. Something about that gave me a chill.

"How'd you convince him?"

He took another swipe at the shaving cream.

"Grown-ups talk things out in our own ways. Don't worry yourself about it." He turned to the other side of the fella he was shaving and left me to my own devices. I went back to sweeping and tried real hard not to be freaked out by the nicest fella in town. I was getting paranoid, that was all.

I was almost all done and ready to run out the door when I saw a car pull up that I recognized, though it took me a bit to remember from where. Then I saw the Florida license plates and I realized it was the car that had been at the airfield in Birmingham. The same short guy that had hurried the lady away from Tommy came in.

Mr. Thomassen almost dropped his razor when the fella opened the door.

"Sam Thomassen?" the short guy said, his voice about five times lower than anyone I'd ever heard before. He didn't bother taking off his sunglasses, either, even though the sky was dark enough that you wouldn't hurt your eyes at all.

"Can I help you?" Mr. Thomassen said.

"I'm looking for someone. I don't have a name, but he is an amateur radio enthusiast. May have just come into a lot of money as well."

Mr. Thomassen shook his head. Everyone else in the room was quiet. Like I said, we don't cotton to strangers in Cullman.

"I haven't heard of anyone like that," he said.

"I need you to think. Anyone at all. Recently acquired radio equipment, perhaps? Spending a lot of time on his own."

"That could describe just about anybody that lives in the hills and valleys around this town. I couldn't begin to guess," Mr. Thomassen said, and went back to shaving. "Why do you think they're here, anyway?"

The man pulled his wallet out and showed a badge that said "CIA" on it.

"I have my reasons," he said.

Mr. Thomassen stopped shaving and wiped off his hands. He took the badge and looked closer at it.

"What's your name again?"

The short guy told him, but I honestly don't remember it. I just called him Short-Guy in my head from then on.

Short-Guy looked over at me.

"What about you? You heard of anyone like that?" he said.

Now, I'm pretty sure it's against the law to lie to a CIA agent. Pretty sure it's even more against the law to cover up the fact that the fella he was looking for was my own pa. Except for the coming-into-money part. We was still as poor as Job's turkey. So maybe it wasn't Pa. I worked off of that.

"No sir, I ain't seen nobody like that."

He stared at me for a few seconds, like he was trying to give me a telepathic lie detector test, and then he took his badge back from Mr. Thomassen.

"If you hear anything about anyone like that, would you give me a call?" He gave him a business card.

Mr. Thomassen put the business card next to his cash register. The agent left in the car, and I wondered how in tarnation he was connected to the lady that had given Tommy the envelope. I finished sweeping up and decided to put it out of my brain so I could focus on the fight.

By the time I left Mr. Thomassen's shop, the sky was already thundering and getting dark. It was mighty hot, too, and muggy as a locker room. I hurried and made the trek out to Mount Vernon Cemetery and met Willie. He was looking at the clouds too.

"I hope we can get the fight in today," he said.

"We will as long as all them fellas get here on time," I said.

He got his tape recorder set up so he could do the sportscasting and I started working on roping off a square for the boxing ring. We was in there with all them headstones and dead bodies, and I was trying real hard to not think about them grave folk casting their own bets on who was going to win.

"I sure hope the spirits don't get too tore up over us being here," I said.

"You talking about ghosts?" he said. "There ain't no such thing."

I was surprised by that.

"You *don't* believe in ghosts? I thought all—" I stopped myself.

"You thought all black kids was scared of ghosts? Heck no. Science, Johnny. I believe in science."

I didn't say no more about it, but I wasn't as sold on science as he was, so I kept getting the creepy crawlies.

The first of the boxers to come around was some of Willie's friends, including Russ. He didn't say too much to me, but they all went over and started joking around with Willie.

"When we going to get the fight started?" Russ asked. "I've been practicing on a car tire for three days." A car tire. That was a good idea.

Willie told him we was waiting on a few more people to come. Didn't tell them they was white people. I hoped he was right that it wouldn't be a big deal.

The clouds was getting even darker, and I started smelling the rain coming. I was beginning to think none of the fellas from my school was going to show up. The air went from hot to cold, just like it does when you are about to get haunted real good. I looked around for any graves getting busted or any headless white ghosts coming walking through the yard. Instead, all them white boys from my school showed up in a group.

And I wished they hadn't.

As soon as they all got there and they saw Willie's friends, and as soon as Willie's friends saw them, it was plain as day that I'd been right to be concerned. They all got real quiet and just stared at each other for a few seconds. Eddie was leading the fellas from my school. He came over and spoke to me extra loud to make sure all Willie's friends could hear it.

"It ain't often you see spooks in a cemetery. Are the Tiggers leaving or staying?"

Before I could tell him to keep quiet and not say that word, especially when they was right there, Russ came over and stood up real tall over Eddie.

"I'm going to give you a chance to rethink that question," he said.

"Back off, Sambo," Eddie said. "We were invited here for a boxing match. So y'all need to find another place to loiter at."

"We're here for a match too," Russ said, then he gave me a look. "The same match? You invited them to our match?"

"Well, it's really all of our boxing match," I said, and I could tell that didn't sit too well.

Willie came over to try to clear the air. Which was good, 'cause I had a feeling it was going to be filled with raindrops pretty soon.

"We invited all of y'all to fight each other." When he put it like that, it didn't sound as fun. "There ain't no reason it should turn into something about color, is there?"

Eddie looked at Willie, then back at his friends.

"Well, this one's a cripple. You know what they would have done with a crippled Tigger back in the good old days?" he said.

Russ didn't give him no time to finish his joke. He shoved him into his friends.

"Shut your mouth and go home," he said.

Eddie brushed himself off all over his porky little body.

"Did you just put your hands on me, boy?" he said.

"I'll put more than that on you if you don't get out of here," Russ said. "Don't much matter to me which white boy I wallop today."

The fella that was mad about his cousin losing a job five years before stepped in between them.

"You're all the same, ain't you?" he said to Russ.

"If you mean that we can all whip your—"

Thunder clapped real loud and drowned out the end of Russ's sentence, but I think we got the idea. I hurried and tried to push them away from each other. I probably shoved them both harder than I should have. Russ lost his balance and crashed into a real big tombstone and cracked it a little. The other fella tripped over a root and went rolling down the hill into a fence.

And that was all the spark them two groups needed to start fighting. And not in a civilized manner that would win me some money, either. Nope, this was more like Gettysburg all over again.

They was swinging and shoving and swearing at each other,

kicking and scratching and acting like they meant to do some real damage. Some of the white fellas saw Willie's tape recorder and grabbed it, talking like they was going to smash it. I ran over and punched one of them in the ear, then took the tape recorder and put it under a broken gravestone.

One of the fellas had knocked Willie down and was kicking him. Russ ran over and swung a stick at him to get him off. The fella grabbed Willie's crutch and swung it back at Russ.

More thunder clapped and I felt a raindrop.

The fella I'd knocked into the fence ran back up the hill, and he was winded. Which meant he couldn't do much damage with his fists. He picked up a rock and tried to throw it at one of Willie's friends. He ducked and the rock busted the wing off an angel statue.

The rain started pouring down, and the wind started to pick up. I looked for Eddie, but he'd already run off. I had to hand it to him, at least he knew he wasn't no good for a fight.

I got in there and threw a few solid punches to try and make a good point that civilized folk shouldn't be fighting, and I took a couple myself, though I wasn't completely sure what point those ones was supposed to make. Willie got his crutch back and went looking for his tape recorder. I didn't have no time to tell him where I'd stuck it, 'cause my mouth was getting battered at the moment.

One of the fellas from my school was on Russ's back, choking him. I went and pulled him off and we went rolling halfway down the hill. A big stream of mud had already started flowing, and we both got covered in it. I bit his shoulder to get him off of me, and he went running. He didn't stop at the top of the hill but kept going from there.

I'd gotten a big glob of mud in my ears and couldn't hear nothing, though I wasn't really paying no attention. I was too busy dodging a tree branch one of the other fellas from my class was swinging at me. Knocked my legs out from under me and then was going to bash my head in, I reckon. But then Russ clobbered him and helped me up. He said something to me, and that's when I realized I wasn't hearing. I cleaned out my ears and finally heard the sheriff's car coming up on us real fast.

I was sure he was there to run us all in or something, and I think any other day he would have been, but instead he was yelling at us all to get on home. He said the storm that was coming our way was a real bad one, and if we got caught in it we might get hurt from debris. I didn't bother to point out that we was already hurt from debris we'd made ourselves. Didn't seem like the time for jokes.

All the other boys had already taken off to go back up to Cullman and Colony, and it just left me and Willie. One look at Willie's face told me that he was hurting real bad, so I didn't tell him that I'd seen this whole problem coming but hadn't said nothing 'cause he was so smart. Which really made it all his fault, 'cause I would have said something if he hadn't been so smart.

The sheriff gave us both rides up the mountain to our houses, and Willie didn't say nothing the whole way. I reckoned he was trying to figure out how he was going to explain the bruises and bleeding he had going on his face and, I was pretty sure, around his ribs. Or maybe he was worried what would happen when his pa found out we'd caused the biggest race fight in Cullman County history. There'd been a bigger fight once, but that was called the Civil War. Which was about states' rights. And maybe a little about race.

After a bit in the car, I leaned over and asked Willie what was wrong.

"I left my tape recorder at the cemetery," he said, looking out at the rain that was starting to come down real hard.

"Maybe it'll be all right," I said. "I covered it up with a gravestone."

"If it gets wet, it's ruined," he said. "Ain't no gravestone going to change that."

There wasn't no consoling him on it, and when the sheriff dropped him off at his house, Willie got out and went in as fast as a kid with a crutch can go. I felt real bad for him, but there really wasn't nothing I could do.

The sheriff drove over the mountain and let me out at my house. I peeked around back before I went in and saw that Pa was in the shed. I went inside the house.

It took me a few seconds to realize that the phone was ringing. I almost went for the one in the living room, then I remembered that it was outside, so I ran into the kitchen and picked up the set in there. Willie whispered at me.

"I'm going back to get my tape recorder."

"How you going to do that?" I said. "Somebody going to take you?"

"I was hoping you would," he said.

I couldn't help but laugh at him.

"You want me to carry you or something? In the rain? I ain't up to that."

"You told me that you drive your pa's truck when you go fishing, didn't you? Drive me back to the cemetery."

"I don't care if you don't believe in them or not, I ain't going back to see them ghosts trying to clean up their resting places after we done busted them up. They ain't going to be happy about that for nothing. Plus I don't never drive in the rain," I said.

"Johnny, please," he said, and it sounded like he was about an ant's tail away from crying. "I can't lose my tape recorder. There ain't no way I could buy another one. I'm begging you."

Now, there's a lot of things I've been okay with in my life, but making a cripple beg wasn't one of them. I agreed and hung up. I went to the washroom where Pa kept the truck keys hanging on a hook and took them, then I went out and started the engine.

It was raining so hard I almost had to turn the wiper speed all the way up just to see in front of me. I put it in reverse and looked over my shoulder. Why didn't they put wipers on the rear windows? Plus there wasn't no headlights back there. Still, thanks to the fact that I knew our driveway about like I knew my own room, I was able to inch out onto the road and go down to Willie's house.

He came out of the back and got in.

"My ma thinks I'm in the bathroom," he said. "Let's make this fast."

"She's going to think you're unloading a week's worth of meals, even if we go as fast as a delivery truck. And I ain't going that fast," I said.

"I can always apologize to her later," he said. "I need to get my tape recorder."

There wasn't no arguing with him, and I was already in too deep to get out, so I put the truck into gear and started on down the road. The rain was falling even thicker than before, and I wasn't as used to driving on the road to the cemetery as I was going out to the lake, so I had to move slower than I'd planned.

There was a good number of times that I had to stop as we was going, 'cause I was afraid the sheriff was coming up behind us. But it was usually just somebody trying to get home in the rain, and after a while we got to the gate that said MOUNT VERNON CEMETERY. By the time we got there, it was coming down like a cow peeing on a flat rock, and there wasn't no way Willie could get out and run to get his tape recorder, if it wasn't washed away or something, so I jumped out and ran back to where I'd stuck it under the gravestone.

It took me a bit to find it 'cause it had slid down the hill in the mud, but the stone had slid with it and wedged onto some rocks so it was somewhat protected from the water. I was trying real hard to not look around, 'cause the last thing you want to do is make eye contact with a ghost. I wrapped the tape recorder in my shirt, though I don't really know what good it did, and I slopped through the mud back to the truck. I could have sworn I stepped on a few arm bones and such on my way, but I said a prayer every time, so I don't reckon they'll be able to come into my dreams or nothing.

As soon as I got into the truck, Willie grabbed the tape recorder and started wiping all the gunk off of it. I got us turned around and headed back home.

"It don't look like the inside got too mucked up," he said. "It might still work."

I didn't say nothing back. I couldn't, I was too busy focusing on the road in front of us through the window that was starting to get all fogged up, I reckoned 'cause the ghosts was breathing on it. I was trying to figure out how to drive without getting the both of us killed. All the wipers was doing was tossing the water into the air off the sides of the windshield, but they wasn't clearing enough for me to see nothing. And the wind was starting to blow too, so hard that I thought we was going to get knocked off the road.

We got away from the cemetery and was on the road that would take us up to our houses, and just when we was a little bit out, I heard something that made me want to go faster. It was the sound of a thousand spirits, howling in torment over the condition of their souls.

Then I realized it wasn't. It was the tornado sirens going off.

They was wailing away out there, letting us know that we was the two biggest idiots in all of Cullman County. Them, combined with the pounding rain and the rumbling thunder, filled my ears so bad that I couldn't hear too much of anything.

I was trying to get us to our mountain as fast as we could go, and I thought I was doing a pretty good job considering I couldn't see or hear anything. But then, just when we was coming around the bend of the road that had the biggest overhanging branches, Willie started screaming bloody murder. The reason he did that was 'cause there was a pair of headlights that was coming straight at our windshield.

I slammed on the brakes and tried to swerve, and when I did that we slid and skidded all the way to the other side of the road. I jerked the steering wheel in the other direction, and that was all the truck needed to spin on out of control and take us over the edge of the road and down into a great big ditch that was lined with trees. We hit one of them trees real hard.

I was about to tell Willie he could stop screaming, but then I realized that I was screaming just as much as him. Once we both calmed down, I told him to open his door. He couldn't. It was wedged against the tree we'd slammed into. I tried to open mine, but then the lightning cracked and the wind blew so hard it shook the truck. A big limb from the tree got knocked off and it crashed down right onto the truck, then down against my door. I couldn't get mine open either.

"Oh my gosh, we're stuck. We can't get out," I said. "What if we can't never get out? What if we die out here?"

"Open the window," Willie said. "You could probably climb out and go get help."

"Oh, right." I rolled down the window and water poured in over us like we had jumped into the shower. I rolled it back up. "Maybe we could wait till the rain calms down."

He nodded, and then the lightning cracked and the thunder made the truck shake a bit. Another bad gust of wind came through and the tree right in front of us blew over. Some of its branches landed on the hood.

"Of course, I guess we could die out here," he said.

That got us both to being quiet, and we listened to the raindrops like they was bullets knocking on the lid of the truck, trying to get in at us. Then we both realized that it wasn't rain we was hearing, it was hail. The tornado sirens blaring off in town made the both of us realize this was probably the worst storm either one of us had ever been in.

"I took five dollars out of the collection plate at church," he said all of a sudden. "Never gave it back, neither."

"Why'd you just tell me that?" I said.

"'Cause, if we're going to die, I don't want there to be no secrets I'm holding on to when I get to Heaven."

The thunder rumbled again and them tornado sirens almost seemed like they was getting louder.

"My only good math grade last school year was 'cause I copied Martha Macker's test paper," I said. I wasn't sure how much I believed what Willie was saying about Heaven, but I didn't want to risk getting kicked out over a math grade.

"I ripped the arms off my sister's doll last year and told her the white kid that lived over the mountain did it," he said.

"Wait, that's me."

"Oh, yeah," he said, grinning. "That might be why she don't like you."

That about did it for his secrets, I guess, 'cause he acted like he was ready to meet his maker. But I still had one thing that was weighing on my conscience.

"I lied to a CIA agent today," I said.

"A what?"

"A CIA agent. He was looking for a fella that's doing radio stuff, and I said I'd never seen nobody like that. But really, I have," I said, and then I went ahead and told him about what Pa was doing. I got so caught up in spilling the beans, I spilled about Tommy not being in Korea, too.

"Wow," he said. "That's a lot more than you probably needed to share."

That made me feel really stupid. I tried to change the subject.

"Do them sirens sound like they're getting louder to you?"

He listened for a bit.

"Yeah, they do," he said. "That's weird."

Then we heard brakes and an engine. I rolled my window down again and we both took to hollering in spite of the gush of water that was falling in on us. We saw a flashlight and heard feet working their way into the ditch we was in. After a few seconds, the sheriff came over to us, covered in a rain poncho, and he shined his light in at us.

"Johnny Cannon? Didn't I already take you home once tonight?" he said.

"Yes sir," I said. "But that time it was from the cemetery. So it's sort of different this time."

He didn't really buy that, but he still rescued us from the ditch. He pulled both me and Willie out of the window and helped us get into his cop car. He said he'd have the fellas at Gorman's Auto Shop, the second of three businesses in Cullman that Bob Gorman owned, come tow our truck up to the house. Provided it was still there the next day.

He drove us through the rain to Willie's house, and he didn't let Willie go back in the way he'd snuck out. Instead, he walked him on up to his front door and told Mrs. Parkins all about what we did and how he got us out of the truck in the ditch. And he didn't even finish telling the story before she was grabbing Willie by the ear and dragging him into the house for what was guaranteed to be the finest whooping he'd ever gotten in his life.

The sheriff drove me up to my house, and the whole way I was dreading the can of butt whooping I was going to get from Pa's strap. I hadn't been lit up real good in a while, and I was sure Pa would cash in his rain check for all them missing beatings with this one.

We hurried to the porch and the sheriff banged on our door. There wasn't no answer. He banged some more. Still no answer.

"Is your pa home?"

"Yeah, but he's a heavy sleeper," I said, then I had an idea. "You want me to have him give you a call tomorrow?"

The lightning flashed and the tornado sirens kept sounding.

"Yeah," he said. "That'll do. Just get somewhere safe as soon as possible." And he ran on back to his car.

I went inside and there wasn't no sign of Pa. I looked out the back window and could see a light coming from his shed. I didn't know what was worse, having him yell and scream at me for what I did or having him not even notice that I was gone. I went on up to bed before I could make up my mind, which was not the safest place to be if a tornado was going to hit. But I didn't much feel like being safe. Getting blown away by a cyclone seemed better than dealing with the mess I was in. Anyway, my head was hurting too bad for me to even think of staying awake.

A few hours later, thunder cracked real loud and I woke back up. I could see that the rain had actually died down outside. It was just a drizzle. Then my stomach started rumbling and I realized I needed a real good midnight snack.

I went downstairs to the kitchen and I saw the shed outside was still lit up. It dawned on me that maybe I ought to go check on Pa, what with the storm and all. I went out there to the shed, and when I got right outside the door, I heard a voice. But not one speaking in English. I opened the door, and the voice was barking and yelling and carrying on. Yet, there Pa sat in his chair, fast asleep like he didn't hear the voice at all.

The notebook that was in Pa's lap had a whole mess of Spanish copied from Tommy's textbooks in it, with the English translation written under it. And when I looked at it, I could figure out what the voice was saying based off the phrases written down.

"*¿La invasión comenzará mañana?*" the voice said, and what it was in English was, "The invasion starts tomorrow?"

That got me a bit worried, and I was hoping to hear what whoever the voice was talking to was going to say, but nobody answered. The voice spoke again.

"*¡WX5RJ! Habla conmigo. ¿La invasión comenzará mañana?*" I didn't get a chance to look that up, 'cause Pa stirred at that. I ducked behind the door so he wouldn't see me. He picked up the microphone in front of him, looked at the notebook, and then he spoke into it.

"*Lo siento,*" he said in the worst Southern-tinted Spanish I'd ever heard. *"Sí, la invasión comienza en la mañana. Primera parte de la Operación Pluto."*

I couldn't help but notice that last part. It sounded like he said "Operation Pluto." Who the heck was Pa talking to?

"Gracias, WX5RJ. Su cheque llegará pronto," the voice said. Pa looked at his notebook again.

"Gracias," he said. And then they didn't talk no more.

Pa stretched real good and got up off his chair with a smile on his face the size of Texas. He grabbed an umbrella he had by him and stepped out into the drizzle, looking like a man that just made a million bucks.

I didn't know what Operation Pluto was, but I had a real bad feeling that my Pa was telling folks that wasn't American about it. I knew I shouldn't jump to conclusions, but Pa helping out un-Americans sounded pretty bad to me. Even if it did mean he got a cool name like WX5RJ.

Maybe losing our house wasn't the worst thing we had coming.

Dadgum, taking care of Pa was the hardest job I'd ever had.

CHAPTER SIX
DIGGING THROUGH RUBBLE

The next morning I woke up to the sound of a bird twittering outside my window. It sounded like he was laughing at something, though I wasn't sure what. Maybe 'cause he'd had the sense to get out of the rain and I hadn't. Dumb bird.

I shut my window and went downstairs. Right off, I was struck by three things that was real unusual. The first was Pa sitting at the table, reading the paper. He had spent every waking moment out in that shed for the last few weeks, ever since our talk about the money problems. Now, here he was, eating a bowl of cereal and sipping his coffee while he read the *Cullman Reporter*.

He had it folded over, and the part that was showing to me was the main headline, which was the second real unusual thing that struck me. The headline said TORNADO DESTROYS HALF OF TOWN. The part that I could read, which was difficult since it was upside down, said that a tornado had run right through Cullman, on the side of town opposite us. It mentioned that the airstrip had been hit real bad, as well as the church and a few houses and such. Turns out we'd been lucky.

The third thing that struck me was the story on the side Pa was reading, which I saw when I went around him to get me some orange juice. It wasn't a main story, it was buried down close to the bottom. But its headline said, CUBAN AIRFIELDS ATTACKED. Underneath, it told that a whole mess of planes and such had been damaged at some airfields in the middle of Cuba, and that the Cuban government, mainly Fidel Castro, was claiming the Americans was involved. But our government was saying we wasn't.

There was a picture with the article of the damaged planes and such, and Pa was staring at it like it was the most important thing in the paper. I got my orange juice, poured some cereal, and sat down next to him.

"What's that you're looking at?" I said.

He blinked and put the paper down.

"Nothing. Just the picture from Cuba. All that destruction brings back memories from the war." He sighed and took a bite of his cereal. "I sure am glad Tommy's safe in Korea."

Except he wasn't. He was in Nicaragua. But that lady back at the Birmingham airstrip was from Cuba. Weird.

"The article there says that the US wasn't involved," I said after I did some reading. "Reckon it's true?"

"No, we weren't involved," he said real quick. "This is just a bunch of Cubans trying to overthrow their government."

"Wow, it ain't much of an uprising then. One airstrip."

"Oh, they're not done," he said.

"How do you know?"

He looked nervous from that question and didn't answer me. He put the paper away and started rinsing out his bowl. Then he saw the trail of mud coming from outside that I'd left from the night before.

"What's that? Was you out in that storm last night?"

I swallowed real hard. Had to come up with a good story.

"I was sleepwalking." Nope, that wasn't a good story. "I walked halfway to the Parkinses'."

"And the rain didn't wake you up?"

"I—" I had to get better at my story-making skills. "—had me an umbrella."

He set the bowl down in the sink and gave me a full-on stare.

"So, while you was sleeping you had the sense of mind to grab you an umbrella," he said, and looked at the footprints again. "And your boots, but you can't never remember to put the milk away?"

I shrugged. "Maybe I ought to make my breakfast when I'm asleep."

He chuckled and I prayed something would come along and change the subject for us.

There was a knock at the door and my prayer was answered. Pa went to see who it was, and I heard Bob Gorman's voice.

"Sheriff had me bring your truck up."

Oh, dadgum it, I should have said I was sleep-driving, too.

"Johnny!" Pa yelled. Here it came. I went in there to where he and Bob was.

"Yes sir?" I said.

"What happened to my truck?" he said, and I looked out at the tore-up hunk of metal that was attached to the back of Bob's tow truck. The top of the cab was all banged in from the big tree branch, the windshield was busted and cracked all over, and it was covered from top to bottom with mud.

"Got it stuck in a ditch," I said. Couldn't get no more honest than that.

"When?"

Bob answered for me.

"Sheriff said it was last night, right in the worst part of the storm. He picked up Johnny about a quarter mile from the bottom of this mountain. Good news is it still runs."

"What was you doing driving all by yourself in the middle of a storm like that?"

I wasn't by myself, and I waited for Bob to tell him that, but he didn't. I wondered if the sheriff had kept that part back, since being out with Willie would be about five hundred times worse than being alone.

"I came home and you wasn't here," I said. "I drove in to see if you was in town." That wasn't the honest answer that was probably necessary, but since I could tell the paddle was coming soon in my future, I felt the need to preserve my backside as much as possible.

His face flinched like my words had slapped him across it. He looked at the truck again, then changed the subject for a spell to keep Bob out of our family business. He turned to talk to Bob.

"Why didn't you have one of the boys at the shop bring that up? Ain't you got work at the airstrip to do?" he said.

Bob let out a groan.

"You haven't read the paper yet? The tornado last night tore up the airfield and wrecked my planes. Half the town is down right now, so we're all pitching in to help whoever we can."

"Everyone's helping out?"

"Everyone but you two, so far," he said. Pa nodded.

"All right, reckon you can give us a ride into town? I can't do much, but my boy here is strong and can do the work for both of us."

Bob reached out and grabbed his hand and shook it something fierce.

"That's mighty white of you, Pete," he said. "There's some folks that are digging through their homes and trying to salvage their personals. And the church is leveled too."

"Which one?"

"*The* church."

"We got ties with two churches," I said. Bob scowled at me.

"Of course the Colony and the church that's in it didn't get hit. Those savages probably cast some voodoo magic to keep the storm away or something. But the real church was destroyed."

"Let's get going, then," Pa said as he grabbed his hat. We both went out and hopped in the tow truck. Bob unhooked our poor pickup and then we headed into town.

It was something, driving through the town that just a day before hadn't had no litter or nothing on Third Street, the main street that went down the middle of town. Now it looked like the whole town had been a bunch of Tinkertoys that some bratty kid had come and kicked over for a temper tantrum. Broken buildings and trash was everywhere, glass was all over everything, along with downed power lines and overturned cars. Folks was out there working together trying to make piles of trash and digging what they could out of what was left of the town. Some folks was picking up their pictures and books off their front lawns, crying as they stared at what was left of what they had.

We drove past the church most of the town was members of, or at least where it used to be. It was flat to the ground, with a few pews stuck on top of cars and the steeple lying in the middle of the street. Bob slowed down until he saw that there was folks from Colony and Reverend Parkins's church out there helping the white folk get their church cleaned up. He sped up to pass on by.

We got out to Bob's airfield, and it was tore up pretty bad too. Not as bad as the town, but since the only folk out there to clean up was us and Bob's family, plus a couple of the fellas that worked at his auto shop, it was bad enough. The top of his hangar was ripped off, and all three of Bob's planes was turned over on top of themselves with their tails plucked like chickens and flung out into the field. I reckoned his air show was done.

All the fellas that was out there working on cleaning up was on one of the planes trying to turn it back over. I ran over and hopped in line next to Eddie, who wasn't really doing no lifting but was acting like it so he didn't get yelled at by nobody. I put my shoulder into it and the plane started to move.

"It's a shame we don't have some of your friends from the Colony out here to help turn this thing over, ain't it?" Eddie said. "This is just the kind of work they're made for."

"Shut up or I'll let this fall on your head," I said.

He looked at my back pocket, where I'd rolled up the paper and stuck it.

"When did they come take pictures of these busted airplanes?" he said. He grabbed the paper out and looked at the picture more closer. "Oh, never mind, that's down there in Cuba," he said, and gave it back to me. "Say, when you going to reschedule that fight?"

"Wouldn't mind giving a preview right now, if you'd like," I said, and that shut him up.

I looked at the picture he was talking about. Just like that I realized we was connected, us and them folks in Cuba. They was probably going through the exact same cleanup we was. Sure, their disaster was made by men and ours was made by God Himself, but I didn't know which one was worse. It was one thing to think that some angry people was gunning for you, but to think that the Almighty had an itchy trigger finger was pretty darn scary.

We got the plane turned over and started working on the next couple, when a white Cadillac pulled onto the strip. Mr. Thomassen was driving it and he rolled down his window.

"There's a lot more work that needs to be done in town," he said. "Your muscles could be better served there."

"Who cares *where* we're cleaning?" Eddie yelled at him. "As long as we *are* cleaning?"

Bob reached over and hit him on the back of his head.

"Pay respect," he said, then he said louder to Mr. Thomassen, "What if I send three of these boys to help?" He motioned for me, Eddie, and one of the fellas from his auto shop to get in the car.

"Not Eddie," Mr. Thomassen said. "He'll do more good here."

I tried to hide my laugh and got into the passenger seat of the Cadillac. Two of the fellas from the shop got in the back and we headed into town. Mr. Thomassen drove us over to the church and we all got out to start digging through rubble. It seemed like most everybody had showed up, from Cullman *and* Colony, to help out. Even Willie was there. I went over and started working next to him.

He checked to make sure nobody was listening to us.

"I think the government is behind it," he said.

"What in tarnation are you saying?" I said. "The government can't make no tornadoes."

"No, the thing that happened in Cuba, in the newspaper you got. I'll bet it's us messing with Castro's people."

I thought about that while I carried some pieces of the wall over to the pile of trash. When we was alone again, I told him how stupid his idea was.

"Why would our government do that?"

"Cuba's a pretty good target these days."

It was funny, hearing him talk about Cuba like that. Whenever I thought of Cuba, I didn't think of all the trouble they'd been having with turning Commie or none of that stuff. I reckoned things was different when you was talking about a place you used to live.

"I was in Cuba for a while," I said. His eyes got real big.

"You was? In Havana?"

"No, Guantánamo Bay, the Navy base we got down there. Lived there all the way up until my ma died, when I was six. *That* happened in Havana, in a car crash that I was in. Almost died, too. It's how I got my scars."

I pointed at my neck. He looked at it like he hadn't never seen it, then he patted his bum leg.

"At least yours don't keep you out of sports," he said.

"Yeah, but folks sure feel uncomfortable with their eyes. They ain't sure if they should stare or look the other way. It's kind of like being—"

"Black?" he said.

I nodded. I was actually going to say it was like being a purple dwarf driving a spotted elephant on the wrong side of the street, but his answer sounded less strange.

We talked off and on about having scars and about Cuba while we worked for the rest of the day, stopping only to eat some sandwiches under the only tree that was still standing. That was when I realized that folks was keeping their distance from us, black and white folks alike. Took a quick glance around, we was the only two fellas of different colors that was working together. Everyone else was grouped either Cullman white folk with white folk or Colony black folk with black folk. People pointed at us and whispered to each other, and I could only imagine what they was saying. I tried to ignore them, but deep down I knew. We was breaking all the rules in Cullman County. Well, except for the rule about not spitting on the sidewalks. We was spitting, to be sure, and there wasn't no telling where the sidewalks was, but we was real careful to only spit on the debris that was on top of the sidewalks.

Folks was trickling away, and I tried my best to convince myself it wasn't 'cause we was making them uncomfortable. Mr. Thomassen told us they was digging people out of houses and such, and you never knew what you might see coming out of the rubble. After a while, it was only me and Willie at the church working. We didn't come anywhere near getting all the mess cleaned up, but the sun started going down so most of the folks agreed to meet back there the next day.

When Pa and I got home, I was half expecting him to chew me out once Bob left. Instead he pulled me into a hug.

"I'm so glad you was safe last night," he said.

"You ain't mad at me for going off on my own?"

"I reckon I've forced you to do that a lot lately," he said. "But that's all changing now. Starting with our money problems. I got some money coming our way, should be in any day this week. And it'll cover our mortgage, believe you me."

I thought about saying something to him about how he got the money, and asking him who it was coming from. But if I wanted him to give me an honest answer, I might should give him one myself. Not going to happen. Anyway, it was probably too late. I just hoped that CIA fella didn't catch wind of it.

I had a hard time sleeping that night, at first from the noise inside my head from all the worries I had going on. But around midnight or after, I was put off by a mess of noise coming from our backyard. I reckoned it was a raccoon or something trying to get at our trash, so I tried to ignore it. Even raccoons have to eat.

But then I heard the sound of something heavy hitting something soft and a swear word barking at the hard thing that done hit the soft thing, and I knew it wasn't no raccoon. Or, if it was, it was a talking one and I was going to be rich. Unless it was shy, like that frog in them cartoons that only sang when nobody was looking. He'd only pull that crap on me once and he'd have been at the end of a fishing hook singing "Maple Leaf Rag" to a big-mouth bass.

And don't get me started on what I'd do to that rabbit.

I got up and went out to check on the noise. Pa was dragging stuff out of the shed and putting our old stuff back in it. He didn't notice me, 'cause he was trying to drag the deep freezer all by himself.

"What you doing?" I said.

He jumped up in the air like a burglar that got spotted by a cop.

"Dadgummit," he said. "You about killed me. Why ain't you in bed?"

"Why ain't you?"

He laughed at that.

"Well, I reckon that's fair. I couldn't sleep with this hanging over me, and since we're going to help out again with the cleanup tomorrow, I wanted to get this done tonight."

"You're getting rid of all that stuff you bought?" That'd make hiding it from Short-Guy easier. Maybe we could put it all in Eddie's closet. Kill two birds with one pile of radio junk.

"I reckon I'm done with it," he said. "About time I put more work in and take some off you. So, go on back to bed and I'll get this all cleaned up." He went back to dragging the deep freezer as best he could. I got behind it and started pushing. It went a lot faster than it had been.

"I can't sleep either," I said. "Too much going on."

We argued a bit more while I helped him get things moved back in, but he finally gave in and let me help him out. We got all the stuff back into the shed and he had me help him carry his radio equipment around to our trash can. He was going to fill it and then some, but he said he'd call the folks that picked up our trash to make a special trip.

He was carrying a box with all his notebooks that he said he needed to burn in the driveway, and I was going to watch him do it, but I saw a folded-up piece of paper fall out of the box. I almost told him about it, but I stopped myself before I did. When he got away from me, I picked up the paper and looked at it.

It was a map of part of the Gulf and the Caribbean. I knew that 'cause there was Florida's sagging butt hanging over the big island that I recognized as Cuba. All around Cuba, there was arrows and little boats drawn. One of the arrows was pointed into a little inlet on the south side of the island and the letters *B.O.P.* was written above it. Up near where Havana was, there was a little explosion drawn. I wondered if that was where the airstrip had been.

There was numbers around them arrows too. The arrow pointed at the explosion had a 15 next to it. The arrow pointed at the little inlet had a 17. I tried hard not to ask myself why Pa had that map. Tried real hard.

I folded up the paper and hid it until I could get up to my room. I stuck it in my sock drawer and tried to go to sleep. I couldn't let myself worry about what Pa was doing anymore. I had a busy day to look forward to.

While we was all working the next day, I had trouble focusing. I was too darn worried. Worried about Pa spilling the beans on Operation Pluto, whatever that was. Worried about the bank saying they might come take our house. Worried about the folks that was stuck underneath their own. Even as we was cleaning up the town and helping folks figure out what they was going to do with their lives without their house to go to, all I was thinking was whether Tommy'd ever get to come home to his.

Then we got word that they'd found an old couple dead under their roof. Then we all remembered why we was cleaning. After that there wasn't no more worrying, only working. Me and Willie was glad we was working on the church, 'cause there wasn't probably no dead folk to be found there.

Sunday night I tried to sleep, but I couldn't. That darn map kept haunting me all night.

Eventually the rooster crowed and I got up. I barely picked at my toast and grapefruit before I took off to school, I just didn't have it in me to eat.

Mrs. Buttke came to school that day using a cane. Apparently her leg had gotten stuck under a beam 'cause of the tornado, and it was making her go extra slow. At least she made it.

There was a lot of kids missing from school that day. I'd heard a few was off with relatives since their houses was gone. Others might have been hurt, there wasn't no telling. I think we all was worried that they was dead, thanks to that old couple putting it in our heads.

Mrs. Buttke went up to the board and started writing.

This Day in History: April 17, 1961—The Bay of Pigs Invasion.

It took me a second while I was copying that down to realize that she'd written today's date up there on the board. I raised my hand while she was starting the prayer. She made me keep it up in the air till she said "Amen."

"Yes, Johnny?"

"What's the Bay of Pigs invasion?"

"It's in the paper today. I'll bring in the newspaper after lunch and we can discuss it this afternoon." She pulled out her teacher's books for the day and winced, like it hurt for her to pick them up. "Before we start this morning, however, I'd like to talk about the storm we had on Saturday."

Turns out, even with all the damage we'd done seen in town from the tornado, not a one of us kids had any idea just how bad it had really been. There was folks out in the hills that had their lives completely destroyed from it. There'd been a couple of other towns in the county that had damage done to them, too. Just about the only towns that got off without a scratch was Colony and Arab, which was where Martha and her ma had gone to stay while her pa fixed their house. A tree had busted right into Martha's bedroom window. I hoped losing a ponytail wouldn't seem as bad after that.

All that talk about the tornado kept putting off the talk I really wanted us to have, about the Bay of Pigs invasion. Seemed like everyone was so caught up in our own mess, nobody cared about the folks in Cuba. I'd learn to expect that as time wore on. Didn't matter that we was closer to Cuba by a hundred miles than we was to New York, it might as well have been another planet. Or Colony. Folks always had something better to think about than the people that was in their own backyard.

Still, I cared. I really wanted to know what the Bay of Pigs invasion was.

I raised my hand and asked to be excused to the bathroom. Once I was out in the hall, I took off to the school office. I'd seen the newspaper in there the last few times I'd gotten in trouble, so I figured they'd have that day's edition.

I got to the front office and asked to see the paper. They was shocked, but happy to oblige. I looked at the front page, and almost dropped it. The headline read:

CUBA INVADED BY SEA, AIR. CASTRO BLAMES U.S. FOR "ANOTHER PEARL HARBOR."

The article told about how a few thousand Cubans, whether they was escapees or disgruntled citizens it didn't matter, got up in arms and tried to overthrow the government. They was coming in from someplace called the "Bay of Pigs," and they was shooting everything they could set their eyes on. There was some bombs getting dropped, tanks getting rolled out, and planes fighting in the sky.

The article said there wasn't no Americans involved at all, and that we was just as surprised as anybody else over it. Except I wasn't surprised one bit. I just knew this Bay of Pigs thing was another name for Operation Pluto, and that Pa'd had his hand in part of it. Which meant there was at least one American involved. I read the whole article and then some to see if I was right.

After a while Mrs. Buttke came to get me. She about had a heart attack when she saw the paper in my hands.

"You couldn't wait till after lunch?"

"How much have you heard about this thing in Cuba, ma'am?" I handed the paper back to the secretary.

"I read the paper and listened to the news on the radio. I'll tell you all about it this afternoon." She marched me out to the hallway and toward her classroom.

"Do you think we had something to do with it?"

She stopped.

"Well, the Russians say we did. But the ambassador to the UN has said we didn't, so I reckon we should believe the ones that don't make a practice of lying."

I assumed she meant to trust the American folk, though she wasn't very specific. I kept quiet after she said that, 'cause I didn't want to spill the beans about what I knew of Operation Pluto and how Pa told some Spanish folk about it. You never knew who else Short-Guy might have given his number to, and Mrs. Buttke had sent me to the principal's office enough times that I knew she couldn't be trusted with that kind of a secret.

We went back to class and she went back to talking about diagramming sentences. I kept my survival guide out on my desk for when she'd get to talking about the event. I had to wait all the way until about an hour before school was done before she did.

"Today there began an invasion in Cuba to overthrow the government," she started, and I hurried and opened the guide so I could write down my notes. "It was only two years ago that Fidel Castro and his followers overthrew the established government in Cuba. That government was friendly to the US government, but Castro's government has not been. Why are the people trying to overthrow Castro's regime?"

"Well, you told us on Friday that folks tend to get mad when they're being ruled by tyrants," I said, looking at my notes. "Maybe it's 'cause Castro's a rat-fink leader. *Sic Semper Tyrannis*, like you said." I thought for a second. "But why would any Americans want to help out the invasion?"

She shot me a look. "I thought I told you before, our government has said they were not involved."

"Right," I said, but I wasn't done. "But what about any other Americans? Why would they?"

She looked down at her notes, and I could tell she was thinking about my question.

"Well, when Castro overthrew Cuba, it affected a lot of US businesses. A lot of money was lost, as well as a lot of property owned by American citizens. Allowing something like that to happen affects your credibility internationally. So, perhaps, if we were to get involved, that would be why."

After school I went over to Mr. Thomassen's, even though I didn't figure he'd have any sweeping for me to do. Sure enough, he was using his barbershop to be a place for folks to get food and drinks while they was working on cleaning up the town. I was about to duck out the door, but he grabbed me and offered to pay me to help him hand out lemonade. It was going to be the second easiest money I ever made. The easiest was when I sold little Billy a fake Duke Snider card I'd made from a Wheaties box.

With all the people coming and going, I got to hear a whole lot of conversations. They was all about the tornado, of course, and about the cleanup and such. There was only one fella talking about the Bay of Pigs. Mr. Thomassen.

"I hope they take it straight down Castro's throat," he said to one of the fellas that was sitting down. "Stick it to him the way he stuck it to so many others."

The fella nodded along, I don't think he was even half listening, but I had to know more.

"Why are you so tied up in it, Mr. Thomassen?" I said.

"I believe in justice," he said. "And what the revolution did to so many business owners nearly broke their backs, some of them. It wasn't right, and somebody should pay. Castro should pay."

"Still, I ain't never seen you so bent out of shape before," I said. "It's almost like you was one of them business owners in Havana."

He didn't say nothing but hurried and started talking to somebody else. Which was how grown-ups admitted to something they didn't want to admit to. It was as sure a sign as a tail between a dog's legs.

I figured I'd get the truth when the place was empty.

"I lived in Cuba for a while," I said. "Even went up to Havana once with my ma."

"That's nice," he said while he was stirring the lemonade jug.

"Wonder if it was when you was living there," I said.

"Maybe, when was it?" he said, then he caught himself. "I mean—"

"It's all right," I said. "I won't tell nobody."

He sighed.

"Yes, I lived in Havana. I owned a little club. Casablanca, we called it. After the movie. Lived there for fifteen years, the best fifteen years of my life."

"A club? What'd you do, cut hair for folk?"

He laughed.

"No, it was a nightclub. With jazz music playing every night, and dancing, and parties. We even had a craps table and blackjack. It was wonderful. But then that devil Castro ruined it."

"Wow, so you had a casino?"

"Did I say casino? No, I didn't. The casinos were owned by the families, and they were too big for me. I liked keeping it small. There was less dirty work involved."

"Dirty work?"

"Collecting, mainly," he said, and his eyes had changed. They was darker, somehow. "When you let men gamble with you, they tend to lose more than they should. The bigger places knew how to get their money out of men's kneecaps. I couldn't ever do that. I was terrible at collecting." He leaned against his counter where he had his hair-cutting stuff. He rubbed his razor, I don't think he even knew he was doing it. "I've gotten better lately, though."

I watched him for a second, letting my mind make all the connections.

"Bob Gorman," I said.

He got all kinds of shocked.

"What did you say?"

"Bob owes you money, don't he? That's why you came to Cullman. Why he does whatever you tell him to, including making Eddie offer me fifty dollars. How much does he owe you?"

Mr. Thomassen raised his eyebrows at me. I think he was impressed.

"Forty-five grand. Not all in one night, of course. He was a frequent customer at my club, and a frequent loser. He and his air show came to Havana quite often. We let him keep coming back because he was a heavy drinker. It wasn't until I was kicked out of the country that I wished I had gotten my money from him."

I filled up some of them little Dixie cups he had with more lemonade and thought for a bit.

"Dang, there sure are a lot of folks from Cullman that went to Cuba, ain't there?"

He chuckled.

"Havana was paradise," he said. "Everyone went there. Honey-mooners, lovers, celebrities. It was where you went when you needed to escape where you were from."

"So, if Havana was Heaven, what does that make Cullman?"

He opened his mouth to answer but then a whole new group came in for drinks and snacks. I wondered if it was weird for him to give out free drinks considering he'd spent so much time charging for them back in the day, but I didn't ever mention it to him. In fact, we didn't talk about it again that afternoon.

When I got home that night, Pa was sitting at the table with an envelope in front of him, and he had a smug smile on his face. He patted the chair next to him, so I sat down.

"What's going on?" I said. He slid the envelope over in front of me.

Vega Suministros Médicos the return address said. I opened the envelope, which he'd already opened, and pulled out a check. Soon as I saw the total on it, I dropped it like it was a hot potato.

The check was for thirty-five thousand dollars.

"Told you I'd take care of things, didn't I?"

"Holy cow, Pa. What'd you do?" I picked the check back up to see if it was real. Sure looked real.

"Don't matter how I got it. Just take it to the bank tomorrow."

"No, actually it *does* matter how you got it," I said. "It ain't easy to get this kind of money doing honest things."

He got real indignant at that.

"Listen here, I've about had it with you acting like you're the pa and I'm the kid around here. I earned that money fair and square, no bones about it. Now, you do what I say and take that money to the bank. Or I'll tan your hide and remind you of your place."

We both stared at each other, and it was plain as day that he planned on winning the standoff, so I grabbed the check and headed up to my room without another word. I knew enough math to put two and two together, and I didn't like the four it was making. Pa had told some Spanish folk about Operation Pluto, and now here we had a check from some Spanish folk. And Short-Guy had said he was looking for a radio operator that had come into some money. And now, here my pa was a radio operator that had come into some money.

I shook my head. Just 'cause there was evidence piled up a mile high didn't mean Pa was guilty. This was America, after all. You was innocent until you got caught. Or something like that.

I rolled the check up and stuffed it in my sock drawer right next to Pa's map.

The next few days made me get more and more nervous about everything. The papers was going on and on about what was happening in Cuba, and how many of the invaders was dying, and what a terrible losing cause it was. And through it all, they claimed that America had been behind it. And through it all, Pa kept insisting they was wrong, but I had a bad feeling they was right.

I had to know the truth. It was one thing if Pa ratted out a bunch of Cuban exiles for money, if he did, but ratting out American troops was the sort of thing that got you hanged. I started reading everything I could get my hands on, and listening to the radio, and even watching the news. It was terrible, seeing how all them folks was getting killed. It was like hearing about World War I while you lived in France. This was happening in the same air we breathed. So to speak.

Of course, the mess that was actually happening in our own air from the tornado was making everything seem about fifteen times worse. A lot of people that had lost their homes decided to leave town for good, and it was real solemn watching the moving trucks pulling what few things had been salvaged down the highway as folks relocated their lives. The bank manager and his family left, and so did one of the teachers, which meant we had to share Mrs. Buttke with another grade till the end of the school year. To do that, they combined our class with the fifth graders. A whole mess of little twerps came in that thought Eddie Gorman was the coolest kid they'd ever seen. He was turning into the king of their little jungle.

With the bank manager being gone, I kind of hoped that all the business about our house would be put on hold until the new manager got himself situated. That way I could come up with another plan to make some money without using that check of Pa's. If I didn't deposit it, then it was like it didn't exist.

I went down to the Parkinses' house just about every day and me and Willie would compare notes on all that was happening. I didn't tell him about the check, though. Or the map. I figured that was too heavy for a kid with one good leg to bear. Somebody had to look out for him. I really wished the Captain was around, looking out for me. I felt like he could give me some real good advice. Or, at least he could show me how a real pa would handle everything.

I wished that on Thursday. On Friday, I regretted it.

I got called into the principal's office right after lunch. The lady that was filling in for the usual secretary didn't know my family at all, so it was an honest mistake when she'd told Mrs. Buttke that my pa was there to see me. But it wasn't.

It was Captain Morris.

He waved at me when I walked into the office.

"Hey, Johnny!" he said. I just about fell over.

"Captain? What are you doing here?"

"You're going home early, kid," he said. "I got to talk to you and your pa. Together."

I had a real bad feeling this was about the radio shack and the money. We went and got in his truck, and as we drove to the house I tried to get the truth out of him.

"You here on account of the CIA?" I said.

"Lord, no," he said. "Why? Should the CIA be here? I know it's a disaster area, but I don't think you can blame the tornado on Commie spies."

Now I was real confused. My stomach was starting to feel real sick, too.

"So this ain't got nothing to do with the radio shack, or Cuba, or nothing?"

He got quiet.

"Why'd you put those together in your brain?"

"Got my reasons," I said.

"Well, forget your reasons. And no more questions," he said. "Wait till we get to your house and I'll explain everything."

We got to the house and Pa was out mowing our lawn. He didn't never mow the lawn. I reckon he was feeling like twice a man on account of that money he'd made. The Captain told him to go inside with us and we all three sat down in the living room.

"What's going on?" Pa said.

"I wasn't planning on coming back so soon," the Captain said. "But then I got word of something that I hate to have to tell you. But I'd hate it even worse if you heard it from somebody else."

That sick feeling in my stomach was getting worse.

"What's going on, Rick?" Pa said.

"It's about Tommy," the Captain said.

"What happened?" I could tell Pa was getting excited, 'cause his voice was threatening to get all high and squeaky.

"There was an—" the Captain started. "That is, he was flying and—" He sighed and pulled something out of his breast pocket.

"This is a copy of the letter they're going to bring to you two tomorrow, I'll just read it," he said, and cleared his throat.

"'Mr. Cannon,'" he read, "'the Secretary of the Air Force has asked me to express his deep regret that your son, Corporal Thomas Cannon, died in a training exercise at Fort Humphreys, Korea, on April 17, 1961. He crashed into the ocean, and they have not had any luck in finding his body. The secretary extends his deepest sympathy to you and your family in your tragic loss.'"

He wiped his eyes after he read it and started apologizing real hard to the both of us. But I didn't listen to him anymore. I felt like somebody'd just socked me in the face with a sledgehammer. Pa wasn't breathing, he was so shocked. Part of me was afraid that he was going to die and join Tommy.

I shook my head. Tommy was dead. But it didn't make no sense. He was the best pilot I knew, the best pilot anybody knew. He had been taught by the legendary Major Harrison. He wouldn't have crashed in a training exercise. Not in Korea, especially.

'Cause he wasn't in Korea. He'd told me so himself.

I started convincing myself like that, 'cause my brain was giving me a ton of questions to think about. Why did they say he was in Korea when I knew he wasn't? He was in Nicaragua. And I didn't think he'd been in a training exercise, neither. He was already a danged good pilot.

So, basically two thirds of that letter was a lie. What if the whole thing was a lie? What if they just wanted us to think he was dead? What if they fooled the Captain into thinking it?

But why would they do that?

What if he *was* dead?

I shook my head again. I wasn't going to believe it. Not until I saw the body.

I reached over and patted Pa on the back and he started crying. Captain Morris came over and hugged on him.

I didn't cry. I'd save it and cry at the funeral, if we ever had one. And I didn't think we would.

CHAPTER SEVEN
ALL BLOOD NO BODY

It was funny, what with the news of Tommy dying, that whole Bay of Pigs thing stopped seeming so important to me or Pa. Or to anybody else for that matter. Folks just sort of stopped talking about it once the week was up. It'd be in the paper every once in a while, but that was about it. I didn't see Short-Guy poking his nose anywhere either, so I reckoned maybe we was in the clear.

Captain Morris stuck around for the next few days to give me and Pa his support. It was real nice of him to do that. He went with me into town a few times. Sometimes he'd go off on his own and strike up conversations with folks like a regular Cullmanite. He seemed to get along with Bob Gorman a lot better than me or Pa ever did. He avoided Mr. Thomassen like I avoided eating onions, though. I thought that was a bit odd, but then again, Pa was avoiding most everybody anymore. So maybe that's just what grown-ups did when they was sad.

He wasn't there when the petty officer came to deliver the official letter, same as the one the Captain had given. And it didn't take a genius to see that this fella was lying about the whole thing. Either that or he was the worst truth-teller there'd ever been.

Oh, sure, he did make it all official and made us feel real important. He told us that it was a crash off the coast of Korea, and they couldn't never find Tommy's body no matter how hard they looked. Told us he was a real hero, though, never saw nobody he wouldn't help out. Loved his country like he'd loved his ma.

And through it all I knew he was lying through his teeth. Even if he didn't know it.

After the officer left, Pa called our pastor so we could get started preparing for a funeral. Since there wasn't going to be no body, the pastor suggested we make a memorial of some of Tommy's personal belongings we had around the house. Pa agreed, and we set to finding the perfect things to symbolize who Tommy was. The Captain offered to help out, but Pa didn't think Tommy would be too keen on that, so he said it was just a family project. I felt real bad for that, and I think it hurt the Captain, too, 'cause he said he had business to take care of somewhere else anyway, so it wasn't no skin off his teeth. He left town again after that. I didn't enjoy watching him go this time at all.

Me and Pa went into Tommy's room and dug out his keepsake box. There was a stack of comic books, some baseball cards, his Captain Midnight decoder ring, and a photo from the newspaper of us with the two biggest fish anyone in Cullman had ever caught.

There was also newspaper clippings from all his air shows, and the photos from his graduation from boot camp. We grabbed it all for the funeral.

At the bottom of his shoebox there was a newspaper article written in Spanish dated July 16, 1955. A folded-up piece of paper was clipped to it with what I figured was the translation of the article. I grabbed it and read it while Pa was looking through some other things.

The story was from the newspaper in Havana, Cuba. It was the story of the accident Ma and I had been in. I hadn't never known the details, never really cared, but reading it all of a sudden made me realize just how bad it had been.

Ma had been in the passenger seat, which was the side of the vehicle that got hit by a truck at the intersection. I had been in the back. It didn't say who had been driving, in fact, it made it seem like the reporters didn't know. What they did know, though, was that the little boy who had been in the back was lucky to be alive. Lucky that someone had taken him to the office of Dr. Raúl Vega, the best surgeon in all of Cuba.

See, the same impact that had crushed my ma to death had also crushed me, the article said. It had sent metal into my body from head to toe, and it had broken most every bone in my body. It about near destroyed some of my organs and even crushed in my skull, they was pretty sure that meant my brain was damaged. But Dr. Vega wasn't just a surgeon. He was a miracle worker. That's what the article said. And somehow he was able to save my life.

I read that whole article and couldn't believe how much of a miracle I was. Nobody'd ever told me that, but there it was in black and white. Close to the end of the article, it mentioned the company that Dr. Vega owned, the company that I owed my life to. I thought my eyes would pop out when I read it.

Vega Suministros Médicos.

The people who sent Pa that check.

Pa looked over and saw me reading the article.

"Oh, wow, I didn't know Tommy kept that," Pa said.

I nodded.

"I ain't never read this," I said, then I got a question in my head. "Who was driving?"

He scrunched up his forehead.

"What do you mean?"

"Look, it says they didn't know who the driver was."

He came over and read it.

"Well, I'll be. I always assumed your ma was driving. I was too tore up to get all the details."

"Why was she even in Havana?"

"Oh, she was meeting a friend there," he said. He looked at the picture in the article of the car all messed up. He shivered. "Still can't stand to look at it."

"Who was the friend?" I said.

"I don't remember. Some girl she'd met in New Orleans that flew down every once in a while for a shopping weekend. She enjoyed the little vacations, and she loved taking you with her most of all."

"She didn't tell you the girl's name?" I said. I was pretty sure that friend was the driver, I just knew it.

"She did, but I don't remember it."

"But you know it was a girl?" I said.

"Well, she had a girl's name, so I reckon so." He sighed. "Anyway, I reckon we should get this stuff to Pastor. We can talk about that another time when we ain't getting ready for another funeral."

By Wednesday we was having the funeral without a body, so it didn't feel like nothing more than a social get-together. The old women from the church even brought their roast chicken, same as they did for the Fourth of July. Pa cried, which helped remind me that there was supposed to be a body to be missing, but if I tried real hard, I could imagine that we was all just waiting for Tommy to come home on leave.

Waiting for him to come back and start taking care of me and Pa again.

I decided to do it like that, for my own sake, and keep quiet about it, for everyone else's.

It was nice to see the Mackers come to the funeral. Tommy'd made a habit of helping Mr. Macker get drunk at the bar, so he was real sad. Martha cried too. That was my lot in life. Even dead, Tommy was still better with the girls than I was.

We went on out to Mount Vernon Cemetery to where we was

putting his gravestone, right next to Ma's gravestone. Since I hadn't hardly ever visited her, I sort of forgot where it was at. I was real thankful it was on the opposite side of where our fight had been at. I wouldn't have wanted her to know I'd been fighting.

Everybody had something to say at the graveside. I figured they felt freed up for talking since nobody'd had to dig the hole or carry a casket. The preacher went on for longer than I'd ever heard him. By the time he was done, he'd preached Tommy so far into Heaven I could imagine him hustling poker with Moses and the disciples.

They asked me to tell something, but I couldn't think of nothing serious to say, so I declined the offer. That ticked Pa off more than usual. He shot me that look that said I'd better be ready for the fires of Hell when we got home. It helped me finally get upset like folks wanted, which was a good thing, 'cause the rest of the funeral went off without a hitch.

When we got home, he was too mad to even yell at me. He sent me to my room and went straight to the living room to turn on the news. After a little while there was a knock at our door. I could see out the window that it was Willie and Mrs. Parkins. Pa got to the door before I could and told them that we needed some space for a little while. I tried to catch Willie's eye from the window, but his ma rushed him off the porch, leaving a basket of food in Pa's hands.

I'd made it through that day pretty good. It was the following Monday that did me in. We only had a few weeks left to school, and as soon as I showed up, everybody acted all quiet and sad, and

I knew those few weeks was going to be the longest I'd ever gone through. Nobody would talk to me, nobody'd even look me in the eye. I'd walk down them narrow halls and everybody'd just turn and walk the other way. If I thought having no friends was lonely, I was wrong. Having folks' pity was worse.

In class, there was notes passed around that wasn't meant for me, and when I tried to read them, the other kids would just tear them up and look real sad. It didn't matter that I believed my brother was still alive, they was all doing their best to convince me he was dead. By the time the last day of school came around, I was almost starting to believe all of them, and that was ticking me off something fierce.

I hadn't been paying no attention to the *This Day in History* at all until that day. Mrs. Buttke wrote up on the board *Lindbergh Baby Found Dead.*

I started copying that down, but then I realized that everybody was looking at me, like the Lindbergh baby was my brother or something. I closed my notebook. There wasn't no use writing nothing down. Might as well just let the vultures pick off my bones.

About an hour before the last bell rang in the afternoon, we was all sitting in our classroom, listening as Mrs. Buttke was giving us an end-of-the-year lecture on how the world might end over the summer from all the missiles. She showed us a map of the world, she called it the "Map of Enemies," and was explaining that every continent besides North America and Australia was gunning for us.

I wasn't paying no attention. I was only interested in running out the door. In fact, Mrs. Buttke made me jump the gun at the end of her talk. She said, "Well, I suppose I've bored you all enough."

I grabbed my books and stood up.

"Sit down, Johnny," she said, and a few of the girls giggled. "I want you all to discuss with each other what we just spoke about. Pair up and ask each other, 'What will you do if the Soviets attack us this summer?'"

It was one of them things I always hated, 'cause most everybody already knew who they'd pair up with except me. Usually me and Eddie did it, but he was too busy being the god among little idiots to even consider joining me, and I was too busy hating him to consider it myself. Which probably meant it would be me and Mrs. Buttke talking. Which meant summer was an eternity away.

Martha turned around in her desk.

"Will you pair with me?" she said.

I forgot how to breathe and started exhaling before I inhaled.

"I—uh—I," was about all I could muster.

She put her hand on my arm. Dadgum, now I'd have to shower with my arm wrapped in a trash bag for the rest of my life.

"I'm so sorry about Tommy," she said.

I nodded. My tongue felt three times too big for my mouth. Like if I'd gotten stung by five hundred bees or something.

She started to say something else, but my dadgum brain and dadgum ears picked up on some whispering coming from behind, and what was being said grabbed my attention something fierce.

Dadgummit. If I could, I'd go back and slap myself to keep on listening to Martha.

But, no. My brain decided to listen to Eddie.

He was whispering to his little fan club of fifth graders.

"I mean, can we really say he's a hero if he couldn't even fly a routine training exercise?" he said to the little people, and they all giggled under their breath so nobody'd hear them.

I heard them.

I snapped my pencil in half and stood up in the middle of Martha saying something about us seeing each other over the summer. I wish I would have sat back down. Heck, even Mrs. Buttke tried to get me to sit down. But I didn't.

Instead, I turned to Eddie's desk and slapped it, just to get his attention.

"What was you saying about Tommy?"

He snickered and looked at his friends. "We was saying how much of a hero he is, to all of us."

His buddies covered their mouths with their hands to hide that they was laughing. I nodded at him and tried to think of what the right thing to do was. All the Sunday School teachers had always taught me about the Golden Rule, that you do to others what you want them doing to you. Well, if somebody ever heard me mouthing off like an idiot and badmouthing my brother, the way Eddie just had, I'd hope they'd smack me in the mouth.

So that's just what I did for him.

I blasted my fist right into his nose, and it was like turning on a faucet, he was bleeding all over his desk. His buddies jumped up and tried to throw their own punches, but they wasn't near fast enough, and they was all nursing black eyes and bloody noses themselves before too long.

I was primed to give Eddie another wallop for good measure, but Mrs. Buttke grabbed my arm mid-swing and dragged me away from him.

"See, that's what socializing with Tiggers will do to you," Eddie hollered, little blood droplets spraying all over my shirt. "You start turning into a dadgum savage."

I almost pulled back out of Mrs. Buttke's arms, but she pulled me past Martha and out of the room to the principal's office. On our way, we passed the trophy wall, where Tommy's name was printed on half the stuff they was showing. I started to feel sick to my stomach.

They called Pa, and he came to pick me up. He preached me a sermon on the way home, with an altar call and everything, and I couldn't muster up the courage to explain myself. All I knew was that I missed Tommy like crazy, more then than anytime before. He usually had a way of letting me know I wasn't alone when Pa was laying into me as bad as he was.

I went up to my room and read all my comic books again, even though there wasn't a one of them that I hadn't read at least five times. After a while, I heard somebody at our door. I looked out and Mrs. Buttke was there. I was sure that she was telling Pa all about how bad of a kid I was, and maybe aiming to get me another whipping or something. She handed him a big book, and then she left.

He came up to my room.

"Your teacher said she wanted you to have this book." He handed it to me. "She said she's never had another student as interested in that as you've been this school year."

The book was called *365 Days in History*. I opened it up. Every single one of Mrs. Buttke's *This Day in History* posts was in there, along with ones for all the other days of the year. I couldn't believe she'd given it to me. It was perfect, I could catch up on any of the days I might have missed.

Pa left me alone with the book and I started digging in to copy things over into my survival guide. I corrected some of my dates, got some of the facts better, and even changed some of my notes after I saw that I'd gotten all the facts wrong. And I also read some of the other days' events. And through it all, I was beginning to learn one really important fact. I even wrote it on the first page of my survival guide in big letters.

There ain't nothing, good or bad, that sticks around.

I reckoned that was as good a lesson to learn that day as any, and I took it to heart. I had to believe that the next day would be a day further away from all the junk that had happened to me. And that might mean it was a day closer to good things.

I woke up the next morning drooling on my best Superman comic, my flashlight dimmed out from being on all night. The first day of summer was coming in through my window, and it was the first thing I'd seen that told me everything was going to be okay. The birds was singing like they only do in Cullman County, the air had the smell of wildflowers, and there was a rooster crowing somewhere down the way.

I rolled out of bed, breathed in the sweet breeze, and figured I'd get some chores done before I went to see what Willie was up to. I closed my eyes and tried to get my bearings on the day. I could hear Pa downstairs cooking onions and eggs for breakfast. The milkman was dropping off our milk outside, whistling "Dixie." A little farther away, I could just barely make out the sound of that momma cat in our backyard screeching at her kittens.

It was finally a normal day.

I ran downstairs, fearsome hungry, hoping Pa might have made me a plate, but he didn't. He'd only cooked enough for himself. I grabbed me a piece of toast and sat down.

He was reading the paper, and the biggest news of the day was that the city had decided to start summer baseball sign-ups on schedule, which was that day. There'd been talk about postponing it due to the cleanup, but the mayor said we needed to get our lives back. So it was going to be a big event downtown. It'd be nice to get something going normal again, and there wasn't nothing more normal than throwing fastballs like Whitey Ford.

I hurried and finished my breakfast and asked Pa if he could take me into town, but he reminded me that our truck was still illegal to drive, thanks to me and the tree branch that busted up the windshield. I didn't reckon Willie was going to the sign-up, since Colony had their own baseball team and he wouldn't be one for playing on it anyway. So I hopped on my bicycle and rode into town.

The sign-up was down at the courthouse, and I was looking forward to seeing all the boys there and arguing about baseball while we stood in line. I was the only Cincinnati Reds fan around, so we usually got into some friendly scraps. They liked to say that the Reds was a bunch of Commies, but I knew that wasn't true. Anyway, a whole mess of them liked the New York Yankees, and the worst thing to a fella in Cullman was a Yankee. But it didn't affect their loyalty to that stupid team.

I was primed for the arguing to start. There wasn't nothing like a good fight over baseball to set the summer up right. It might put all the conflict we'd had during school behind us.

When I got there, nobody'd talk to me. We stood in line, and nobody tried to convince me to be on their team. There was a kid who'd been in a wheelchair up until a week before the end of school, they tried to get him, but not me. It didn't make no sense.

Then I got to the sign-up table and it dawned on me. The man in charge of the Cullman Baseball League was Bob Gorman. I tried not to look him in the eyes and grabbed the first clipboard I could get my hands on. He snatched it out of my hand before I could put my name down.

"Boy, I think you best take this summer off. What with your loss and all."

I couldn't believe what I was hearing. "But, I really want to play. And there ain't a better pitcher in Cullman, sir, and you know that's a fact. You got to let me play."

He looked me square in the eye and laughed. "I ain't got to do nothing but stay white and die. Now, move on so these good boys can sign up to play ball."

My ears was burning, but I couldn't think of nothing to say. If he'd been closer to my age, I would have just called him outside so we could let our fists finish the talking. Still, there wasn't no arguing with what he said, and even less with what he hadn't. A quick glance around the room at the eyes of all the dads that was trying to keep their sons far away from me proved what I already knew was true.

I'd done been labeled a Tigger-lover.

I left the courthouse and tried to find something else to do. I was able to scrounge a few pennies outside the Laundromat and took them to the soda shop for a root beer. It wasn't near as much fun drinking alone, so I gulped it down and figured I'd head back home. The bike ride was real lonely.

When I got home, Pa was still sitting in his seat, reading his paper. I looked at the kitchen sink and it dawned on me that nobody had done any dishes in a week of Sundays. Of course, dishes wasn't one of the chores on my usual list, but I figured there needed to be a peace offering made between me and Pa, so I went to take care of them.

While I was scrubbing the pots and pans, I heard something hitting the kitchen window. Then it happened again, and I saw it was pebbles getting thrown from outside. I looked and saw Willie hiding behind the tree in our yard. I wiped off my hands and went out.

"What you doing over there? Just come up to the door," I yelled at him.

"Wasn't sure if I was welcome anymore," he said. "It's been a real long time since we talked. And your pa said you needed space."

"I've had about all the space I can stand. What do you want?"

"First I wanted to say that I'm sorry about your brother." He actually looked sad, which was nice.

"Seems like everybody's sorry he died," I said.

He nodded. "I was also wondering if you was playing baseball this summer."

I shrugged. "Not this year."

"Why not?"

"They didn't want me. Ain't no problem. I guess I'll do some reading or something." I winked at him. "Maybe some science books, for once."

He laughed. "Yeah, that'd be good." He pushed a rock around with his foot. "But, the reason I was asking, if you still feel like playing baseball, my pa told me he'd love to have you throw for our team."

"On the Colony team? Ain't that against the law or something?"

"Nope. We can have whoever we want. And we want you to be our pitcher."

I had to admit, being a pitcher on any team was better than not being one at all. Of course, the Colony baseball team only played half the games Cullman teams did, but they played one big one at the beginning of the season against last year's champion from Cullman. That'd be fun, but what if joining them got me permanently labeled a Tigger-lover?

"Have you got any other white kids on your team?"

"Cody Fannon. He's on second."

That killed the deal. "Cody Fannon's trash and everybody knows it. Anyway, y'all don't need me. Russ is a good pitcher."

"He broke his finger," Willie said.

"In a fight?"

"No, practicing piano. His cat jumped on the lid and slammed it on his hand."

I couldn't help but chuckle. "I thought he wanted to be a boxer."

"He does, but his grandma wants him to play music in front of folks some day. Scares the bejeezus out of him. He'd rather get his brain bashed in than have folks hear him play the piano." We both laughed at that.

"Still, I don't know," I said. "Seems like, the more I try to ignore our colors, the more it blows up in my face. So, even if y'all do need me, I don't think I need that."

He shrugged and started to leave. "Maybe. But Pa thinks maybe you do. He says you need *somebody*, and we might as well be the somebodies for you. If you change your mind, we practice down at the church field."

I watched him hobble his way back down the road and it struck me how much effort he'd put into coming up there after me.

"Willie, stop!" I yelled.

He turned around.

"You're right," I said.

"So you will join the baseball team?"

"Well, I still ain't sure about that," I said. "But you're right, we haven't shown you how welcome you are around here. So, how about if you stay the night?"

"Are you serious?" he said.

See, in all the history of Cullman County, there hadn't never been a time when a black kid and a white kid stayed civilly in the same house without one being a servant and the other a master. Heck, they couldn't even be in the same city limits, let alone in the same residence. For him to stay up there with me was breaking all the rules folks had been following since forever.

And the first rule of surviving history I ever wrote down was, *If you want to stop history from repeating itself, stop repeating yourself.*

It made a lot more sense to me at the end of the school year than it had at the beginning.

"Yeah, I'm as serious as sin," I said.

"Wow, that's pretty danged serious," he said. "I guess I need to call my ma and get her to say it's all right."

We went inside so he could use the phone and Pa was still sitting, reading the paper. He looked up at us and smiled at Willie.

"Good to see you, boy," he said. "I hoped you wasn't too put off when I said we needed space. I didn't realize till I said it that it might have seemed a mite bit color-minded of me."

Me and Willie both had the same puzzled look in our eyes.

"Well, you know, on account of the plantations and all that. Space, you see. Room. Land spread out that's ours and ours alone. Like what the white folk had in the old days."

"Pa, I think you're overthinking it."

He nodded. "Anyway, good to see you."

"Willie's going to spend the night," I said.

Pa had the look on his face that every other person in Cullman would have had if they knew about it. "Don't you reckon you ought to get some permission first?" he said.

"He's going to ask his ma."

"Okay, what about *your* pa?" he said.

"Hadn't thought about it," I said.

"Oh," he said. "Well, it's all right with me."

"Like I said, I hadn't thought about it." Don't know why I felt like sassing him, but I did. He winced a little and I felt bad, but I wasn't going to apologize in front of Willie.

Mrs. Parkins gave the okay and I went over to get some of his things to take to my house. I made sure to get his tape recorder, which he'd said was working just fine except for a crackle in the speaker. I also grabbed his comic books so we could trade. And also his science book.

When I came back, he told me he didn't know how to shoot a gun. I decided it was time he learned.

We unloaded all his stuff in my room and then I went and got my hunting rifle out of the front closet. We went out to the backyard and I showed him how to load it and how to keep from killing somebody unintentionally. I ran him through all the same gun safety lessons Tommy'd done. Don't point it at nobody, carry it pointed down to the ground or up and away from you, if there's a safety on it make sure you keep it on, blah blah blah. He was soaking it up, though.

"Why ain't you ever shot a gun?" I said.

"I'm a preacher's kid," he said. "Folks don't think preachers' kids should be playing with guns. Especially black preachers' kids."

That made sense. After I made sure he understood the safety side, it was time to get to the shooting side. With his bum leg, we was kind of limited in the positions he could be in to shoot from, but I made him a bench out of some firewood and he got to where he was aiming it proper. I took some limestone and drew a big X on our shed and told him to shoot it.

First shot he took, he didn't even hit the shed. The recoil from the gun knocked him plumb off the firewood. He looked like a dead deer with its legs stuck up in the air.

I tried to hide my laughing, but I didn't need to, 'cause he was busting his gut. He got up and got back on the firewood and tried again. He hit the roof of the shed.

"Dadgum, if you keep that up we can give the woodpeckers and termites the rest of the year off," I said.

We kept it up for the next couple of hours, and by the end of it he was getting pretty good. He was actually hitting the shed, and he was getting pretty close to hitting the X. We both finally realized how hungry we was, so we went inside. Willie wasn't yet ready to stop holding the gun, so I let him take it up to my room with us. I made us some sandwiches and we ate upstairs.

We stayed up real late trading comic books and listening to Willie's SuperNegro radio shows, and I had to admit that he made stories as good as any that was in the comic books. I also showed him my guide to surviving history and the book Mrs. Buttke'd given me. He thought it was interesting, but he said he had something to show me in his science book that was just as interesting. Maybe more.

"You remember when you told me that history shows us how things ought to be? Well, science does just as good. Here, look."

He opened his book to a page that showed some flowers and the places they'd grow best.

"See, this flower here can grow real good if you plant it in the right place, give it good sun and water, and even give it plant food. But, what do you think would happen if I took another of the exact same flower and planted it in the desert instead? Didn't give it no water or food or nothing?"

"It'd die, I reckon," I said.

"Does that mean that flower wasn't no good? Got a bad seed or something?"

I shook my head.

"Exactly," he said. "In science, we call that an environmental variable. And it's pretty easy to see when you got two of the exact same flower. But let's say the flower we planted here in Cullman was a yellow carnation and the one we planted in the desert was a red one. And the red one died. You know what some folks that didn't understand environmental variables would say? They'd say that red carnations was more prone to dying than yellow ones."

Made sense to me.

"Okay, so what's the point?" I said.

"The point is it wasn't the color of the flower that turned it out the way it did. It's the place it was planted and the care it got that did it. Just like with people."

I had to process that a bit.

"Eddie Gorman says Negroes got different biology than white folk," I said.

"He's an idiot." Willie grabbed my hunting knife and cut his hand. He squeezed it till some blood started dripping out. "Look at that blood. It ain't no different than yours. And I promise there ain't no separate medical books for doctors to operate on black folk."

I took the knife and cut my hand. Dadgum, it sure looked like we bled the same.

He grabbed my hand and put his on it. He smeared our blood together.

"See, we're brothers now," he said. "Don't matter the color. And together, we can change the dirt we're planted in."

There was something real sacred about that moment, and I felt it in my gut. Then I farted and the moment passed into us both rolling in laughter.

We fought falling asleep for as long as we both could, but after a while our conversation got slower and slower and the spaces between sentences got farther and farther apart. He had been sitting on my bed, and before I knew it he was sprawled out, snoring. I laid on my rug and fell asleep myself.

A loud crash outside woke me up. I looked at my clock, it was two in the morning. There was some more noise from outside. The only thing louder was Willie's snoring. It was rafter-rattling. I went to look out my window. I accidentally kneed Willie in the gut on my way.

"Holy Jesus!" he said as he shot up in the air. I grabbed him and covered his mouth.

"Shhhh! Did you hear that?" I said.

"Hear what? You trying to kill me like some freak show?"

I heard the bang outside again, and he heard it too. It sounded like it was coming from the shed. We looked out the window, sure enough, there was some kind of shadowy figure moving around our shed.

"I'm going to see who that is," I said.

He nodded and started to get up. "Okay, let's go."

"No, you stay here," I said. I grabbed my rifle and handed it to him. "Watch out the window and if it looks like I'm in trouble, shoot."

He got wide-eyed.

"You want me to shoot you?"

"Not me," I said, "whoever's out there. Though, based on how you did earlier, maybe aiming at me would be the safest."

I went down and snuck out the front door, then walked around the house as quiet as I could be. I got all the way to where I could see the intruder, digging through our tools and such. Whoever he was, he was wearing black pants and a black shirt, with a black toboggan hat on. I aimed myself at his shoulders and took off running.

I tackled the intruder like a linebacker. He swung around and clipped me in the chin.

I grabbed his toboggan hat and yanked it off.

It was Short-Guy.

I let go of him 'cause I was surprised. He kicked me in the gut and jumped up to run away.

I jumped at his ankles and brought him down again. He rolled over and clocked me right in the forehead. Almost made me let go of him again. But that wasn't about to happen.

"Let go of me, boy," he said. He grabbed a hammer that had

come out of our toolbox and swung it at my head.

I let go of him and blocked it, then I punched him right in the chest. I caught him just right and he lost his breath and took a step back.

A shot rang out from my bedroom window and he dropped down to the ground.

"Dadgum it, Willie," I yelled. I hurried to check to see if he'd killed Short-Guy. Short-Guy was holding on to his arm right above the elbow, and blood was all over him.

"You okay?" I said. He glared at me. I pulled his hand away from his arm, but there wasn't no bullet hole or nothing, looked like he'd just gotten grazed by it. I looked at the shed, and there was a bullet hole there. Right in the middle of the X.

"I knew he'd hit it eventually," I muttered. I helped Short-Guy get up to his feet. "I'm sorry, I thought you was a burglar. We need to get you to a doctor."

"I'm fine. Just let me go."

"No way. You're bleeding 'cause of a bullet from my gun. That's probably arrest-worthy, especially if you die or something."

He sighed. "Do you have a first aid kit? Needle, thread?"

"Yeah, inside."

"Then take me inside."

I helped him walk in through the back door and I fished out our first aid kit. He sat at the kitchen table and started doctoring himself up. Willie came downstairs, and he was about as white as a black kid ever could be.

"What's going on? Who is that?" he said.

"That's the CIA agent you just shot," I said. His jaw dropped.

"Wow. Maybe preachers' kids *shouldn't* have guns."

"He'll be fine," I said.

He was running a needle with thread into his own arm to close the gash the bullet had left when it grazed him. He grimaced at me while he did it, so I reckoned I could wait till he was done to ask any more questions.

"I got a tip that your dad had a radio shack up here," he said.

Willie gulped and I elbowed him something fierce.

"So what if he did?" I said. "I didn't know it was against the law to do amateur radio."

He reached into his pants pocket and pulled out a folded-up piece of paper. He unfolded it and put it on the table in front of us. It was the exact same map that Pa had dropped when he was emptying out the shed. The same map I had up in my sock drawer, with arrows and the boats, all headed for Cuba.

"I made this map based off what I overheard someone, WX5RJ, broadcasting over the airwaves. It's a map of the Bay of Pigs invasion, code-named 'Operation Pluto,' and WX5RJ was selling it to the Cubans before the invasion took place. I analyzed his frequency and determined there was only one location that could be generating the signal strength at that time of night, and that's right here in Cullman County." He tied off the knot on the string in his arm. "WX5RJ is here, I'm sure of it. And I'm going to find him."

CHAPTER EIGHT
BLOOD MONEY

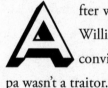fter we convinced Short-Guy to leave and to forgive Willie for shooting him, I had a whole new task of convincing to do. I had to convince Willie that my pa wasn't a traitor.

"You told me he was doing radio, and that he was telling stuff to folks in Cuba," he said. "And here I am assisting a criminal, a traitor. They hang traitors, you know that?"

"He didn't do that," I said, and my mind was scrambling. I knew right then that it was either protecting Pa or myself, and I knew what I had to do. "I lied to you. Made it up to sound interesting."

"Or you're lying now."

"I ain't." I tried real hard to get a sincere look on my face. "Come on, look at my pa. Does he look like the type to do that? I just wanted you to be as impressed with him as I am with *your* pa. And

I got the idea when Short-Guy showed up at Mr. Thomassen's. I made it up on my way to the cemetery."

"That's a real dumb thing to do," he said.

"Maybe that's why I ain't so good at keeping friends."

"Maybe," he said. Then he grinned. "Good thing we're blood brothers now."

That was close.

"Yeah, good thing."

"Anyway, I don't reckon you'd have been willing to get your nose punched in if your pa was coming in to money."

"Wait," I said, "I thought you was sure I was going to win that fight."

"Miracles happen," he said.

I nodded. Now I just had to keep the check and the map hidden for the rest of my life. I sure hoped he didn't ever need to borrow no socks or nothing. I needed to think up a better hiding spot. Like my underwear drawer.

At any rate, there wasn't no going back to bed after that incident. We stayed up reading our comic books till Mrs. Parkins came to fetch Willie for church. After he left, I collapsed and slept until Monday.

I almost slept through Mrs. Parkins honking her car horn to pick me up so we could head down to the ballfield in Colony. I reckoned that meant I'd agreed to play.

When we got to the ballfield, or at least what they called a ballfield,

I almost backed out. It was more like a dead patch of forest with tall weeds growing in the deep mud. There was a stump that nobody had pulled up which was supposed to function as third base. The other two bases was wherever the boys guarding them decided to stand for the play. And if the batter hit the ball into left field, it was an automatic home run 'cause there was two mean dogs sitting out there waiting for their dinner.

It was honestly pretty hard to take it seriously. But, man, did those kids ever take it seriously.

It helped that the mayor had decided to make the Cullman-Colony game a big event, the first game of the season, with tickets being sold to finance the rebuilding of Cullman's downtown. He didn't make no big deal about the fact that it would be the white team against the black team. Didn't have to, the folks in both towns was doing that themselves.

And the story that was leading it all, apparently, was that the Colony team was going to have a Tigger-loving white kid as a pitcher.

"Well, if it isn't Whitey Ford," Russ said as soon as I got out of the car. His hand was all bandaged up. "Come down to help the lowly Negro rise to the challenge."

Some of his buddies laughed. One of them, who had a buck-tooth, chimed in.

"Yeah, if it ain't the Great White Hope."

Before I could say anything to that, Russ smacked him across the head.

ISAIAH CAMPBELL

"You birdbrain," he said, "the Great White Hope was the boxer they picked to try and defeat Jack Johnson, back in 1912, because they didn't like having a Negro boxing champ. It doesn't make sense for this, 'cause Johnny's down here to help us win."

Dadgum. Russ liked history.

"You know," I said, "it's sort of funny about that story. Johnson used to beat them white fellas so bad, the government was afraid people watching the reels would haul off and start a riot."

Russ nodded. "That's why they made it illegal to transport them reels across state lines," he said.

We eyed each other for a second and, without saying nothing, both agreed that maybe there was a spot between us we could meet at peacefully. He went and sat to watch us all practice and I took my place at the pitcher's mound.

It was funny, I don't reckon I'd ever been as tied up and nervous about my life as I was that week. Worried about Pa and what he'd done. Worried about money and about losing our house. Worried about Short-Guy. Just everything. But, when I got on that pitcher's mound, it all sort of seemed to fade off behind me.

I told Willie about that, and he said it was 'cause I was sublimating my anxiety into a right good activity. He said it was something Dr. Freud would be happy with. I thought it sounded pretty promising until he explained that there wasn't no money in it. So I didn't give no more thought to sublimating and got focused on playing baseball.

Still, there was always the times I wasn't out there playing, and those times I was fearsome nervous. Nervous that Willie would find out the truth I'd been hiding, or worse that Short-Guy would get the last clues he needed to run my pa into jail. After a few days, something happened that I thought might spill the beans from both sides to the other. And, of course, it was Pa's fault.

Me and Willie was up in my room looking at some comic books. Just when we was all into arguing over whether it was really possible for Wonder Woman to block every single bullet with her bracelets without having super speed, Pa yelled up the stairs for me. And he sounded real mad.

I went downstairs and asked him what was wrong.

"Did you drop that check off at the bank I gave you?" he said.

"Which check was that?" I said.

"We got a notice from the bank that our home is getting auctioned in a few days," he said. "That wouldn't have happened if that check was in our account."

"Reckon they lost it?" I said.

"You lost it?"

"No, they did," I said. "I mean, maybe they did."

"Maybe you never dropped it off. Where is it?"

I couldn't keep lying to him no more.

"Okay, it's up in my underwear drawer."

He didn't even have to tell me, I headed on up and got it. I grabbed the pair of tighty-whities that I'd stuck the check in and headed out my door.

ISAIAH CAMPBELL

"What happened, you have an accident?" Willie said.

I didn't say nothing back and ran downstairs. When I brought the check to Pa, he snatched it without saying nothing. I reckoned he knew he couldn't say nothing without killing me. He put it in his pocket and started to leave.

"We can't use that money," I said, and he stopped. "It's blood money."

He glared at me.

"What you mean?"

"You sold information about the invasion to the Cubans. Folks died 'cause of that. That puts their blood right on your hands."

He thought about what I said, and I could tell it hit him right in the face. He put his hand on the table and leaned on it.

"You ain't got no idea what you're talking about."

"I got more idea than you know."

He stood there for a bit, staring at me like he wasn't sure if I was lying or telling the truth, and he wasn't sure which one he wanted. Then he went ahead and walked on out.

I watched him going for a second, and then I heard somebody breathing behind me. I spun around and caught Willie just before he got going back up the stairs.

"I was going to get a drink of water," he said.

"How much of that did you hear?"

He swallowed. "Enough."

I nodded. "I reckon we ain't brothers no more, are we?"

He stood still for a bit, then he headed toward our door.

"I got to go," he said. I grabbed his arm.

"You can't tell nobody," I said. "He didn't know anyone would get hurt, I'm sure of that."

"No, but you knew. And you still lied to me."

"Wouldn't you to protect your family?"

"I wouldn't have to," he said, and then he left. He didn't even bother saying good-bye. I reckoned he was real mad at me.

I felt like I was drowning or getting buried alive. And the worst part was, it was in a hole that I was digging around me, deeper and deeper. I watched as many movies on TV as I could stand to get my brain back in order, but every dadgum one was either about two fellas that stopped being friends or about the CIA coming down on the Commies. Finally, just as it was starting to get dark outside, I decided to stop by Willie's house, to try and make things right with him.

"He said he's not feeling well," Mrs. Parkins told me. "I'm sorry."

I nodded. I didn't blame him.

"Could you just tell him I'm sorry for what I did?"

She told me she would, and I headed to leave. She came out on the porch and stopped me. "I've been wanting to talk to you for a while now, but it seems like now is the time. Come sit with me." She patted the spot next to her on the porch swing. I came and sat down.

"I think you need to know a little more about Willie's story."

ISAIAH CAMPBELL

"Ma'am, I appreciate it, but I got a lot going on right now." I started to get up. She pulled me back down.

"I know you do." Her eyes told me that she knew a lot more than I wanted her to. "And that's exactly why you need to listen."

I nodded.

"Willie's brother was killed when we lived in Mobile, about four years ago. He was a strong, handsome boy. An athlete. Willie looked up to him like he was a superhero." She took a deep breath.

"But then they got him. The Klan, they was the ones that did it. He'd been running around with a white girl he was convinced was in love with him. But then she got pregnant and claimed that he'd forced himself on her. So they lynched him outside of our church." She stopped, and her eyes started crying. "It was in the news for a week." She sobbed a little and wiped at her eyes. I didn't much know what to do when a woman cried, so I patted her back.

"I'm sorry, ma'am," I said.

"So am I." She took a deep breath. "Now, Willie had always loved the news. He listened to his radio every single day, almost all day long. There wasn't much else for a kid who couldn't run with his friends or play outside to do. And he wanted to be a newscaster. But, after his brother died, he listened for every single mention of the event. And every news story that spoke of death, Willie took it personally. It was like he thought all the problems of the world were his own."

"I can understand that," I said.

"At his brother's funeral, Willie told me that he wanted to change the world someday. He wanted to see it become a better place. And it scared me, because everyone knows what they do to a Tigger who dreams big."

"You ain't supposed to say that word," I said.

"No, *you* ain't," she said. "So I told my husband we had to leave that town, had to go someplace where Willie could just be a kid, and not be surrounded with all these problems that he'd want to fix. I heard about Colony, and I could tell it was a place we could be safe. So we resigned the church and came to Cullman County."

"I remember when y'all came, it was right before my grandma died."

"She was a good woman," Mrs. Parkins said with a nod. "And this was a good place for what we were looking for. A place that Willie could just be a kid. He made friends here, friends who were interested in baseball and sports, friends who he could play with after church. And he was happy. But then he met you."

I didn't know quite what to make of that, so I apologized.

"He's started talking about changing the world again," she said. "Because of you. Because you've become his new superhero. He got hope that he could do more than the average man, that he could actually save people's lives and futures."

"I don't know where he came by that," I said. "I ain't putting them thoughts in his head."

"No, he's trying to put them in yours."

I hated to admit that he'd been pretty successful.

"Oh well, so what if he's got hope. What's wrong with that?"

"He's a crippled Tigger from Alabama. He doesn't have any hope."

"I'm sorry," I said again.

"Sorry ain't enough. You've got him all tied up in your affairs, and in the affairs of folks that are bigger than you. And that kind of attention, that kind of mess isn't going to leave my boy in good shape. So you need to stay away from him. Leave him out of it all."

What she was saying was sinking in right to the middle of my heart, and it was hurting. I'd spent my whole life without a friend and I hadn't cared none. But now the only friend outside my family I had was getting taken away, and it hurt worse than a broken nose. I was used to not belonging in Cullman, but I didn't know what to do now that I didn't have no place in Colony either.

She stood up.

"I'll still cook dinners for you and your pa. But you leave my boy out of your life, you hear me?"

I got up and I wanted to tell her what I thought, but it wouldn't have been any different from what she'd already said. She was right, I was bringing more trouble than I was worth into everybody's life around me. It was better for Willie if we stopped being friends.

Still, as I went up to my house, I couldn't help getting mad at her. And mad at Pa. And mad at the whole dadgum world that Willie felt needed changing. Why did everything and everyone have to be so unfair about everything? Why was I stuck holding everybody else's secrets? And why in tarnation was it such bad luck for me to get friendly with anyone?

When I got to my house, I was so mad I needed to tear something up. And it struck me that the best thing to tear up was sitting up in my sock drawer still, that dadgum map that had caused so much trouble. If it was a dog I'd shoot it dead.

So I went and dug the map out, took it to the back, and I nailed it onto our shed, right over the big X. Then I got my hunting rifle and had me a little target practice.

I sat up and took my time aiming, at first, and I shot it right through the center. Then I shot it again. And again.

I ran out of ammo before I ran out of anger, so I went in and dug Pa's pistol out of his closet. Went back out and unloaded it at the map, filled it so full of holes there wasn't no way you could see what the truth was about it.

When I was done, I wiped my forehead from the sweat I'd just done put out. I started feeling a bit better 'cause I'd actually accomplished something with my time. I went to pull the map down and reckoned I'd burn it in our fireplace next. I turned around to head inside.

Short-Guy was standing there.

"So, you *are* hiding something from me," he said.

CHAPTER NINE
HOME RUN

I needed to think fast. Faster than I'd ever done in my life.

"Uh," was all I could muster. He even gave me a second to come up with something. "Uh," I said again. My brain must have been stuck in the mud.

"That's the same map I showed you, isn't it?"

"Uh," I said, "I don't know. Is it? I ain't no cartographer." Dadgum my brain. It could think of the word *cartographer* but it couldn't come up with a decent lie.

He came over and pointed at Cuba, which I'd put two bullet holes in.

"It doesn't take a cartographer to recognize that."

"Huh. Well I'll be darned." My wheels was spinning faster than a semi-truck. "I found this in the trash. Down by Eddie Gorman's house." I finally caught some traction in my head. "Come to think of it, there was some fancy equipment there too.

You don't think maybe he's the fella you're looking for, do you?"

I didn't wait for him to answer, I hurried up and walked away.

"Where are you going? We're not done talking," he yelled at me.

"I got to go to the bathroom real quick." That was my go-to lie. Got me out of everything. Nobody didn't ever follow you to the bathroom, and you could spend as long as you wanted in there. The longer you was in there, the less they usually wanted to be around when you came out.

But he followed me.

I walked through our back door to head upstairs, and he didn't even let the screen door slam before he was inside with me.

"What you doing?" I said. "You ought to go over to the Gormans' and dig around in their trash."

"Not until we're done talking."

"Well it might be a while," I said as I went into the bathroom. "I had a big lunch."

I closed the door and sat on the bathtub. Pa had a collection of books in there, mainly Charlie Brown books and such, and I reckoned I could spend the next hour or so reading them. I could wait out anybody.

After about ten minutes, I heard the screen door slam. I went ahead and flushed the toilet, just to make it seem realistic, and I came out. Sure enough, he was gone.

I went up to my room, relieved and worried all at the same time, and figured I should stay holed up for the rest of the day. At least he'd be off bothering Eddie for a while. That made me feel a little better.

When I walked into my room, I realized that I wasn't nowhere near out of the woods with Short-Guy yet. He'd been in there, and he'd taken the liberty of going through my things. My drawers had been rummaged through, my closet was dug open, and my clothes was picked up off the floor. It almost looked like I'd cleaned, which was the creepiest look my room had ever had.

Then I realized something that took me from being creeped out to feeling like I'd gotten kicked right between the legs.

He'd taken some of my stuff.

Specifically, he'd taken my surviving history notebook, the history book Mrs. Buttke had given me, and the article about my accident from my desk. And one of my jackets. I reckoned he'd felt chilly.

I ran over to my window, hoping he might still be outside. Maybe if I offered to go with him to Eddie's house he'd give me back my stuff.

But he was gone.

Dadgummit, I'd been robbed by the government. And it wasn't even Tax Day.

I wasn't quite sure what to do, and the hole I'd punched in the wall before stood there making fun of me, so I punched it again. Then I screamed, on account that I just about busted my knuckles in half.

I sat on my bed, feeling like there wasn't no place in the world I could hide from nobody. Then I saw the silver dollar Tommy'd gave me sitting on my desk. In all Short-Guy's cleaning and robbing, he must have dug it up, I reckon he wasn't interested in taking my money, only my valuables. I picked it up and went outside to our backyard. I stared up at the moon that was coming out, rubbing that silver dollar between my fingers. It seemed like the whole world was crumbling around me.

After a while of sitting and listening to the crickets that was starting to come out, I got up and went around the house to see if there was any lightning bugs I could catch. I hadn't caught no lightning bugs yet that year, and it seemed like a darn shame at that moment. I chased a few and put them into a jar. I took them up to my room and watched them all, lighting up and bouncing off the lid.

After a few minutes, I started to feel bad for them. Here they was, with all that light to spread, and I was keeping them tied up in my room. I opened my window and let them go.

The next morning, I went downstairs and got myself some breakfast. I looked out on the porch. Pa was sitting out there, whittling a stick. At first I thought about going out the back, but then I realized how dumb it was that he and I wasn't talking. We was family. He was the only person on the planet who wouldn't never leave me. I went out and sat down next to him.

"I reckon you deposited that check?" I said after I took a bite of my cereal.

He nodded. "Yeah, but they only let me get a hundred out right now. We've got to wait before the rest goes on our account." He put his knife down and fished a twenty-dollar bill out of his pocket. He handed it to me. "Here, I reckon I owe you this for all you've had to do lately."

It was blood money. I couldn't bear to look at it. I stuck it in my pocket.

"So, that means we're still in a heap of trouble with our house?"

"No, I checked. We should have the money to pay it off before the auction."

"That's good." I tried to think of something else to say to keep the conversation going civil, but there wasn't nothing. So I finally decided to take the conversation to honest instead. I was done with secrets.

"Wonder why they didn't make the check out to WX5RJ," I said.

Pa stopped whittling.

"Where'd you hear that?"

"That was your call sign, right?" I said.

"Yes, but I don't recall ever telling you that."

"You didn't," I said. "The CIA agent did."

"Boy, that ain't funny," he said.

"No it ain't," I said. "It also ain't funny that he told me how you made that money, by selling secrets about the invasion to the Cubans. And it ain't funny that, after you spouted off about God and country, you went and did a dadgum thing like that and made me dadgum glad that Tommy ain't coming back from Nicaragua." I caught it right when it came out, and I tried to stop it. "I mean, Korea."

Pa's voice got real quiet.

"Why'd you say Nicaragua?"

"I don't know," I said. Then I took a deep breath. If I was done holding on to secrets, I might as well be done with them all.

"Korea was a lie," I said. "He told me that the night he left. He had a secret mission in Nicaragua to attend to. Not sure what, but I reckon that's where he crashed at."

His eyes got big and his hand started trembling. "A secret mission? In Nicaragua? Did he say what kind?"

"No, he just said a whole mess of people was counting on him to help them out."

He clutched at his chest. "Oh God. Oh dear God. And the CIA is investigating. That means we *were* involved. Oh dear God, Tommy—"

"Well, now, don't get no heart attacks." I reached over and patted his back. "There ain't nothing to worry about that CIA fella. I reckon I've done got him barking up a different tree."

He got up, still clutching his chest. He headed inside.

"I have to make a phone call," he said.

"Don't use the living room phone, something you did in moving it made it not work right," I yelled after him. He went and used the phone in the kitchen, and I could hear him barking at every person he talked to, trying to get connected to a certain number. I was plumb tired of the whole thing, so I blocked his voice out of my head. But, I had to admit, it felt good to finally get all that stuff out in the open.

After a bit, a station wagon drove up to our house. Mrs. Parkins pulled into our driveway and right up next to our porch. She didn't get out, but Willie did. He was carrying his tape recorder.

"'Lo," he said to me.

"Hi," I said. Mrs. Parkins was watching me like a hawk. "I thought you and me wasn't allowed to be around each other no more."

"We ain't," he said, looking over his shoulder at his ma. "At least, not as friends. But Pa wants me to interview all the players from the team before tonight's game in Cullman. So that makes this business."

I couldn't help but smile.

"So, you're finally going to get that interview you was wanting?"

"Yeah," he said, then he made a big deal about moving around the porch and listening to the air at all corners. He said, real loud, "There's too much noise out here. We'll have to do the interview inside." He looked back at the car, and Mrs. Parkins nodded at him. We went inside.

As soon as the door was closed, he started talking.

"I'm so sorry, Johnny," he said.

"Sorry for what?"

"For telling my ma."

I'd figured he had. Hoped he hadn't, but figured he had.

"Why did you?"

"I didn't know what else to do," he said. "Finding out that about your Pa, it was just the sort of thing she always said we wasn't supposed to get into."

I couldn't hold that against him.

"What's done is done, I guess. He still says he's innocent. I reckon I'm supposed to believe him," I said. "Do you think she'll keep quiet about it?"

"Are you kidding me? She's been grilling me every fifteen minutes that I need to forget the whole thing. She's terrified of people finding out that we know."

Just then, Pa got to yelling again in the kitchen.

"And you thought it was loud outside," I said.

He grinned. "Well, there ain't no going back out there to record. We best find a decent spot in the house." He looked around. "How about over on the couch?"

We went over and I took a seat. He went to set up his microphone stand on the little table by the couch. When he did, he bumped the telephone, and the part you hold fell off the table.

"Dadgummit, Johnny!" Pa yelled from the kitchen. I hurried and hung that phone back up and put it back on the table.

Willie turned on his tape recorder.

"Here, let's get some test questions done. What's your name?" he said.

"Johnny Cannon," I said.

He stopped the recorder and rewound it. He put on his headphones and listened.

"Dang it. I can hear some other voices in the background."

I bent over the table and listened.

"Yeah, it's coming from the phone. Pa messed with it when he brung it back inside from his shed and it won't hang up good. I'll have to fix it once Pa's off the line. Do you want to wait?"

"No, let's just get this interview done," he said. "You got a habit of never cashing a rain check."

He had a point. "All right, let's do it."

He started his tape recorder again.

"Johnny Cannon, you're the pitcher for the— Oh no!" he said.

"What's wrong?"

"This is Pa's sermon tape from Sunday."

I looked at the reel that was spinning around. Sure enough, it was labeled *Reverend Parkins, May 14.*

He hopped up and ran to the door.

"I need to go get a new tape," he said as he went to the porch.

His tape recorder was still going. I didn't want to mess with it 'cause my luck had been so bad lately, so I went and followed him.

"Can I come with you?" I said.

"I don't know. I got to go all the way into town," he said.

Mrs. Parkins got out of the car.

"What's wrong?" she said. I think she thought I'd gotten her son into the middle of another CIA mess.

"I need a new tape. We got to go into town," Willie said.

"Can I come along?" I asked. She seemed to hesitate. I stuck my hand in my pocket and felt that twenty Pa'd just given me. "I'll pay for the tape."

"We don't need you to pay for the tape," she said.

"Ain't it the least I could do?"

She thought for a bit.

"Fine. But this is only for the baseball team. That's all."

We went into town and it felt good to be hanging out with Willie. Even though Mrs. Parkins was watching us like a hawk, we was able to sneak in some fun. He picked up his tape that he needed and we also got some Butterfingers and MoonPies, and then we went back to the house. Pa was gone when we got there, so the house was good and quiet. Willie changed out the tape and we did the interview.

After the interview, Willie had to go so he could catch the other players before the game. I decided to take my time and do all the chores around the house. I even did some of Pa's usual too. I wanted there to be nothing hanging when it came time for the game. There was still a part of me that wanted to see Pa in the stands. To see him proud.

After a while, it was time for me to go and Pa still hadn't come home. I got into my cleats and my ball cap, grabbed my glove, and wrote him a note telling him where and when the game was.

I decided to stop by Mr. Thomassen's shop first 'cause I hadn't stopped by in a couple of days. I hoped he wasn't upset about that.

When I got to his shop, the front door was locked and the lights was out. There was a sign up that said CLOSED UNTIL FURTHER NOTICE.

I peered into the window. I noticed a light coming from under a door, way in the back.

I went around to the back side of the building, where his dumpster was. He had a door at the top of some rickety wooden steps that led into his back room. I headed up them steps to try the door. I accidentally stepped on a cat's tail. He went squawking and ran off to Lord knows where.

It was a good thing I wasn't trying to be sneaky.

I got to the door and reached down to turn the knob.

It opened before I touched it.

Mr. Thomassen peeked out and saw me, then he slammed the door in my face.

It almost hurt my feelings, but I could hear him talking to somebody inside, saying something about "those pesky possums tearing into stuff," and I heard the racket and rattle of a bunch of bottles getting tossed into a trash bag. Next thing I knew, the door opened again and Mr. Thomassen came out with two big trash bags full of beer bottles. He closed the door behind him.

"Johnny," he said. "You shouldn't be here." He started down the steps with the trash bags.

"I just wanted to drop by and—"

"I've closed shop, didn't you see the sign?"

"Yeah, I saw it." I grabbed one of the bags from his hand and helped him heave them into the dumpster. "I just wanted to invite you to my ball game."

His breathing got real fast. He grabbed me and pulled me into the shadow of the dumpster, out of view from his back door.

"I can't tonight. And neither should you," he whispered to me. "The agent is here, been staying in my shop. He said he knows for certain that radio man is in Cullman."

"Why don't you call the cops?" I said. I remembered something from my history books. "After all, the Redcoats tried that kind of stuff, but George Washington kicked their butts over it. He can't make you let him stay."

"Who could I call?" he said, and I could tell he wasn't expecting an answer. "He's the CIA. They do what they want."

It was just starting to sink in how big of a mess I was in, and now Mr. Thomassen was in it with me. If I just told him that WX5RJ was Pa, maybe he could go back to operating his shop and making his money. But that would make me the worst son ever. Didn't even matter that Tommy'd told me to take care of Pa. It wasn't never right to turn in your kin to the government.

As much as it killed me, I had to keep the secrets.

"Why you?" I said. "There's about a thousand other places he could stay, why's he so stuck on you?"

He sighed. "Because I had a hand in the invasion."

He couldn't have shocked me more if he'd tried.

"What do you mean by that?"

"The invasion was done by Cuban exiles, as you know. One of their leaders was Dr. Raúl Vega, a frequent visitor at my club in Havana. He and my bartender, Carlos Martí, were cousins. When I was driven out of the country, Carlos came with me. And," he said, and looked over at the door, and then he whispered twice as quiet as before, "Carlos joined Dr. Vega in the Bay of Pigs invasion."

I didn't much care about his buddy Carlos, but Dr. Vega was in the invasion? Dadgum, this plot was getting thick enough to make a pie out of it.

"But you said you had a hand in it. That means more than just that you knew one of the fellas."

He looked like he didn't want to say no more, but that he knew he had to.

"I told you Bob Gorman owed me big, right?"

I nodded.

"I came here to Cullman to kill him," he said, and he let that sink in. "At least, that's what I told him. He begged me for anything else, so I told him I'd cut his debt in half if he connected me to the best pilot in his air show. I wanted to make sure the invasion had the best chance it could, and that meant they needed the best pilots giving air support."

"Tommy," I said, and my head started hurting again. "He gave you Tommy, didn't he?"

"I contacted Carlos, and he convinced Dr. Vega to have the CIA recruit some pilots from the Alabama Air National Guard. They asked for your brother by name."

"So he flew for the invasion? But they said we didn't give no air support or nothing. We wasn't even involved, according to the government."

"Tommy contacted me the day before the invasion from a pay-phone in Nicaragua and told me that everything had gone to hell. Vega had defected to Cuba and President Kennedy had called off the full air support," Mr. Thomassen said. "I suspected both those things might happen. Vega was always crooked, and Kennedy doesn't have the stones for the job, not yet at least. Which was why I was glad I had my own man down there. My own pilot."

"Tommy flew anyway," I said, and I knew it was true. That was Tommy's style.

He nodded.

"He flew anyway. I didn't even have to ask, he told me that was what he was doing. He said the exiles couldn't handle another betrayal."

"And he got shot down?"

"I'm sorry."

My head was swimming. I couldn't look Mr. Thomassen in the eyes no more. It was his fault, this whole dadgum thing with my brother. I couldn't say nothing to him, couldn't breathe the same air he was breathing no more. I ran off before he could say nothing else. I got on my bike and headed to the only place that seemed like normal. The ball field where the Colony team was playing the Cullman team.

I tried to shake off what I'd just learned so we could start pitching around, but my brain wasn't really in it. I missed three catches and Reverend Parkins kept asking me if I was okay. I didn't let on nothing, just told him I had the jitters, and we got ready to start the game.

We was pitching at the top of the first inning, and when I took the mound I looked over to the bleachers to find Pa. He wasn't there. My first pitch was a strike, but it wasn't a pretty one. It only got worse. I walked that kid and the next two to load up the bases. Reverend Parkins came out to the mound to talk.

"What's going on, son?"

I shook my head. "It's taking me a little to put my head in it. I'll get this one."

He patted my shoulder. "I hope you're right."

He left me out there, and I closed my eyes to focus. I decided to listen to the crowd for Pa's voice. Maybe he wasn't in the bleachers yet.

I strained to listen, but I couldn't find it. Instead, I heard a whole bunch of Cullman folks talking about the white pitcher for the used-to-be-colored team.

"Who knew that Cannon boy was a Tigger-lover?"

"Gorman said this would happen, didn't he?"

"He ain't going to pitch nothing worth hitting. That's the problem with integration."

"Somebody ought to teach them colored folk to keep their hands off good white kids."

"Why hasn't the Klan done something about this yet?"

I opened my eyes and shook my head to get all them voices out of my ears.

The batter was ready for me, but my brain wasn't ready for him. I tried to focus on the top corner of the catcher's mitt, tried to plot the perfect fastball. I had to block out all them folks and their chattering, all the problems I was having with Pa, everything that had been going on lately.

I threw the pitch and it was a line drive straight to the batter's kneecap. Dadgummit.

Reverend Parkins came running out after the batter hobbled to first and the fella on third walked in for a score. I was scared he was going to cuss at me, or at least say whatever preachers said whenever they was cussing at folks. Probably quote the names of the twelve disciples or something.

Instead, all he did was ask if I was okay. I shook my head, there wasn't no sense in trying no more. I wasn't good for nothing, especially not baseball. He went ahead and sent me back to the dugout and called up Russ, whose pitching hand had healed up good enough to play a minuet, according to his grandma. Russ smacked my butt and told me I'd do better next time. I didn't say nothing back.

Everybody in the stands was staring at me so hard, I reckoned I should find a place to hide. I ran around behind the bathrooms and right into Willie, who was looking like he'd just seen a whole mess of ghosts line dancing to a Hank Williams song.

"You need to listen to something," he said. He was carrying his tape recorder.

My head was splitting and I didn't feel like playing along.

"I can't listen to nothing right now," I said. "I just want to find a hole I can bury myself in."

"You can do that anytime," he said. "But, you need to listen to this right now. It's the tape from your interview."

"I was there. Why should I listen?"

"Not the second tape, the first one. I left it recording when we went for a new tape, and it recorded your pa's phone call that was coming over that telephone in your living room."

"So?" I spied something, or somebody, hiding out under the bleachers. I couldn't really see what it was. But it looked like it was waving at me.

"He spills everything, him and the person he was talking to. And it proves that he ain't as guilty as you thought he was."

"Wait, what?" Now he had my attention. "You're saying he didn't help the Cubans?"

"No, he did. But he got tricked into doing it. He didn't know he was selling to the bad guys and he didn't know the folks he was ratting out had ties with America. He just thought he was solving y'all's money trouble. Here, just listen to it," he said as he pulled out his headphones. "It explains everything."

I nodded, and just almost put on them headphones, but then I heard a whistle. Whoever was under the bleachers was whistling at me.

"Tell you what, let me go shut up whoever's making that noise and then I'll listen," I said.

"But this is important!"

"And I want to give it all I got. So let me go wring the neck of the whistler."

I didn't give him no time to protest. I took off running to the bleachers. Right up to the shadow.

Right up to Captain Morris.

He was leaning on a trash can and, judging by the half-drank bottle of whiskey in his hand, he was running on a full tank.

I ducked into the dark right next to him

"Captain? What are you doing here?"

"I'm a big baseball fan," he said, then he giggled. "Plus I needed to talk to you. Alone. To warn you."

"Warn me? Of what? That I'm going to throw the worst pitches of my life tonight?"

He had a sad look in his eyes, and he quieted down a bit.

"They're coming for your dad. Tonight. Now. They're going to arrest him."

My chest got super tight.

"Who?"

"The Feds. He did something he shouldn't have. I can't tell you any more than that." He took another swig from his bottle. "I'm sorry, son."

I felt like somebody punched me in the chest.

"They're wrong," I said. "He didn't mean to rat out Operation Pluto."

He straightened up and got sober, like he'd just swallowed five gallons of coffee.

"Where'd you hear about that?" he said.

"I heard Pa telling some Spanish folks about it. But he wasn't doing it to hurt nobody."

He didn't say nothing for a bit.

"How much about that did you hear?"

"I don't know. Most of it, I guess."

He pulled out his tobacco and shoved a glob into his cheek.

"You probably ought to get down to your house. They might not let you see him once they take him away."

He didn't have to say another word. I left a cloud of dust in the shape of Johnny Cannon and ran off to get on home. I probably should have gone back to Willie and listened to the tape, but I didn't think of that. All I could think of was my pa getting dragged out of our house in chains, with about a million guns pointed at him. Maybe there'd be a helicopter involved.

I rode my bike faster than I'd ever ridden it up the mountain. I was so all-fired focused on making it home, I wasn't put off at all that it was as dark as a boar's underbelly. I was just going on instinct. I reckoned that would help me manage all the bumps and twists in the road.

But it didn't make up for the stick that got shoved in my spokes about halfway up the hill. I got thrown off my bike and went rolling for a good six feet, then I jumped up and got ready for a tussle with whoever or whatever thought it was a good time for a prank.

It was Mr. Thomassen. He stepped out of the bushes and turned on a flashlight.

"Gosh danged it!" I yelled, though I actually yelled something else. Then I realized who I was yelling at. "I'm sorry. I'm just—"

"What? What are you doing?" he said. He got more stern than I'd ever heard him.

"I'm trying to hurry home. I need to talk to Pa before they take him off."

"And do what?" he said. "That agent is hell-bent on finding WX5RJ. And he knows your father is WX5RJ. He finally told me that right before he headed to your house."

"But my pa wasn't—"

"Your pa dropped off a check at the bank yesterday for thirty-five thousand dollars. The bank flagged it and contacted the agent," Mr. Thomassen said. "That's pretty damning evidence."

"But, he was tricked into it." I picked up my bike and started to get back on. Mr. Thomassen stopped me. "I can prove it," I said.

"Do you have the evidence? With you? Because that's the only thing that will stop him."

I looked up the mountain. I could just barely make out the lights of Short-Guy's car that was parked up there.

"No, I don't," I said. "But, maybe he'd wait and let me get it. Let me put things together so he can let my pa go free."

Mr. Thomassen bent over and picked up something I could just barely make out in the dark. It was my jacket that Short-Guy had taken from my room.

"How'd you get that?" I said.

"I stole it out of his suitcase at my shop," he said. He pulled my survival guide out of the jacket pocket. "And I read this. December 6, 1884. Remember what that one is?"

I had to think real hard.

"Ain't that the day the Washington Monument was completed?"

"Exactly. Do you remember the story?"

The lights from the car started to move.

"Dadgummit, they're leaving," I said.

"The story. What is the story of the Washington Monument?"

I sighed.

"They started it in 1848 and they got up about a third of the way. But then a whole mess of stuff happened, arguing and corruption among the folks doing the building. They stopped building ten years later and the monument was the laughingstock of Washington. It wasn't until 1879 that they started building it again, and then they finished it five years later."

The car drove down the mountain on past us and I don't reckon they saw us in the dark. Then they disappeared around a bend.

Pa was gone.

I was officially all alone. I picked up a walnut off the ground and threw it as hard as I could at a tree.

"And what's the lesson you wrote down for this day?" Mr. Thomassen asked me again.

"No disrespect, sir, but this ain't school," I said. "Don't you got any idea of what just happened? I just lost my pa. Lost it all. Probably lost my house, too. My whole dadgum life is ruined."

"No worries. He's taking your father to Birmingham for processing. I cashed in a favor and he'll hold your father for up to a week. There's plenty of time. Now, the lesson. What is it?"

I tried to visualize the page.

"That Eddie's got a million jokes about tall pointy things."

He chuckled.

"The *other* lesson," he said.

"That it don't much matter how your story starts, it just matters how it finishes."

"Exactly. And the agent's story is ending the way he wants it to, by catching the bad guy. If you can't offer him an ending as good as that, then he's not going to be interested."

The sound of the crickets filled my ears as I processed what he said.

"How do we do that?"

"By finding the real bad guy," he said.

That made sense. And I knew how we'd do that too.

"Willie's got a tape," I said. "Pa was talking to somebody about the whole thing. I'd bet you a silver dollar that whoever he was talking to knows who the bad guy was, if he wasn't the bad guy himself."

"Now you're thinking. Let's go get that tape from Willie," he said. He handed me my jacket. "Here, you might need this."

I put the jacket on. It was getting a little chilly, either that or I was shivering from loneliness. I'd probably tell folks it was chilly.

"Why are you so fired up about helping us?" I said.

"When your brother left, he made me promise I'd take care of your family."

Tommy was good at that.

"Yeah," I said, "he said something similar to—"

I heard a truck coming up the road that stopped me in the middle of my sentence. We saw headlights coming around the bend. Me and Mr. Thomassen both stepped off the road to make way.

Mr. Thomassen noticed who was driving. He stepped forward and shielded his eyes to see better.

"Is that—" he started.

Then the car swerved and slammed right into him.

He went flying off the road, rolled down the ditch, and smacked right into a tree. He was out cold.

I was screaming.

Then the door to the truck opened. Captain Morris got out.

"Oh my God!" I screamed. "You done killed Mr. Thomassen!"

He came over and put his arm around me. He looked down into the ditch.

"No. He's not dead. I don't think." He squinted his eyes. "Nope, not dead. Not yet, anyway. He's still breathing."

I was still hollering. Couldn't stop. Not even if I wanted to.

"Johnny. Johnny." The Captain started shaking me. "Stop. You need to listen to me. You're going to get in the truck and we're going to go away. Okay? Everything's going to be okay."

I shook my head.

"No. No it ain't. It ain't at all."

"Come with me," he said.

I jerked out of his hand.

"I can't. I can't."

He grabbed me and flung me around. I felt something sharp go into my neck.

"That wasn't a request," he whispered in my ear. "You're coming with me."

Everything went dark.

CHAPTER TEN
IT'S COLD INSIDE

I probably won't never understand how you can smell something and it brings back a whole mess of memories, like smelling biscuits and remembering your grandma cooking breakfast, or smelling fried catfish and thinking of your brother's graduation. But, if I'd ever doubted how powerful of a memory-producer a smell could be, I stopped when I smelled the air as I was waking from the long nap I'd just taken.

The air wasn't nothing you could smell in Cullman, or in Alabama at all. In fact, I'm pretty sure you couldn't smell it anywhere in the country. There was only one place where you could smell bananas and fish, mixed with gasoline and wood smoke. Havana, Cuba. And smelling that brought back a whole mess of memories, memories that had been dead and buried for a real long time.

Memories of life before I had my scars.

They was memories of playing in the sun, under the palm trees.

Memories of walking down the streets of Havana, carrying a stuffed dog, holding hands with the prettiest woman I'd ever seen.

Memories of Ma.

And I remembered how it used to be, how she and I would fly to Havana from our home at Guantánamo Bay Naval Base so she could meet her friend from New Orleans for a weekend every couple of months. And I realized why Pa had said the friend was a girl, 'cause the name was a girl's name if you said it, though when you spelled it, you saw it for what it really was.

Gene, a doctor who Ma was having a relationship with.

Of course, if I'd seen him now, I would have called him by his full name.

Captain Richard Gene Morris.

But back then, he was Uncle Gene, and me and Ma met him at his favorite club in Havana, where they'd let me sit by the band while they danced. They even got me my own special drink, called *Batido de Trigo*. It tasted like the milk after you ate three bowls of shredded wheat with five scoops of sugar in it. It was great, and I'd drink it and watch my ma be five times happier than she ever was back home with Pa.

And I remembered them meeting Uncle Gene's business partner, Dr. Vega. They had a private practice together there in Havana. Uncle Gene and Ma would have dinner with him and his wife. And I remembered the night Dr. Vega and his wife got in a big fight 'cause he'd seen her kissing the bandleader, Dr. Vega's cousin. And Uncle Gene had lost a ton of money at the poker table, and he was rip-roaring drunk, and he snuck me and Ma out the back door so he wouldn't have to pay his money.

And as he drove off, he was so drunk, he didn't see the truck that was coming up on the intersection he was crossing. I remembered looking out the door and screaming, but Ma was asleep and Uncle Gene wasn't paying no attention.

And the next thing I knew, I was in the hospital. And I couldn't remember nothing.

And Ma was dead.

Some water splashed on my face and woke me from all them memories.

"Hola, chico. Bienvenidos a La Cabaña," somebody said. I bolted up and realized I was in a heap of trouble.

I was on a dirt floor, surrounded by yellow-brown rock walls. There was bars on anything that was opened to the outside. Sunlight was shining through, making shadows that danced on the walls with the movement of the palm trees outside. And the air was filled with that intoxicating Havana smell.

The fella that had thrown water on me was sitting next to a bowl on the ground. He was real dirty, his clothes was tore up and had bloodstains on them. One of his arms was in a sling, and both of his hands was all bandaged up. He had a beard that was long but matted to his face, which was all swollen and puffy. But his eyes was piercing through the puffed-up slits they had to look through, and somehow I recognized him.

"You're the bandleader, ain't you? From the club?" I realized he probably didn't speak no English. "I mean, *You el bandleader-o from el club-o?*"

He grinned, and some of his teeth looked like they'd been freshly beaten out of his mouth.

"*Sí*. But that was a long time ago." He laughed a little and started coughing. "You must have a very good-o memory-o."

"It ain't so good, it's just fresh." I wiped my hands off on my pants, which didn't do nothing to clean them, and I held one out to him. "My name's Johnny."

He showed me them bandages and didn't take my hand.

"I'm Carlos. Carlos Martí."

That name rang a bell.

"Hold on a minute. You was Mr. Thomassen's fella, wasn't you?"

Now he looked really surprised.

"*Sí*. I worked in his club."

"So that was Mr. Thomassen's club where you was kissing Dr. Vega's wife?" I shuddered. "You was kissing your cousin? Dang, I heard that kind of thing only happened in Arkansas."

"Raúl is my cousin, and I would never kiss him," he said, and wiped his mouth off with his bandage. "But, how do you know all these things?"

I told him all about my memories, and he looked like he was reliving a part of his own life that he hadn't remembered in a while.

"Those were wonderful days," he said.

We didn't get the chance to talk no more about it, though, 'cause a couple of big fellas dressed in green uniforms carrying big guns came over to our door. One of them pointed his gun in our general direction while the other one unlocked and opened the door.

"*¡Levántate!*" the one fella with the gun said.

"He wants you to stand," Carlos whispered to me. "And he's very serious about it."

I got up. I figured it was a good idea to listen to him since his gun was so big.

"*Sígueme,*" he said.

I looked at Carlos for the interpretation.

"Follow him," he said. "And then, maybe later on, learn some Spanish."

I walked behind the fella and we went out into a real big open space that was surrounded by rock walls. There was a mess of other fellas with guns and green outfits on, and I was starting to realize they must be the Cuban soldiers that worked for Fidel Castro. I figured I was right when I saw who they was taking me to.

They was walking me up to Fidel himself. Next to him was a fella with a wild beard and a hat on, next to him was a fella with glasses, and next to him was someone who made my heart almost stop.

It was the Captain. And the way he was laughing with them fellas, it didn't look like he was a prisoner.

The fella walked me up to them and I shot the Captain a death glare.

"You was the fella on the other side of Pa's phone call, wasn't you?" I said.

"I can explain," he said. "And I will, trust me. As soon as I can."

The guard poked me in the back with his gun and made me step toward Castro. He nodded at the Captain.

"He wants you to pledge your allegiance," the Captain said. "Do that and you won't have to go back to that cell. You can stay with me."

I thought about it for a bit. Didn't seem too hard. Did it all the time at school. I put my hand over my heart and I started.

"I pledge allegiance to the flag of the United States of—"

The fella with the wild beard backhanded me right across the face. The Captain winced. Don't know why, 'cause it was me that got hit. I could taste the blood in my mouth to prove it.

Castro put his hands on the sides of my face.

"To Cuba," he said in English. Didn't know he knew English. He had an accent, but still, he was understandable.

"You want me to pledge allegiance to Cuba?" I said. "After he just walloped me like that? You got to be halfway to crazy-town."

Castro looked at the Captain, confused. I guess he wasn't as good at English as I thought.

"Él quiere una disculpa del Che," the Captain said.

Castro looked at the fella with the wild beard and nodded at him. Didn't seem to sit too well with that fella.

"Lo siento," the wild-bearded fella said.

Castro smiled.

ISAIAH CAMPBELL

"Che Guevara apologizes," he said. "Now. Pledge to Cuba."

I nodded. I knew what to do. What Tommy'd do.

I put my hand on my heart.

"I pledge allegiance to the flag of apple pie, and Superman, and girls like Martha Macker, and heroes like my brother, Tommy. To the dadgum United States of dadgum America. And if you think I'm going to change my mind, you can all go—"

This time Che punched me right in the nose. I fell down on the ground, my face, jacket, and pants getting soaked from the gusher of blood I was producing. But it was all right. It was for God and country.

The Captain dropped down next to me and started poking at my face.

"I think your nose is broken," he said. He yelled at Che, *"Se rompió la nariz."*

The fella with glasses got down and looked at me with Captain Morris. He grabbed my nose and snapped it back into place.

I might have screamed a little.

Okay, I screamed a lot.

In fact, the guard that had his gun pointed at me took to giggling at how bad I was screaming.

"Gracias, Dr. Vega," Captain Morris said, and shook his hand. So that was Dr. Vega. Saved my life and saved my nose. I'll be.

"If you'll pledge your allegiance to Cuba," the Captain whispered in my ear, "then you can be free. We can be free together. It's just words."

"No it ain't," I said. "It's blood. And it's loyalty. Something you don't know nothing about. How could you sell out my pa like that? Especially after you was having an affair with my ma? You tricked him real bad."

He looked real surprised by that.

"How did you know about that? The affair, I mean. Did Tommy tell you?"

"Nope, he didn't. He knew?"

He was watching Castro and Che like he didn't want them to hear nothing we was saying.

"Not important. Now, listen, Pete Cannon is an idiot. Always was, even back in the war. Your mother knew it, and she wanted out. She wanted to be with me. Which would have been fine if he had died in the hospital like he was supposed to, but he didn't. He got better and she stayed with him. I had to settle for having her on special occasions."

"And you hated my pa for it."

"I did," he said real matter-of-fact-like. Cold-blooded. "But I respected your mother. No, I loved your mother. Then she had you, and I loved being with you. I hoped, someday, that she'd finally get the courage to leave him and marry me. Then she and I could raise you together."

"But then you drove us into a truck."

He winced.

"Yes. And then I lost you both."

Dr. Vega was talking to Castro now. He was pointing at me, but Castro was shaking his head.

"So, what, you reckoned you'd just go betray your country out of spite or something?"

"No." His eyes looked real concerned. "I did it for you. You deserve a better life than what you had in Cullman. So, if I had to pledge to help Cuba to get the life for you that you deserve, I was willing to do it."

I didn't know what to say to that.

"You betrayed your country for me?" I thought for a bit. "You betrayed all them exiles? For me?"

He nodded. "When Castro heard that the Cuban exiles were planning an invasion—"

"How'd he hear about it?"

"Oh, he reads the *New York Times*," he said, "Anyway, when he heard about the invasion, he wanted to make sure he could crush it decisively. To make a point to Cuba and the world that his regime was not one to be taken lightly. So, I volunteered to acquire that information for him."

"Why'd you use Pa?"

"That I did out of spite," he said. "But, in helping Castro, I negotiated for a new life for myself. For us. It's what your mother would have wanted. She loved you so much."

That made me mad.

"Tommy was her boy, too. And now he's dead 'cause of what

you did. 'Cause there wasn't no air support besides him during the invasion. I'll bet Ma wouldn't have done that."

"No, she wouldn't," he said. "But she wouldn't have saved Pete Cannon's life in the hospital, either. She begged me to let him die, to end his suffering when she saw how bad he was in New Orleans. And I wanted to. But I couldn't. I was the idiot who saved his life. And she cried the day he survived. Because that was the day our dream together died."

That was awful romantic talk about my ma, and it was making me sick.

"I didn't even get to say good-bye to my brother," I said. "Didn't even see his body. So you want me to thank you 'cause you didn't kill my pa, even though now you got him in a heap of trouble? Ain't happening."

He looked a mite bit hurt from that. He hollered over to them fellas.

"El primer ministro, tengo que mostrar el cuerpo del piloto a este muchacho." He shot me another glance. *"Es su hermano."*

Fidel Castro came back over to us and looked me square in the eyes. He seemed like he was looking for something he might recognize. Finally, he nodded at the Captain.

"Sí, every boy should see his brother one last time."

Before I could ask what he meant by that, he'd motioned for a couple of soldiers to come over, and they took me and the Captain out through a great big archway to a yellow car that was parked

ISAIAH CAMPBELL

among a mess of military vehicles. We got in—one of the soldiers kept his gun trained at my head—and we drove off.

We made our way through the streets lined with buildings that looked like they was still suffering from whatever battles had been fought around them. We drove past folks riding old cars and horse-drawn wagons. Everybody moved out of the way for us, like they knew that we was automatically more important than they was, and we went straight to the heart of the city. It was weird, 'cause I remembered it being the perfect place full of money and music. And it used to have a whole mess of white folk everywhere. Not anymore.

"Where are we going?" I asked the Captain.

"To see your brother."

That sort of made my heart skip.

"So he ain't dead?"

He didn't answer.

My heart went back to beating its normal way, pumping blood, pain, and suffering through the carcass I called my body.

We pulled up in front of what must have been the capitol building and I couldn't believe my eyes. I swear, it looked just like the Capitol building in Washington, except with palm trees. We got through the security and went inside the most amazing entrance I'd ever walked through. Great big golden chandeliers and shiny tiled floors, it looked like the opposite of everything else I'd seen there in Cuba. If I squinted my eyes, I might have thought I could see President Kennedy coming around the corner. Except, what with all them Cuban guards that was walking around, I don't think it would have been good for the president's health if he did.

We made our way all through the building, down hallways and past rooms that was decorated real nice. We got to a big metal door that was near what I figured was the kitchen. One of the soldiers opened it and a blast of cold air hit my face from the hallway that was behind it. He motioned for us to walk down it.

This hallway was made of concrete and steel, and the further we walked down it, the colder I got. I was getting goose bumps so bad they was goose mountains by the time we got to another door. There were some thick snowsuits hanging on a hook outside of it.

Captain Morris picked one of them snowsuits off the wall and handed it to me.

"What is that, a door to Antarctica?" I said.

"You want to see your brother? He's in there."

I put on the snowsuit. I also had to put on gloves that was thicker than a catcher's mitt and a scarf that would cover my face. He did the same, and so did the soldier that was with us. Then the Captain opened the door.

Didn't matter that I had all that extra clothes on, I started shivering.

We walked into a room that was covered in ice. It looked like we'd stepped into a deep freezer, only there wasn't no meat or nothing in there. There was just the walls of ice, the floor of ice, and a box the size of a coffin.

I had a bad feeling I knew what was in there.

The Captain motioned for me to come over to the box. It didn't have no lid. I walked over and looked in.

It was Tommy.

He was lying in the box still with his uniform on. He had blood matted all on him, frozen like red ice-cream stains. His skin was blue. His lips was split open, but there wasn't nothing coming out.

"When they shot down his plane," the Captain said, his words making clouds in the room, "they went and recovered his body from the wreckage."

I couldn't barely talk. I didn't feel much of nothing yet, 'cause it was too much for my little brain to take in. Like algebra.

"Why didn't they bury him?"

"They wanted to preserve it so that he could be buried by his family."

I nodded. Not 'cause I understood what he was saying, but because I was accepting it.

"So he is dead, then," I said.

"I'm afraid so."

I pulled the glove off my hand. Dadgum, it was so cold it started hurting almost instantly. But I didn't care. I reached down and touched my brother's cheek, right next to his mouth. I didn't care if it was sappy or nothing, I needed to be close to him. I wished

I was alone so I could tell him how crappy of a job I'd done with taking care of things. And there he had been, doing an amazing job taking care of them Cuban fellas in the invasion. He'd always been a billion times better than me at stuff like that.

I noticed a lump in his chest pocket. I opened the flap and pulled out what was in there.

It was that Superman action figure I'd given him.

He'd promised he'd give it back.

I'd promised myself in Cullman I wouldn't do no crying until I saw the body. Now that I saw the body, there wasn't nothing stopping them tears.

The Captain let me cry, and it was awful good of him to do it. Then he pulled me away after a few minutes, and that was good of him too, 'cause my tears was starting to give me frostbite on my face.

We went back out to the hallway and worked on getting out of them snowsuits. None of us didn't say nothing while we did that, I reckon they felt like I needed my space. They was right.

I was getting my foot out of the left leg of the snowsuit and realized just how hungry I was. I started to ask if we could get some food, but I stopped myself. I remembered where I was. In the middle of a Commie country, at gunpoint, with a man who tricked my pa and had tried to take away my ma. Heck, he was the reason she was dead.

I kept quiet. I could eat when I was free again.

After we got all ready to go, we left the building and got back into the yellow car.

"So, now do you trust me?" the Captain said.

Not one bit.

"I reckon them last words he told me was his last words ever," I said. "'Take care of Pa.' How am I going to do that if I'm here?"

He didn't like that question too much.

"Pete Cannon," he said through clenched teeth, "will be fine. He'll be in a federal prison where they'll take care of him. Two hots and a cot."

"What if they kill him?"

"Kennedy won't kill anybody."

I clenched my fists.

"I can't believe you'd do a rat-fink thing like that to my pa. He ain't never done nothing to you except loved the same woman you loved."

"I can't believe you want to protect him so much," he said, and he was halfway to yelling. "He's never taken care of you. Never done what a father ought to do."

"What's that supposed to mean?" If that fella didn't have a gun to my head, I'd have socked the Captain in the jaw.

"He didn't bother giving you the life you deserved. Never taught you how to be a man. Plus the bills, the money problems, everything he let fall on your plate." He looked about fit to be tied. "Why, he never even explained the birds and the bees to you."

"Birds fly and bees make honey. I don't need him to tell me that."

He rolled his eyes.

"How are babies made, Johnny?"

He stumped me with that.

"I don't know. I ain't never really cared."

"A man and a woman make the baby, and she's pregnant with that baby for nine months. When is your birthday?"

I knew that one. "July 6, 1948."

"When did Pete Cannon get let out of the hospital in New Orleans?"

"It was a Christmas present. December 25, 1947."

"How many months are in between?"

I had to do some counting, and I didn't like the number.

"Only six and a half. But, if it takes nine months from the time a baby's made till a baby's born, and Pa wasn't out of the hospital but six months before I was born, then that means—"

The Captain reached over and grabbed my hand real eager. It was like he'd been waiting for that moment for a while.

"Son. I wanted to tell you."

Yeah, that was the straw that did it. I yanked my hand out of his and balled it up and I socked him right in the eye. The fella with the gun yelled at me and put the barrel right up to my forehead.

The Captain waved him off. He was rubbing his eye something fierce.

"Fine. Fidel was right, you aren't ready. Maybe after you've sat in a cell for a while, then you'll realize that this isn't a bad turn of events for you."

We didn't talk no more while we drove back to the fortress. They dragged me out of the car and threw me back into the cell with Carlos. And the whole time, I was trying to not think of what I knew was the truth.

Pa wasn't my pa. The Captain was.

CHAPTER ELEVEN
REMEMBER THE MAINE

Welcome back, Johnny," Carlos said to me. "Did you enjoy your big adventure?"

I sat down in the dirt and really started feeling how bad things was. I couldn't answer him or nothing, I just started blubbering.

Dadgummit, I'd gone almost seven years without doing no crying, and now I'd done it twice in one day. Maybe it didn't count as much since it was in Havana.

It was funny, just a few days before, I would have paid money for Captain Morris to be my real father. But now, knowing that polecat's blood was running through my veins, I felt like I needed an IV of Palmolive dish soap.

Nobody tells you what to do when you find out you ain't blood related to your own flesh and blood. But they do tell you what to do when you find out you've been duped. At least, they do in Alabama.

We call it an Alabama Beat-Down, and Captain Morris was due about five of them. I just had to stop the waterworks first.

I buried my face in the dirt so Carlos wouldn't see me and I let my tears come out until they was all gone. I barely noticed that he'd come over and was patting me on the back.

"Oh, *chico*, it's going to be all right."

After my eyes was all dried up and I'd made a mudpie with tears, I rolled over and looked at him.

"I'm sorry for making a mess of myself in front of you," I said.

"It's okay," he said, and he looked real sincere. "Around here, crying is necessary for survival."

"Well, that ain't what I usually do." I had to change the subject. We was getting too touchy-feely for my taste. I looked at his banged-up hands again. "What do you do? Or, what *did* you do? In the invasion, I mean."

He leaned back.

"When we were in Nicaragua, I was the radio operator. I sent information about our training and preparations to a man who Raúl told me was sending it to Washington." He sighed. "Only later did I learn he was actually sending it to Che Guevara."

"I think you was talking to my pa. WX5RJ?"

He looked real shocked.

"He didn't know he was doing nothing wrong," I said. "I swear. He got tricked same as you. And he's in a heap of trouble now, same as you."

He processed that for a bit, then nodded.

"It's a small world, isn't it?" he said. "During the invasion, I was a gunner for an American pilot. The only one to fly for us."

"My brother, Tommy."

Now he didn't look shocked no more. He looked excited.

"You are Corporal Cannon's brother? And WX5RJ's son?"

I looked out at the Captain.

"Yeah, I'm Pete Cannon's son, so to speak."

"And you know Mr. Thomassen?"

"Yeah, I do."

"Then," he said, and sat back, his whole face changing, "the universe has given us hope."

I looked at Castro, Che, Dr. Vega, and the Captain all standing together next to a pillar in the middle of the clearing.

"What do you reckon they're talking about?" I said.

He came and looked at them with me.

"What to do with you, I would imagine."

I tried to hear them talking, but it didn't do no use. Even with that Superman in my pocket, I didn't have no superpowers.

"I thought they was going to keep me in this cell," I said.

"That is not a permanent solution," he said. "I overheard them discussing it while you were sleeping. Castro is not willing to hold an American boy captive. He is trying to maintain the image of Cuba's innocence, and keeping you prisoner will tarnish that image to the world. That's why he wanted you to pledge alle-

ISAIAH CAMPBELL

giance to Cuba. Then you would simply be a defector."

"But I ain't going to do that."

"So he needs to decide what to do with you. And those three men have three very different ideas."

I watched them more closer. They was all arguing pretty passionately with each other, and Castro was listening real intently.

"Let me guess, Captain Morris wants to take care of me himself." I figured that 'cause he was pointing at me and then at his own chest.

"Yes. Exiled into his custody," Carlos said. "Raúl, on the other hand, wants to reprogram you. He says he's studied brainwashing techniques and wants to use you as his test subject."

Dr. Vega was drawing circles on his own head and making like there was wires coming off. I really didn't want to know the details of his plan.

"What about Che?" I said. Then I noticed that he was acting like he was shooting a rifle at something. "Never mind, I think I can guess."

He squeezed my shoulder. "No worries. We will find a way. Somehow."

My nose was running and I wiped it on my hand. I left a streak of mud on my wrist. That's when I realized my face had to be as dirty as a riverbank. I felt in my pockets for a hanky or something to wipe my face with. I didn't have nothing but some wadded up notebook paper. I pulled it out and started wiping.

"What's that?" Carlos said.

I looked at the paper more closer.

"It's a paper from my survival guide."

"Your what?"

"I've collected all kinds of lessons from history. Figured it'd keep me out of trouble." I started to wad the paper up. "Reckon I was wrong."

He stopped me before I tossed it.

"What does it say?"

The paper was from February 15.

February 15, 1898—USS Maine *Sunk in Havana Harbor.*

I remembered that story pretty good. The Cubans was trying to get free from Spain, kind of like how we Americans had tried to get free from England. And folks thought we ought to help the Cubans out. But we was staying out of the fight. Then somebody sunk our ship that we had parked in Havana Harbor, the *USS Maine*, and folks blamed the Spanish. So everybody got to yelling, "Remember the *Maine*," and eventually we got in there and helped the Cubans find their freedom.

And the lesson I wrote was real good too.

The closer you stand to a fight, the more likely you are to get punched.

But the other lesson, the one that I wrote down 'cause Eddie'd put a firecracker in my lunchbox, seemed more appropriate.

If you're going to blow something up, you're going to have to run like hell.

I showed it to Carlos. He started grinning.

"That is my kind of plan. We just need to blow something up." He started looking around.

"That don't seem like much of a plan at all," I said.

He looked shocked.

"I thought you said you were Corporal Cannon's brother? He told me you were brave and wild. Not timid like a mouse."

That got my gumption up a bit.

"Yeah, well maybe that was before I saw him dead on the ice. That's when I realized that the bad guys win a lot more than you think."

"They haven't won yet," Carlos said. "That's why he is frozen."

"Captain Morris said he's frozen so his family can bury him."

"That's what they want you to think, *chico*. But really, he is frozen because Castro fears he may still lose."

"How? The Commies won. It's all over."

"He fears America may successfully convince the world that the US was not involved in the invasion. Cuba's victory will seem much smaller if they only defeated the exiles. If they defeated America as well, then they are on track to becoming a world power. Freezing your brother's body means preserving evidence, in his mind, that the US was involved."

"Seems like a lot of trouble," I said.

"It's priority number one to Castro that the world believe Cuba was innocent in the invasion and that America attacked them without reason."

That got my wheels to spinning, and I thought about them Rosenbergs.

"So, if it got out that they was stealing information beforehand by tricking an American into betraying his own country?"

He nodded. "That would be a nightmare for Castro."

That was the spark I needed for an idea.

"Hey!" I screamed out at the soldiers. "I hope y'all enjoy looking innocent while you can. 'Cause I got a buddy with a tape recording that proves y'all was as crooked as anybody else. And I reckon he's going to sell it to your favorite paper, the *New York Times*."

Captain Morris came over.

"What tape recording?"

"That phone call between you and my *pa*." I made real sure to emphasize that last word, and the Captain looked like it stung him good. "Willie recorded it and it shows everything y'all done to trick him. And how Castro cheated his win. You're all a bunch of dadgum liars and cheats. And wait until they hear about how y'all are keeping Tommy on ice. You know that's what movies is made of."

Castro heard everything I said, probably on account that I was screaming it at the top of my lungs. He poked Dr. Vega and motioned him toward me. Vega came to my cell. He glared at Carlos.

"*Siempre estás hablando,*" he said. "*¿Por qué no cuando son interrogados?*"

"*Besa mi culo, primo,*" Carlos said. That must have been real bad, 'cause Vega slammed his fist into our door and called a soldier over. They opened the door and the soldiers grabbed Carlos and dragged him out.

Right when he was going out the door, though, he started throwing a fit. He grabbed it and wouldn't let go. They started beating on him, kicking him and everything. He didn't let go. One of the fellas slammed Carlos's hand with the butt of his gun. Except Carlos moved his hand just in time and the rifle slammed on the cell door, right where Carlos's hand had been.

Right on the lock.

Carlos was as docile as a lamb after that, but them soldiers was super concerned about the cell door. They was fiddling with it and couldn't get it to shut good.

"Está roto," one of them hollered to Che Guevara. Che pointed at him and told him to stand in front of the door.

Meanwhile, the Captain had gone back over and was getting chewed out by Castro. He was going on and on, in both Spanish and English, and I could tell that he wasn't happy at all that there was loose ends back in Cullman. Finally, Captain Morris had enough.

"Fine," he said, and threw his hands in the air. "You want it finished, I'll go finish it. Just get me on a plane back to the States and I'll get that tape recording." He looked over at me and I reckon he wanted to sting me like I'd stung him. "I might even shoot that idiot from Cullman, too."

Him, Castro, and Che all left together. I knew the Captain was trying to scare me straight, but he hadn't scared me none. I was done with that. You can only mess around for so long with somebody from Alabama.

Now I was pissed.

I would have run out that busted cell door right then, but the dadgum guard was watching me like a hawk. Plus, I wasn't faster than no speeding bullets or nothing. Still didn't have no superpowers from that Superman.

I looked over at the other side of the courtyard, where Carlos was getting the tar beat out of him. I reckoned busting the lock was part of his plan, but I didn't know what part him getting whipped was.

Then I saw him grab something off one of the guard's belts and throw it.

A truck that was parked all the way over on the other side of the fort we was in exploded into a ball of flames.

And just like that, I figured out his plan.

Remember the *Maine*.

Everybody went running to put out the fire, or get burned up by it, I didn't much care. Including the guard that was watching me. Now, I had to move fast. I whispered to Superman that, if he could loan me just a little bit of his powers, I'd be much obliged.

I opened the door and ran off to the arch we'd gone out of before. All the guards was so busy trying to put out the fire, they didn't even notice me.

I got out of that arch and took off down the hill, following the road as best as I could until I started imagining them soldiers coming after me. Then I took to ducking through the trees and bushes.

I figured I should run to Havana Harbor, which was the easiest thing to do, 'cause it was right there in front of me. I figured I could hop on a boat or something and get headed to Florida.

It wasn't my best plan, but it was a start. Of course, I didn't have no idea where there might be some boats with refugees heading to America, or even where you might find folks like that.

I reckoned I needed to ask a local for directions.

I ran around, trying to find someplace where I could ask for directions without getting hollered at or shown off to the soldiers. Considering I was one of the only white fellas around, I knew that would be hard to do. But I finally found a place where there was a whole mess of people just standing around, and I decided to try there.

It was a building with a sign on it that said LA PANADERIA. I remembered that word from Tommy's schoolbooks, 'cause it was one of the only ones I'd taken interest in. It meant "The Bakery." There was a line of people stretched out from it, all waiting to get up to the door where they was handing out bags of bread or something. At first I was amazed at how patient they was all waiting, then I realized from their faces that they wasn't being patient, they just knew hurrying wasn't an option.

I ran up to one of them fellas, a plump one with a mustache, and tried to remember anything that Tommy used to say when he was practicing his phrases in his room. Of course, he took a year of French and also of German along with Spanish, so I couldn't be sure which language I was speaking exactly. But I figured I could get my message across.

"Pardonnez-moi, monsieur. Yo no hablo kein Deutsch. Wo ist die baño? Merci."

He blinked at me like I was crazy. Maybe he didn't speak no Spanish, either. I tried using what had worked with Carlos.

"I am *looking-o* for the *place-o* where *el* folks trying to *escape-o* might get on *el* boat. Can *you-o* show *me-o*?" That was the best I could do.

He shook his head. Dadgummit.

I was about to try again, but a soldier driving a motorcycle with a sidecar drove up. I ducked behind the fella I was talking to.

"I don't know if you know Carlos Martí," I whispered, "but I'm his little pal. Hide me."

The fella must have understood that, 'cause he got in front of me better.

"No más pan," the soldier barked at them folks. I think that meant there wasn't no more bread. *"Vamanos."*

The people started shuffling away, some of them grumbling a bit. The soldier yelled at them and they shut up. The fella I was hiding behind tapped me and pointed me at the motorcycle the soldier was on. I wasn't real sure what he meant by that. Then he started hollering at the guard.

"¡Tiranía! ¡Tiranía!" That reminded me of what John Wilkes Booth had shouted after he shot Lincoln, about tyrants. *"Para*

escapar del infierno, ¡nos venden al diablo!" I found out later that he'd said, "To escape from Hell, we are sold to the Devil."

Well, that didn't seem to sit too well with the soldier. He hopped off the motorcycle and came running at the fella. The fella took off running down the street, yelling *"¡Tiranía! ¡Tiranía!"* as he went.

And the motorcycle was just sitting there, still running.

I hopped on that motorcycle and I took off. And, since I only knew one direction to go, I drove back up the hill to *La Cabaña.* I reckon I was hoping Carlos would be waiting for me.

He wasn't.

I pulled up right under a big window, not really sure what to do next. I pulled out my survival guide, which had helped me so far, and opened it to:

December 17, 1903—First Flight by Orville Wright.

What was interesting about that story, I remembered, was that the Wright brothers had called every newspaper in the area to come out and witness it, but only one showed up. Nobody else believed it was going to be big news.

You don't need everybody on your side. You only need one.

Down at the bottom was the lesson I learned from Eddie, 'cause he'd hung a water balloon over my head and dropped it on me during math.

Always make sure you look up.

Just then the window above me busted through and a fella came flying down. It was Carlos. He ran over and jumped in the sidecar.

"Go! Go! Go!" he yelled.

The guards was already shooting at us, so I kicked it into gear like I saw them do in the movies and we took off.

"What'll we do next?" I said.

"We need to go to the airport."

Yeah, flying was probably a much better option than paddling a rowboat to Florida.

He started giving me directions and we moved all through the city. It was actually easier to drive a motorcycle than it was to drive a truck, which surprised me. Maybe I'd get a motorcycle of my own someday. A blue one. And I could put the Superman symbol on it.

I almost ran over a chicken 'cause I was too busy dreaming about my Super-Cycle that I wasn't paying no attention.

"Stop here," Carlos said.

We wasn't nowhere near the airport.

"Why are we here?" I said. He didn't answer.

He hopped out of the sidecar and ran up to the building we was next to. It had boards all over the windows and doors, and there was big signs that said DECLARAR EN RUINA on it. But up at the top, faded and torn up, there was another sign.

CASABLANCA

This was Mr. Thomassen's club.

Carlos ran over to the wall next to the door and he kicked at one of the bricks. It wasn't a brick. It was just plaster. He reached into the hole and pulled out a briefcase and then he ran back to the sidecar.

"What's in that?" I said.

"It doesn't affect you," he said, and looked behind us. "But those men will. Let's go."

Yeah, them soldiers was coming our way. He told me where to go so we could get turned around and we took off again.

We sped through town as best as I could drive and finally made our way to the back side of the airport. It was still pretty banged up from when them folks had bombed it right before the Bay of Pigs invasion. Still, it looked like they was sending out flights and stuff, and I reckoned it was the best bet we had to get back to Cullman.

"Okay, what's next?" Carlos said.

"What do you mean, 'what's next'? I thought we was following your plan."

"I got us this far," he said. "You're the one with the survival guide. What do we do next?"

"It ain't magic, and I ain't no wizard or nothing." I looked out at the airstrips, where there was planes getting loaded up with passengers and such. One plane had a bunch of soldiers around it. I looked closer.

Castro and Che was there talking to Captain Morris, who was getting ready to board.

"He's going to fly home?" I said. "I didn't know planes still flew from here to America."

"Only to transport children," Carlos said. "A Catholic priest in America has arranged for Cuban children to fly to the States until they can be reunited with their families."

"And Captain Morris is joining them to tear apart mine."

Carlos nodded.

"If my cousin, Raúl, has his way, those children are flying to their doom. He's hoping to use the success of defeating America's plans to convince Russia that Cuba is a good place to store weapons. And missiles. All to destroy America."

My chest got tight. Missiles in Cuba? I didn't want to be around if that ever happened.

"Maybe we could sneak onto that plane," I said.

"I'm sorry, Mr. Hitchcock, I think you have me confused with Cary Grant," he said.

"Huh?"

"This isn't a movie. Those guns have bullets that will kill us."

"What happened to all that running-in-with-no-plan stuff you was saying back in the cell?" I said.

"That was when there was no other way. Now there *is* another." He pointed over to another airstrip, where a little airplane was getting warmed up. The pilot was sitting, talking to a couple of other fellas, and they was all drinking some beer together. "Do you see what I see?"

"A free ride to America?" I said.

"And no guns," he said.

We made a pretty good plan, I thought. We ditched the motorcycle and snuck around behind them fellas with the airplane. Then
all we had to do was sneak onto the plane without them seeing us
and, once we was up in the air, Carlos said he could convince the
pilot to fly us to America.

It wasn't until we was halfway up behind them that I realized
the big problem with our plan. There was three of them and two
of us. Even though they didn't have guns, they had more fists
than we could probably handle. Especially with Carlos being all
banged up.

Them fellas was finishing off their beer and Carlos was trying
to get up to the door on the other side of the plane. I didn't know
how to do hand signals in Spanish, so I had to change the plan
without telling him.

I ran at them fellas and tried to tackle them.

And that's when I found out that they really *did* have guns.

They pulled out handguns and pointed them right at me. I
stuck my hands up in the air. They was yelling stuff in Spanish at
me and I really wished Carlos could help me out with it, 'cause I
didn't know what they was saying.

Instead he helped me out a different way.

He ran around behind them and slugged two of them with the
briefcase. The other one was so surprised, he didn't pay no attention when I wound up and landed a zinger right on his chin.

Carlos grabbed one of their guns and tossed it to me and he

took the other two. We both climbed onto the airplane. Once we got in the seats, we stared at each other.

"Well, let's get going," I said.

"Yes, let's," he said.

Neither of us did nothing.

"So, take off," I told him.

"I don't know how to fly."

"You ain't a pilot?" Dadgummit, that made things more interesting.

"No, I assumed you knew how because of your brother."

"I do. But I'm only twelve. I ain't allowed to fly. It ain't safe."

Just then, them fellas we knocked down went off running, hollering at the top of their lungs for any of them soldiers that was standing around.

"Do you know what else isn't safe?" he said. He didn't need to tell me the answer.

I did exactly like Tommy'd always showed me, turning the knobs and flipping the switches. I got us moving on down the runway.

"Could you go faster?" he said. Turns out, there was a couple of jeeps that was heading our way with them soldiers. They was bound and determined that we wasn't leaving Cuba.

"Going as fast as I can," I said. Then them soldiers started firing. "Okay, I'll try to go faster."

At the end of the runway there was a great big old fence, which wouldn't be no big deal since we was going to be up in the air before we hit it. Except for one small problem.

I couldn't remember how to get us up there.

It was the simplest thing, the easiest part of flying, how to lift off of the ground. But something about them fellas shooting and us being in Cuba, and maybe every other problem that was bouncing around in my head, was keeping that simple thing from making any sense to me. I just stared at the yoke that was right in front of me and we headed straight toward that fence.

"Anytime," Carlos said.

"I-I don't remember how," I said.

"Don't you pull back on the stick thing?"

I knew he was right, but I couldn't make myself do it. I was too scared. It all hit me at once, all the panic that I'd been fighting off that whole time. It made me about paralyzed.

He reached over and grabbed the yoke and yanked back on it. We shot up in the air and just cleared that fence. Them fellas behind us sprayed the air with their bullets and a couple hit our plane. Well, I reckon we didn't own it or nothing. So I didn't let it worry me too much.

I took a deep breath and grabbed ahold of the yoke and started steering. Them fellas kept firing, but we was getting away from them faster than they could aim good at us. After a few minutes, we'd done left the land of Cuba behind us and we was over the water. I pointed us north, 'cause I reckoned that was where home was.

"Well, I reckon we're pretty darn close to home free," I said.

"As long as they don't deploy the fighters," he said. "I don't think they will, so no worries. They don't need to draw any more attention to this story than they already have."

His confidence didn't keep me from looking out them windows every fifteen minutes, though. I was waiting for us to get a rocket shot at us.

Now, I ain't going to sit here and lie to you. Flying an airplane is a lot harder than it looks, and even though I'd done helped my brother out a hundred times or more, I really didn't have no idea what I was doing up there. That's why, even though Carlos said the Florida Keys was only about a hundred miles from Havana, we went two and a half hours staring at the ocean below us. We should have hit Florida in forty-five minutes.

See, when you're up there and you ain't got nothing but water below you, and you're depending on a compass that ain't accounting for the wind blowing you around a bit, it's real easy to get off course.

I started getting real nervous and I had Carlos try to hunt a map for us so I could maybe figure out where we was at. And then, to get my mind off of it all, I decided to take a peek inside the brief-case while he was looking underneath one of them seats.

It was filled with bundles of bills. And they wasn't no small bills, like ones or fives. They was five-hundred-dollar bills, all stacked real nice and banded together. I started to try and count how much money was in there, but Carlos closed the briefcase real fast.

"I told you this didn't concern you," he said. He handed me a map. "Now, where are we?"

It really didn't do no good looking at the map, 'cause I didn't have nothing to go by but water. Still, I tried to use my brain like how Willie might and came up with a general idea.

"Well, we're flying at about one hundred seventy miles per hour, and we've been going for nearly three hours. So we ought to be right smack in the middle of Florida, but we ain't."

"Clearly." He didn't look too happy. I had to think some more.

"But, the wind's been blowing at us real hard from the east. So, if I thought we was going north but instead we've been going northwest, then we might be about here." I pointed at a spot in the Gulf of Mexico. It was maybe a hundred miles from Alabama.

Just then the radio that I didn't even realize was on started speaking.

"Attention, aircraft. You are entering American airspace. Please identify yourself."

I reckoned that was a good sign. I picked up the microphone and talked back to them.

"Hi. My name's Johnny Cannon, and I'm from Cullman, Alabama. I'm Tommy Cannon's brother, he's a pilot with the Guard. This here airplane is from Cuba, though. I don't reckon y'all want it up in the States, but if you'd wait till I land before you do anything to it, I'd be much obliged."

They was quiet for a bit.

"Aircraft, did you say you were Johnny Cannon?"

"Yes sir, I sure did."

"Copy that."

We kept on our course and they didn't say much else to us for another good twenty minutes. We could see the land of the good old U.S. of A. in front of us. The radio came back.

"Johnny Cannon, you are cleared to land at Bates Field, the Mobile airport. Your guardian is on his way here and he will take you where you need to go."

I didn't much reckon I knew who they meant by my guardian, but it was something else he said that got me as worried as a cat in a rocking-chair store.

"Excuse me, mister, but I was wondering if you could help me out with something."

"Roger that. Go ahead."

"How do you land one of these things?"

Carlos shot me a look like he was wishing he had a parachute. I sort of wished I did too. The radio was quiet for another good five minutes, and then a different voice came through.

"Johnny Cannon, this is Major Steve Harrison, flight instructor for the Alabama Air National Guard. I taught your brother how to land a plane and I'm going to teach you how too."

The legendary Major Harrison. I was dumbstruck, so I nodded.

"Did you copy that?"

Carlos nudged me. "You have to speak into the little boxy thing."

"I copy that, mister," I said.

Major Harrison started telling me real specific instructions about moving the rudders and changing the speed and such, and I was real thankful to Tommy that I could understand it. As we got closer and closer to Mobile, we started going down and I really felt good about landing that big hunk of metal.

That is, I felt good until I actually saw the landing strip.

Dadgum, it's a whole different story when you're watching your brother bringing you in for a landing on one of them things. It looks plenty big, and plenty long enough, and there don't seem to be no reason to worry.

But when it's you landing it, that landing strip looks like the smallest little piece of concrete with no hope of keeping your airplane on it. I was sure we was going to crash and burn like the *Hindenburg* did back on May 6, 1937.

"Okay, Johnny, you're coming down just fine. Now, keep your nose up."

I looked up at the ceiling. Carlos nudged me again and pointed at the nose of the plane. I pulled back on the yoke. The nose of the plane started to lift up.

"Not too much, now. Not too much."

I kept pulling back. It didn't feel like too much yet.

"No, Johnny, you're going to flip it. Nose down a little."

I sure didn't want to flip it, so I cranked the yoke away from me.

"Not that much!" Major Harrison yelled into the radio.

Too late. We smacked right into the ground like a car hitting a wall.

"Straighten out, you need to straighten out."

I was trying. We rolled a little and our wheels was sparking against the runway. We skidded along the way and I got thrown from the seat into Carlos. Then I thought to cut our engines off.

We finally came to a stop.

"Johnny! Johnny!"

I picked up the radio.

"Yes sir?"

He started laughing.

"Are you still alive, Johnny?"

I felt of myself to make sure.

"Yes sir, I sure am."

"Then that was a good landing. Congratulations."

CHAPTER TWELVE
THE INVASION

W e'd had to sit around at the airport for a while so we could get checked out and asked a whole mess of questions. Carlos had told me to keep as quiet about things as I could, 'cause he said you couldn't never know who you could trust. So I didn't spill nothing about the Captain or Tommy being on ice or nothing. It was real hard when Major Harrison was telling me how sorry he was that my brother had died. I accepted his condolences and left it at that.

After a little while, one of them fellas came into the room and said that my guardian was there. Scared me half to death, 'cause I reckoned Captain Morris had shown up to hog-tie me and throw me in the back of his pickup.

Instead, Mr. Thomassen came in.

Come to find out, he was the reason they wasn't too surprised when I radioed in. After he'd woken up in the ditch, he started calling up every person in the government that owed him money and told them he'd cancel their debt if they found me and got me home safe. Turns out Major Harrison owed him something fierce, so as soon as he heard my name, he got right on it. I was never so glad that folks had gambling problems before in my life.

Mr. Thomassen and Carlos hugged on each other like two best friends would, sort of how I reckoned me and Willie would when we saw each other again. Then, after we got done appeasing the folks there at the airport, we got into his Cadillac to head home. That's when we told him about what had happened in Havana.

"So Dr. Morris is on his way to Cullman?" he said.

"Most likely," I said. "And we got to get the tape to Short-Guy so Pa can get out. We should call him up from Birmingham, and the National Guard, and maybe even the president. Somebody needs to go over and protect the Parkinses."

"Right," he said. He started to say something else to me, but I had to admit, I was starting to fall asleep, so I wasn't listening so good. It had been a real long day.

He grinned in the rearview mirror and turned on the radio. Then he and Carlos started talking to each other in Spanish. I listened to the music and, in two minutes, I was fast asleep.

I must have been real tired, 'cause I slept almost the whole way from Mobile to Cullman County. When I woke up, it was darker than the inside of a skunk's butt.

ISAIAH CAMPBELL

"Where we at?" I said. I interrupted a conversation they was having.

"Fifty miles away," Mr. Thomassen said.

I could have guessed that, actually. I recognized some of them hills as being home. Even though I hadn't been gone but a day or two, it felt like it had been forever since I'd seen them. Sure it was dark, but there ain't no darkness that can hide home from you.

Anyway, there was a light I could see on the horizon. A light I hadn't never seen before.

"Say, what's that?" I said, pointing over to the light.

Mr. Thomassen looked.

"It looks like a fire, by my guess." He watched it for a bit. "Yes, definitely a fire. Look at how it's flickering."

"Do you reckon it's a forest fire?"

"Probably. There isn't anything over there, that I can think of."

I had to swallow real hard.

"No, there is," I said. "That's where Colony is."

"Oh, those poor people. The last thing they need is a fire."

"They ain't got no fire department over there either." I was starting to get sick to my stomach. "We need to go over there and help them."

"We can call the fire department from the shop. We have to find Dr. Morris."

I knew that was the sensible thing to do. I knew we had to have priorities, and I knew that going off track was the worst idea anyone could have.

But somebody had to stand up for Colony.

"Mr. Thomassen, we got to do it. We can't let them poor folk burn."

He let out a sigh, but he didn't argue. He got off the highway and started taking them back roads that you had to take to get to Colony. I wasn't sure if he was mad about it or not, but I was sure glad that he was doing it.

As we got closer to the limits of Colony, it was becoming more and more clear that there was serious trouble. It wasn't so much that there was a wide fire burning. It was that the fire was burning at the most important place in Colony. At least in my opinion.

It was burning the church.

When we got a little closer, I saw Mr. Thomassen and Carlos both get tense, and Mr. Thomassen stopped on the side of the road real short of where we was supposed to be going.

"What's wrong?" I said. "We need to go help out."

"This fire was no accident," Mr. Thomassen said.

"What you mean?" I said, then I saw what they'd seen.

All around the church, watching it burn and carrying torches of their own, was a bunch of fellas with white robes and white hoods on their heads.

It was the Klan.

And that could only mean one thing.

Cullman had invaded Colony.

"We can't get involved in something like this. Not right now," Mr. Thomassen said.

"We can't *not* get involved," I said. "For all we know, Willie and his pa are up there. And maybe the tape."

"Johnny, we should go get the sheriff. This is bigger than we can handle."

I was watching the building as it was falling apart. The flames was starting to reach up to the steeple.

"There ain't no time," I said.

Carlos reached back and squeezed my knee.

"Well then, *chico*, what do you suggest? Something from that survival guide of yours?"

I reached in my pocket. Then I got an idea.

"Superman," I said, and I showed them both the action figure. Mr. Thomassen looked at me in the rearview mirror.

"I think we'd have a better shot getting the sheriff."

I shook my head.

"No, not actually Superman," I said. "Back in 1946, there was a fella that wanted to hit the Klan where it hurt. So he got in there with them and learned all their secrets, every single dirty little thing that they was hiding, 'cause it would make them seem less scary to folks on the outside. 'Cause that's how the Klan gets their power, from folks's fear."

"So, he was Superman?"

"No. He gave all the information to the fellas that was running the Superman radio show. They made a whole series out of it, called *Superman and the Clan of the Fiery Cross*. And the story was that Superman beat the Klan by getting in there among them, drawing their fire, and pulling off their masks. Which is just what the show did to the real Klan, it pulled off their masks. It was the biggest punch in the gut the Klan ever got."

"So you're saying—" Mr. Thomassen said.

"We should do the exact same thing," I said.

We drew straws real fast and Carlos got the short one. I was super glad. I reckoned I'd done faced death enough times for one day.

Me and Mr. Thomassen got out of the car and snuck up to the back side of them Klansmen. I was hoping I could see Reverend Parkins or Willie, maybe, and that they was okay. Or, if they was stuck in the church, maybe we could hurry up and get them out.

But then I saw what the mess of them fellas was doing together, and I completely forgot all about our plan. 'Cause they was all gathered around Reverend Parkins, who was lying on the ground, covering up his head. And they was all kicking him.

It felt like a bone in my brain snapped in half. I started to run out of the shadows, but Mr. Thomassen stopped me.

"Patience," he said. "We'll get him."

The hooded fellas stopped kicking Reverend Parkins all of a sudden and a couple of them tilted their hooded heads like they was hearing something. Then I heard it too.

Carlos was singing some Cuban song as he staggered out of the darkness right in there among them.

"*¡Buenas noches, amigos!*" he said, waving a beer bottle he must have found in the dirt on the way up there. "Beautiful fire." He walked over to Reverend Parkins and held his bottle out to him. "*¿Cerveza, padre?*"

One of the fellas that had been doing the kicking gave Carlos a push.

"Move on. This don't concern you."

Carlos held his hand up to his ear.

"*¿Que?* I'm sorry, I couldn't hear you through your pillowcase."

The fella stepped closer and yelled.

"I said, move on, this—"

Carlos grabbed his hood and ripped it off.

It was Bob Gorman. He started cussing something fierce and wound up to punch Carlos, but then he stopped.

Mr. Thomassen had darted out of the shadows quick as a whip and had his pistol in the back of his head.

"Hello, Bob. It's true what they say, when the cat's away."

Bob raised his hands above his head and got perfectly still. All them other hooded finks did the exact opposite. They all took off running.

"Now, I think we need to have a long conversation regarding your debt," Mr. Thomassen said.

I went to check on Reverend Parkins.

"They took Willie," he said, his voice all raspy. "We heard they were burning the church, so we came down. One of them grabbed Willie while the others attacked me. I don't know where they went."

"Don't worry, I'll find him. Tell me, what did the fella look—"

I heard a kid's voice cussing from the other side of the church. Said something about his bike chain getting stuck.

I jumped up and ran around the other side in time to see a fat Junior Klansman trying to take off on his bicycle.

I tackled him and yanked his hood off.

Eddie started crying immediately.

"Who took Willie?" I yelled in his face.

"I don't know," he blubbered. "It was a stranger we didn't know. This was all his idea."

"A stranger?"

"Yeah. A Texan with a mustache."

Captain Morris.

"Where did he take him?"

"He said something about getting to the house."

I felt all ready to backhand him right across his fat face, had my hand raised and everything, and he knew it was coming 'cause he braced himself for it. But then I saw Carlos helping Reverend Parkins, and Reverend Parkins was looking over at me, and I just couldn't do it. I dropped my hand.

"I knew you was a backstabbing, low-life scumbag," I said.

"But I used to at least think you was human. Now that I've seen what you done this time, though, I know I was wrong. You can't do something like this, to people like them, and have a drop of human blood in your body."

He just kept on crying. I took his bike and headed up the mountain.

It didn't matter to me that the church was ten miles away from Willie's house, or that I was pretty tired from facing them Klansmen, I pedaled harder and faster than I ever had in my life. There wasn't no way I was going to let the Captain hurt Willie, or Mrs. Parkins, or their little girl.

I was almost to their house when I heard screaming. Only it wasn't coming from the Parkinses' house. I heard it coming all the way from my house.

And I could tell the voice was Willie's.

I jumped off the bike and cut through the woods that was between our houses. I ran over the mountain to our backyard and slipped in behind our shed to try and figure out where the yelling was coming from. It didn't take too long.

"Where is the tape?" the Captain yelled. They was in the kitchen. I could see through the window there was some water boiling.

"I ain't telling you," Willie said. He sounded like he'd already been hurt some.

I heard some splashing, and then what sounded like meat getting sizzled.

And Willie screamed bloody murder.

I snuck over to the kitchen window and peeked in.

Willie was tied up to a chair with his pants off. Steam was coming off his good leg, right out of some blisters. The Captain was filling up a coffee mug with boiling water.

"Where is it?" he said. He started tilting that cup over Willie's leg.

Willie had his teeth clenched and he was breathing really hard.

"You might as well just kill me. You ain't getting nothing out of me."

"Murder is too easy," the Captain said, and then he poured out his cup onto the leg.

I had to turn my head, but I knew what was happening 'cause Willie was screaming something fierce.

"I've got plenty of water. And the good news is, I've got plenty of time, too. Nobody in this county is going to come looking for you, not for a while." He jammed a glob of tobacco into his mouth. "So, go ahead and take your time. You'll tell me where it is eventually." He started to get more water into his cup.

I had to do something.

I ran around to the front yard where our busted-up truck was still sitting. I reached through the missing windshield and started honking the horn.

I could hear the Captain cussing. I heard him head through the house and start to open the front door, so I ran around to the back.

I hopped through the back door and went in there where Willie was.

As soon as he saw me he started fighting back some tears. I went over to untie him.

"No," he said, "you got to get the tape first."

"I got to get you out of here." I showed him the cut that was still on my hand. "We're blood brothers, remember?"

"Yeah, and I ain't letting your pa get punished for something he didn't do." He forced himself to smile at me. "I don't wear short pants anyhow. I'll survive this a little longer."

I didn't want to do it. The thought of letting him take all that for me and my pa wasn't right. You just didn't do that for somebody.

Not unless you was brothers.

"Okay, where's the tape?"

"You remember all them holes I made in your shed's roof with the rifle?"

He didn't have to say no more. I bolted out of there, and it was just in time, 'cause I heard the Captain heading back into the house. I went behind the shed and started climbing up the pile of wood that was stacked up. All the while, I could still hear Willie screaming and the Captain doing more pouring. It made it real hard to concentrate.

I got up on the roof and felt around for one of the holes that Willie'd put in there with the gun. I found one, but it wasn't big enough to hold a tape. I moved over a bit and felt for the next one. It was empty too.

I remembered that he'd hit right on the corner with one of his shots, so I inched across the roof to check there. I got to where I could almost feel the hole with my fingertips. But then the roof remembered that it was old and weak. One of the boards I was leaning on fell into the shed. It banged against my bike and made one heck of a racket.

Not to mention that it almost took me down with it.

I heard the Captain cuss again, but I was dangling from the hole I'd just made and couldn't run off or nothing. I tried to hold my breath and be quiet, 'cause he came out the back door to see what was making all the noise.

"This is why I hate the woods," he said. "Stupid beasts get into everything."

Then he must have spied the shed.

"Of course," he said as he went inside. "You hid it in the shed, didn't you?"

"See, that's the sort of thing somebody that don't know science would do," Willie said. "But I know that rain and dirt will really mess up a good tape. Make it sound all funny. So I didn't put it out there."

The Captain went back inside.

"You didn't put it in the shed, you say?" the Captain said.

"Yup. In fact, you know what? I'll tell you where it is. It's out in the lawn. In a hole I dug."

"Come on," the Captain said. I heard him cut the ropes that was holding Willie to the chair.

"Wait, why are we going out back?" Willie said.

"Don't throw me in the briar patch, Brer Wolf," Captain Morris said. "You people all think alike."

They came out the back door.

I pulled myself up onto the roof again and dug my hand into the hole. The tape was in there. I grabbed it and shoved it in my pocket.

I started to crawl back to the other side of the shed.

"What's that up there?" the Captain said. I reckoned he saw my shadow.

It was one of them moments when you know that you only got one shot to do the right thing. One shot to be a hero. One shot to be Superman.

And I was going to be the best dadgum Superman there ever was.

I ran to the edge of the shed and jumped off, both fists out in front of me. I soared through the air, and it almost felt like I was flying. Then I collided with the Captain's face.

That felt even better.

"Get out of here, Willie!" I yelled as I rolled off the Captain. He shook off my punch and tried to grab me.

"I ain't leaving you," Willie said.

I smacked the Captain in the jaw and jumped up.

"What you going to do with one leg?" I yelled at Willie. "Get on home. I can take care of myself."

The Captain grabbed my legs and pulled me back down to the ground. Willie watched for a minute and then he went off around the house as fast as he could.

I gave the Captain a kick in the gut and I braced myself for another hit from him.

He pulled a gun out instead.

"I don't know how you got here. But you're going back with me." He cocked the gun. "Unless you're bulletproof."

I was pretty sure I wasn't. I raised my hands.

He spied the tape that was in my pocket and fished it out.

"You made me swallow my tobacco," he said. "But I'll forgive it for this. Now, get up to my truck. We've got a flight to catch."

I kept my hands raised while he put the gun in the back of my head and we walked around the house to his truck.

"Didn't have to be like this, son."

"I got my hands raised and I'm walking to your truck," I said. "But you're going to need a bigger gun than that to make me listen to you calling me 'son.'"

He chuckled as he opened the door and made me get in.

"My God, you're as full of spunk as your mother."

He got in behind the wheel and got to looking for his keys. They was apparently in the same pocket he'd stuck the tape in, 'cause he fished the tape out and threw it up on the dash. He started the truck and drove us off. He steered with one hand while he kept the gun pointed to my head with the other. I hoped he didn't get the trigger and the turn signal mixed up.

"So, I reckon we're headed back to Cuba, ain't we?"

He turned pretty hard down the road. He was going fast down the mountain. When he turned, the tape slid across the dash closer to me.

"Yeah," he said. "For a little while, until you pledge your allegiance. Which you will. Then we'll go off somewhere else."

The road turned right and the tape slid over to his side.

"Moscow?" I said. "Going to help Che Guevara get them missiles?"

To the left. The tape was right in front of me again.

"Yes, that's the next stop. Then to China, North Korea, maybe into a couple of countries in Africa. It's like a tour of the world. You'll learn things, we'll make Fidel happy. Then we'll settle down in Switzerland." He wasn't expecting the next right turn and the tape hopped across the dash again.

"And what about Pa?"

He grunted.

"What about him? I don't have time to do anything to him, and without this evidence, he'll spend the rest of his days in prison."

I was trying to think of something else to say, 'cause I needed him to be talking when we got to the highway at the bottom of the mountain. That way he'd stop on instinct and I could hop out. But I was having a hard time thinking, 'cause I could hear something unusual coming from behind us.

I figured out what it was.

He came around the last turn, a left one, before the highway. The tape slid across right in front of me. I grabbed it and then I opened the door next to me.

He slammed on his brakes and I almost busted my nose on the dash. We was about five feet away from the highway.

"What are you doing?" he said. "You think if you get out I won't hunt for you? I won't track you down? Do you honestly think I won't shoot you? I'm a doctor, I could stop the bleeding."

"I'd rather take my chances with you shooting me than with a truck hitting me." I rolled out of the door into the ditch.

And I did it just in time.

Right then, a tore-up pickup with a busted-in windshield that had been parked in our yard slammed right into the back of the Captain's truck. Him and his truck went flying out across the highway and off the edge of the mountainside, flipped over, and bounced off a few trees on their way down the hill, until we couldn't see them no more.

Meanwhile, our pickup came to a stop a little bit in front of me. The driver door opened and Willie climbed out as best he could. I ran over to him.

"Turns out there's at least one thing you *can* do with only one good leg," he said.

"Why'd you do that?" I helped him get his balance on the ground.

"We're blood brothers."

I nodded. There wasn't nothing more to say or do about that.

The truck wouldn't start no more on account of the engine getting banged up as bad as it did, so we knew we'd have to walk wherever we was going to go. It wouldn't have been nothing more than a walk in the park to go up the mountain, but Willie was worse off than usual, so we walked along the highway and hoped we'd see a car to hitch a ride with.

After a little ways I was all done telling him about everything that had happened to me. We walked for a bit in silence until a Chevy came around the bend and I hopped in front of the headlights. It screeched to a stop.

"Johnny?" a voice said from the passenger side.

I squinted in the lights.

"Martha?"

Sure enough, it was Martha Macker and her ma. After a little bit of explaining, they let me and Willie into their backseat. They didn't even mention nothing about how beat up we both looked.

"Your hair looks nice," I said to Martha. Then I realized it was the first time I'd ever said much of anything to her. But it did look nice, like Jackie Kennedy's hair.

She blushed.

"I got it done in Montgomery. Right before we went to hear Dr. King speak."

"Dadgummit, I've had a real mess with doctors lately," I said.

That was two things I'd said to her. "They ain't exactly been good for my health."

"No, Dr. King is different," Willie said. "He's a regular Super-Negro."

We was driving down the mountain toward Colony. I was sure thankful the Mackers hadn't been a part of the invasion.

We was coming around a bend on the highway and him and Martha was telling me about what this Dr. King fella was doing, and I just about thought things was finally better. Then Mrs. Macker screamed and slammed on her brakes and we all flew off our seats.

Bloody and all tore up, Captain Morris stood in the middle of the road with his gun pointed straight at all of us inside the car. He looked about halfway to death's door.

"Get out of the car, Johnny!" he screamed.

He wasn't the only one. Martha and Mrs. Macker was screaming too.

"Shut up!" He walked over and tapped the window right next to Martha's head. "Johnny, out."

I didn't move. Didn't know how to.

He hit the window real hard with his gun and it shattered. Then he reached in and grabbed Martha by the hair and dragged her out. He held the gun to her head.

"I said get out, Johnny!"

I could tell Martha was as scared as she'd ever been in her entire life. I opened up my door and stepped out.

ISAIAH CAMPBELL

"Captain, let her go. This ain't about her."

He stepped toward me.

"You're right, it's not. It's about my son. *My* son." He wasn't letting go of her for nothing. "Why can't you just accept the truth? Your mother is dead. Your brother is dead. I'm the only real family you have."

"Your son?" I yelled. Finally yelled at him. "*Your* son died. Back in Havana, I died. When my ma died, when you killed her by driving right in front of that truck. You killed us both."

He glared at me and I thought I saw tears in his eyes.

"So, if you're aiming to put a bullet in somebody," I said, "put one in me. Finish what you started. 'Cause God knows I've already been dead for years."

He flung Martha off to the side and pointed his gun right at my head.

"Maybe you're right," he said.

I closed my eyes. If my brains was about to be roadkill, I didn't want to see it coming. I always said them deers ought to learn how to close their eyes.

Standing there with my eyes closed, it almost felt natural. The crickets chirping, the breeze hitting me. It was the perfect setting to get sent to Heaven in.

Then a shot rang out.

But the Captain hadn't fired.

I opened my eyes to see the Captain falling to the ground with a bullet hole right in his chest. I turned around to see who fired.

It was Pa.

He and Short-Guy had pulled up behind us a ways. Judging from Short-Guy's empty holster, I guessed the gun was his. Pa must have grabbed it.

"Johnny, are you okay?" Pa said as he ran up at me.

I looked back at the Captain, sprawled out there on the ground. My flesh-and-blood father shot by my pa.

"Yeah, I reckon I am."

So it turned out that, while I was sleeping in the car on the way up from Mobile, Mr. Thomassen had stopped at a gas station and called up Short-Guy in Birmingham. Told him we had proof that Pa was innocent and everything. But he didn't get me no snacks. Still, I reckon he saved my life, so I wouldn't hold that against him.

In fact, it was pretty hard to hold anything against anybody after a night that had been filled up with fires and torturing Willie and guns and such. Nothing just seemed to matter too much. Besides that, it ended with three of the best things I'd ever gotten to have in my entire life.

First off, Martha Macker was so dadgum scared after what happened on the highway that she needed somebody to put their arms around her. And her ma got caught up in telling Short-Guy what had happened before they got there and asking for some explaining, so somebody else had to step up to do it. I was sort of scared to offer at first, but Willie told me if he could drag his burned-up legs into a truck to drive it down a dark mountain, I could offer to hold Martha. I had a bad feeling he was going to use that against me for just about everything from then on out. I'd have to draw the line at alligator wrestling. Maybe.

So I got to hold Martha in my arms and smell her hair. And if Heaven is anything like what that was like, I want to say my prayers twice a day so I can go there. Provided it don't have a body sitting in the middle of the road.

The second good thing that came from that night happened after the sheriff got out there. Short-Guy right away flashed his badge and gave him a real detailed account of what happened, except he took the credit for shooting the Captain away from Pa. Which I reckoned was good. Then Short-Guy had the sheriff help him load up the Captain's body into the trunk of his car, 'cause the folks at his office would want to see the body. He also mentioned something about always getting his man. That made me remember what Mr. Thomassen had said about us rewriting the ending to Short-Guy's story. It was starting to sound like maybe we'd done it.

After that, we headed up to the Parkinses' house to get Willie home and get ourselves some hot tea. Mr. Thomassen and Carlos was up there with Reverend Parkins, and he'd done told Mrs. Parkins about how I'd saved him from the Klan. Then Willie told the story about me getting him away from the Captain. Then Mrs. Parkins came over and gave me a hug. And it might have been one of the warmest, tightest hugs I'd ever felt. For the first time in a long time, I knew what it was like to be hugged by a mother.

Life was good.

Right then, the clock on the mantel dinged midnight and we was all super surprised at how late it was.

"Hey, Johnny, it's the first of June now," Willie said. "What's today's thing?"

I thought for a spell.

"Today's the day Benedict Arnold was court-martialed, back in 1779. Which reminds me." I fished the tape out of my pocket and handed it to Short-Guy. "I reckon you need to listen to this."

Short-Guy took it and stuck it in his pocket.

"I'll have to wait until I get back to the office," he said. "Unless you have a tape player nearby."

"Sure do," Willie said. "It's the one I recorded the phone call on."

"Wow," Short-Guy said. "Tapping phone calls and crashing cars. You might just have a future with the CIA, kid."

Willie's eyes got as big as baseballs.

"Seriously? Dadgum, that'd be cool!" He looked at his mama, and Mrs. Parkins was touching her chest with her hanky, her eyes looking like they was seeing the future ahead of her and knowed how many worries she was in for. But she smiled and nodded at him, and then he gave out a little hoot.

"Of course, you'll have to get that tape recorder set up first," Short-Guy said.

Willie hopped up and went to get it. He hooked it up and Short-Guy put on the headphones to listen to the tape.

I sighed. Finally things was coming together.

"Now if only there was something I could do about our house," I said. "The auction's supposed to be coming soon."

Pa put his hand on my shoulder.

"We'll figure that out together. Maybe I can find a desk job somewhere."

Willie cleared his throat.

"I heard the auction happened yesterday," he said.

Well, that wasn't good.

"Did you hear who bought it?" I said.

"Yeah," he said, "but I don't want to say."

Me and Pa both looked at Mr. Thomassen. He shook his head.

"It wasn't me," he said.

"It was Bob Gorman," Willie said.

Nope, that sure wasn't good at all.

"I reckon we might as well pack up our bags and move," I said. "That is, if them Gormans haven't already burned our things."

"Well, maybe Bob will be reasonable," Pa said.

Mr. Thomassen sighed and touched his briefcase that had all that money.

"He can be, if the price is right."

Carlos saw the look of worry in my eyes. He came over and patted me on the arm.

"Fear not, *chico*. It's like my mama used to always say, *'El hombre es como el oso, mientras más feo, más hermoso.'*"

We all was quiet, waiting for him to finish.

"That's real nice," I said. "What does it mean?"

"It means, 'Men are like bears, the uglier they are, the more handsome they become.'" He patted me again.

We was all quiet one more time, processing that.

"Okay, but what does it mean?" I said.

He shrugged.

"I never asked her. It just always seemed to make everything better."

Right then there was a knock at the door. Mrs. Parkins went to go answer it.

"Is Mr. Thomassen here?" I heard Eddie Gorman's voice say. I got up and followed Mr. Thomassen to the door.

"What do you want, Eddie?" Mr. Thomassen said.

"My pa sent me—"

"Where is your pa?" Mr. Thomassen said.

"He's still in the truck," Eddie said. He cleared his throat and started again. "My pa sent me to—"

"Why didn't he come himself?" Mr. Thomassen said.

"He didn't reckon he was welcome."

He was right.

"Go on."

"My pa sent me to deliver this to you, Mr. Thomassen," Eddie said, and he handed Mr. Thomassen an envelope. "He said he hopes you two are square now."

Mr. Thomassen opened the envelope and pulled out what was inside.

It was the deed to our house.

"Yes," Mr. Thomassen said with a grin. "Yes, I believe we are."

Eddie turned and started to jump off the porch, but then he stopped.

"Hey, Johnny."

"Yeah?"

He took a deep breath.

"I got something for you, too," he said, and then he fished whatever it was out of his pocket. "From me."

He handed me what I thought at first was a dead snake all wrapped up in twine. Then I held it and realized it was hair. To be more specific, it was a ponytail.

"Why—"

"It ain't right that I have that," he said. "So I reckoned I'd give it to you." He thought for a second. "Reckon it's my attempt at being human."

I rolled up Martha's ponytail and stuck in my pocket. Eddie left without us saying another word, but I had a feeling things was about to start changing between him and me.

Me and Mr. Thomassen headed back into the living room. Mr. Thomassen handed the envelope to Pa.

"I think you can check 'House Payments' off your list of worries," he said.

Pa looked and saw the deed, and then he grabbed Mr. Thomassen's hand and shook it like a dog shakes a snake.

"I don't know how to thank you."

"It wasn't me," Mr. Thomassen said. "However, if you're still interested in a job, I might have some work for you. As thanks for everything else I've done for you two." He said that last part with a twinkle in his eyes.

Pa looked about ready to pass out.

"But, we barely know each other. Why would you do that?"

Mr. Thomassen grinned at me.

"I know you good enough," he said. "Besides, us Cuba transplants have to stick together."

Willie shook his head.

"Dang," he said. "I think I've about heard enough about Cuba for one year. When did that darn island even become such a big deal?"

Everybody looked at me. I almost started blushing.

"Thought you only cared about science," I said.

He shrugged.

It only took me a couple of seconds to remember the right page from my book.

"October 12, 1492. That's the day that Christopher Columbus, after going sailing west to find a passage to the Indies, landed on that darn island of Cuba."

"So, what's your lesson?" Mr. Thomassen said.

And that's when it hit me. The best thing that happened that night.

As I thought about the lesson, I looked around that room. Looked at all them folks I wasn't blood related to, from Pa to Willie and all them skin shades in between, but who was as close to family for me as anyone. Then I realized that I had something in common with old Columbus.

"The lesson is that you don't always get what you're hunting for. Sometimes you wind up with something better instead."

Everybody got real quiet, letting that lesson sink into their heads. Short-Guy took the headphones off and handed them back to Willie.

"Good job, kid," he said. "That tape makes my job a heck of a lot easier. Now, I'll probably still need a testimony from you, Johnny, but we can get that tomorrow."

I nodded, all of a sudden realizing just how tired I was. That nap I'd took in Mr. Thomassen's car seemed like a million years ago.

"I wouldn't count on that," Willie said. "His rain checks for interviews ain't worth the paper he writes them on."

"Is that so?" Short-Guy said.

I nodded again. There wasn't no arguing.

"Well then, I suppose we could go ahead and record your testimony now. On this junior agent's tape recorder."

I nodded a third time and Willie got the microphone all set up for me. Mrs. Parkins gave me another cup of tea and I woke up a little. Maybe I still had one more story in me.

Willie started recording, I cleared my throat, and I began.

"There ain't much difference between a deer and a dog when you're shooting, but there's a world between them when one lands on your plate."

ISAIAH CAMPBELL

Johnny Cannon
June 16, 1961

The Bay of Pigs Invasion:
The Worst Sooey-cide
Mission There Ever Was

Mrs. Buttke, this here's the report you asked
me for. I just want to say how downright unfair
it is that you made me do this report right
in the middle of the dadgum summer. Claiming
you're doing it so I don't got to be held back a
grade doesn't change the fact that it's ungodly
to make a kid do school in June. Do you know how
many fish I could have caught in the time I was
writing this thing? Anyway.

Cuba is an island about ninety miles south of
Florida, which I reckon is just about spitting
distance. Well, for a world champion spitter,
that is. If the seeds are right. And he's got
a good wind behind him. Maybe it ain't. But I'm
going to say it is 'cause it works real good in
this report.

When Christopher Columbus landed on the island
in 1492, he claimed it for the likes of Spain. I

reckon it was a good thing to do, bringing civilization to the natives and such. Of course, he brought smallpox, too, but nobody's perfect.

Four hundred years after Columbus did that, the folks on the island started getting tired of being ruled by the Spanish. A fella by the name of José Martí, who I reckon was an ancestor of my buddy Carlos Martí, started a group in 1892 that was looking to get Cuba's independence from Spain. Of course, Spain wasn't too happy about that, and that started a war. And, since the war was happening just ninety miles south of us, and since somebody went and blew up an American ship in the Havana harbor, the US got involved. That was the Spanish-American War, which went on until 1898, and it eventually wound up with Cuba getting freed from them Spanish folk.

After all that mess, it was real good for the Cubans to be their own nation and such. They was so thankful for all that America had done that they went ahead and let America have quite a bit of control in their country. We bought up a lot of land, put a whole mess of our business down there, and even started heading down there

ISAIAH CAMPBELL

for vacations. There was casinos and resorts built up, and it turned into a real nice place to visit. Even Walt Disney spent some time down there. Mickey Mouse, too, so you know it was nice.

Well, I reckon it was nice for us. And nice for the wealthy folks in Cuba. But there was a whole mess of folks in Cuba that didn't take too kindly to what was going on in their country. Those were the folks that was seeing all the poor people who couldn't get jobs, and seeing all the bad junk the American mafia was bringing down from the States, like drugs and prostitution and stuff. They also was seeing their own president, a fella by the name of Batista, who wasn't concerned with nothing more than making and keeping money. He even had a solid gold telephone, which sounds real neat until you think of all them folks that didn't have no bread.

Then, in 1953, there was a fella that started listening to all them folks that didn't have no bread. His name was Fidel Castro, and he started preaching that the way to fix Cuba was to get rid of the government they had, get rid of all them Americans, and turn their country into one where everybody got to be equal. Which sounded real good on paper, I guess, but it turned out to be a real bloody revolution that didn't get done until 1959.

While that revolution was going on, there was a bunch of Cubans who had a feeling that things wasn't going to be too good under Castro. They left the country and moved up the ninety miles to Florida, mainly to Miami. They started new lives there, making new businesses, caring for their families if they was able to bring them, and all the while really missing home.

Meanwhile, Castro took over and the revolution that looked so good on paper really started to stink. For one thing, all that property that was owned by Americans, he took it and said they didn't own it no more. Didn't pay them for it or nothing. He also didn't take too kindly to anybody in Cuba being better off than anybody else. So Cuban folks who'd made money or owned property saw theirs get taken away too. And if they spoke up against it, they'd find themselves staring down the business end of a rifle.

Well, all this stuff reached the ears of Pres-

ISAIAH CAMPBELL

ident Eisenhower, and he told his buddies that worked with him that they needed to come up with a plan. But he didn't want no plans that involved US troops invading and taking over the country. He wanted a plan that would be the Cubans overthrowing their own government, 'cause he reckoned that would look better in the papers.

Eventually his buddies put a plan together. They'd recruit all them Cuban exiles that was living in Miami, them bakers and doctors and musicians, to band together and invade Cuba on their own. We'd provide them air and naval support, but the invasion would be theirs and we'd just be assisting our allies. I imagine they all high-fived and patted each other on the back 'cause they liked that plan so much. And President Eisenhower signed off on it, so you know they all started dreaming of big raises.

And that's just what they did, they went to Miami and recruited a bunch of Cubans who was now American immigrants and told them all about the plan. And I'll be a monkey's uncle if that plan didn't look real good on paper, and so a whole mess of them Cubans signed up for it. They all started training there at the Orange Bowl for a while before they got transported down to Narnia, I mean Nicaragua, and really got trained. The bakers was learning how to shoot a man, the musicians how to sneak around land mines. It was a real strange time for them.

But then President Kennedy took office. When he heard about the invasion, nicknamed at that time Operation Pluto, he didn't like it nearly as much as Eisenhower did. So they asked him what he wanted to do about it. But he just hemmed and hawed and didn't make no decisions, and the time for the invasion kept getting closer.

It was finally the week before the invasion and all them Cuban-Americans was ready with their American-American friends to pull off the invasion of the century. The leaders, back in Washington, went to Kennedy to get his final approval. I imagine they handed him a slip of paper that said, "Do you want to invade Cuba, circle YES or NO." And then Kennedy pulled out his presidential pen and circled both of them. 'Cause that's basically what happened.

The invasion went forward, but the American support didn't. All them Cuban exiles went and

attacked a beach and they was confronted by all
of Castro's forces. But they wasn't scared,
'cause they reckoned them airplanes with bombs
would be there any minute. But them airplanes
didn't come. Them Cuban-American exiles got
left like sitting ducks. Or pigs, I reckon.
'Cause they was in the Bay of Pigs.

The end result of the Bay of Pigs invasion
wasn't what they'd been told would happen on
paper. Instead, all them exiles we sent on the
mission got captured by Castro and was held
inside his prisons. Castro used the aftermath
of the invasion to show the world how powerful
and strong he was, and how stupid people was to
attack him. Kennedy eventually told the world
that he'd messed up, and on paper that should
have ruined his presidency.

But, because he was honest with folks, it
actually made him look better. Even though there
was over a thousand Cuban exiles who was sitting
in Castro's dungeon because President Kennedy
had bailed on them, America decided he was still
a pretty cool president. And the world decided
that Castro was a pretty powerful fella. And a
whole mess of people forgot about them fellas in

them dungeons that had just wanted to go home.

But, who knows, maybe they won't be forgotten forever. Maybe putting them down on paper like this is a start.

Well, I reckon that takes me to the lesson that can be learned from the Bay of Pigs invasion:

There's lots of people or plans that look one way on paper, but when you put them in the real world, things turn out differently.

Oh, there's also a lesson I learned from Eddie:

If you want to get your butt whooped by a bunch of girls, put a sign on their restroom door that says BAY OF PIGS.

So, there you go, Mrs. Buttke, that's my report. I sure hope you decide to put me through to seventh grade. When you make your decision, let me know. I'll probably be out hunting.